PUFFIN CANADA

GIRLS' OWN

Sarah Ellis is the author of ten books for children
and young adults, including *Back of Beyond, The
Baby Project, Out of the Blue* and *Next Stop*. She
has won the Vicky Metcalf Award for a body of
work, and her books have been published in five
countries. Her love of reading, writing and talking
about books has led to her present career mix as
a librarian, freelance lecturer, book reviewer,
storyteller and writer for children. She lives in
Vancouver.

GIRLS' OWN

An Anthology of Canadian Fiction for Young Readers

Edited by

SARAH ELLIS

PUFFIN
CANADA

PUFFIN CANADA

Published by the Penguin Group

Penguin Books, a division of Pearson Canada, 10 Alcorn Avenue, Toronto, Ontario, Canada M4V 3B2

Penguin Books Ltd, 80 Strand, London WC2R 0RL, England

Penguin Putnam Inc., 375 Hudson Street, New York, New York 10014, U.S.A.

Penguin Books Australia Ltd, 250 Camberwell Road, Camberwell, Victoria 3124, Australia

Penguin Books India (P) Ltd, 11, Community Centre, Panchsheel Park, New Delhi – 110 017, India

Penguin Books (NZ) Ltd, cnr Rosedale and Airborne Roads, Albany, Auckland 1310, New Zealand

Penguin Books (South Africa) (Pty) Ltd, 24 Sturdee Avenue, Rosebank 2196, South Africa

Penguin Books Ltd, Registered Offices: 80 Strand, London WC2R 0RL, England

First published in Viking by Penguin Books Canada Limited, 2001
Published in Puffin Canada by Penguin Books, a division of Pearson Canada, 2002

10 9 8 7 6 5 4 3 2 1

Copyright © Sarah Ellis, 2001

Publisher's note: This book is a work of fiction. Names, characters, places and incidents either are the product of the author's imagination or are used fictitiously, and any resemblance to actual persons living or dead, events, or locales is entirely coincidental.

Manufactured in Canada.

NATIONAL LIBRARY OF CANADA CATALOGUING IN PUBLICATION DATA

Main entry under title:

Girls' own : an anthology of Canadian fiction for young readers / edited by Sarah Ellis.

ISBN 0-14-130993-8
1. Girls—Juvenile fiction. 2. Children's stories, Canadian (English)
I. Ellis, Sarah

PS8323.G57G57 2002   jC813'.010892827   C2002-901819-6
PR9197.35.G57G57 2002

Visit Penguin Books' website at **www.penguin.ca**

Contents

Introduction

The joys of sincere work and worthy aspiration and congenial friendship were to be hers; nothing could rob her of her birthright of fancy or her ideal world of dreams. And there was always the bend in the road!
L. M. Montgomery, *Anne of Green Gables*

Tim Wynne-Jones once wrote a story with the very short and wonderful title "Ick." In this story a boy called Brody hears the word "boisterous" and thinks it is "boysterous," how boys are. He wonders, "Whoever heard of girlsterous?"

The word "girlsterous," how girls are, could be a very useful addition to the dictionary. But what would it mean? I think the answer lies in a very old story, a story that begins with weapons and bashing and armour and all kinds of guy stuff.

A long time ago, in the time of knights and magic and riddles, King Arthur was riding through the forest one winter day, more or less minding his own business.

Suddenly a huge, mean knight appeared on the path, grabbed Arthur's sword and threatened to kidnap him. The thug was wearing serious armour and carrying a very scary-looking club, so Arthur decided to take this threat seriously. But then the thug gave Arthur one last chance. He told Arthur he wanted him to answer a riddle. If he got the answer right, he could be a free man. If he got it wrong, the thug would hack him to bits. Arthur quite sensibly said he would give the riddle a try. The thug said he would give Arthur until New Year's Day to find the answer. Then he laughed in a particularly nasty way and Arthur got the feeling this was going to be one tough riddle.

Arthur was right. The riddle was "What is it that women want most?"

Arthur went home and proceeded to ask the opinion of all the women he knew. He sent out his knights to search for the solution. The problem turned out to be that there were far too many answers. One woman wanted wealth. One wanted a handsome husband. One wanted honour. One wanted flattery. One wanted fabulous clothes. One wanted wisdom. One security. One goodness. Days went by. New Year's Eve approached. At the thought of that big, scary-looking club, Arthur's heart sank.

One thing I love about this story is that it tells the truth. Women—and girls—come in a huge variety. In this collection of stories, you will meet some of that variety, that variety of goals, wishes and desires. If you could ask the girls in this book to answer the riddle, what would they say?

What Maria and Sweetgrass most desire is to feed their families. Clever-Lazy wants to mix together things that have never been mixed before. Slava wants to be accepted and safe. Deirdre wants to save the ranch. Becca wants to play. Parvana longs for her father to come home. Charlotte longs for her sister to come home. Rebecca wants to be popular, and Eliza wants to fit in. Keely wants to be a hero, if she could only figure out what that means. Lucy wants to obey the rules, if only she could figure out what they are. Madeleine wants to recapture an old friendship; Naomi and Elspet want to make new friends. Julie's goal is to be believed. Molly wants everybody to get along. Maylin wants to make people happy. Penelope's life-long desire is to record the truth. And Coyote? Coyote is supposed to sort out the world, but when it comes right down to it, she really just wants to play ball.

Back to the Middle Ages and Arthur's dilemma: New Year's Day came and he had no answer. He was riding back to meet the thug, however, when he had the great good fortune to meet a wise old woman. Wise old women are good at riddles. She told Arthur the answer and it must have been the right one, because when Arthur told it to that thug of a knight, our Mr. Tough-Guy went into a total snit, raging and sulking, but he didn't hack Arthur to bits. Official score—Arthur: one; big bully knight: zero. Secret score— wise old woman: ten.

So what was that useful answer? This story exists in a number of versions and each has an answer that is slightly different. The punch line I like best is "What a woman most wants is to be in charge of her own destiny."

Welcome to *Girls' Own*, Girl Zone. The girls between these two covers are of every sort. They are shy and bold; obedient and rebellious; clever and slow; subdued and boisterous; fierce and gentle; funny and serious. But each of them is in the process of grasping her future with both hands. That is a very girlsterous thing to do.

Sarah Ellis
Vancouver, B.C.

from

Hero of Lesser Causes

by
Julie Johnston

Keely and her brother Patrick are close. Whether Keely is daring Patrick to stand in Bloodsucker Pond or Patrick is planting a stink-bomb in Keely's bed, they live in a state of affectionate rivalry. When Patrick is stricken with severe polio Keely is convinced that she can bully, cajole and tease him into health, that she can charm him out of the depression that his illness causes. For example, Keely is all in favour of Peggy Doyle, the fortune-telling nurse who predicts that Patrick is about to receive a parcel. But Patrick wants nothing to do with any of it.

Every day I expected a huge package to be delivered for Patrick. Patrick expected nothing.

Whether or not to hire Peggy Doyle came to a family vote Sunday evening. Patrick's vote was an uncomplicated no. Mine was an emphatic yes. Mother wavered on the fence. She had no doubt about Peggy's nursing ability, but this tendency towards fortune-telling, no matter how much Peggy denied any real belief in it, was upsetting. Father reviewed the case for and against hiring Peggy and cast the deciding ballot. "She's helpful, she's cheerful, and from what I've seen, she knows her stuff," he said. "She can't help it if a little bit of the old magic and superstition still clings to her. She's from the valley, after all. It's bred into you up there. I say she stays."

Peggy was hired. I began to regret my vote while Patrick began to forget he had ever cast one. "She's nice and everything," I explained to Ginny, "but does she have to spend so much *time* with Patrick?"

"Well, she's his nurse."

"I know, but . . ."

"You're just jealous."

"I am not."

Patrick was unaware of the tension rising around him. Much of Peggy's time with him was spent bullying him into doing daily exercises. Although she wasn't a physiotherapist, she had worked side by side with physios and knew how to bend and straighten Patrick's arms and legs to keep his muscles toned up and to prevent contractures. "Look at it this way." She said this to me, although it was Patrick with his eyes closed she was aiming her lecture at. "Some of his muscles have nerve fibres regenerating, coming back to life, and some of his muscles don't because what they call the motor cells in his spine were wiped out by the polio germ. At this point we're not dead certain which muscle groups will come back, so we keep working them all. If we don't, his good muscles will atrophy, waste away. Some of his neck muscles are coming along. And so are some of his arm muscles. Patrick," she said, "push my hand away."

"Why should I?"

"To prove you can."

"Forget it. I can't." Patrick's arm was lying limply on the sheet. With one hand Peggy pressed lightly against his forearm. She stretched her finger over and tickled the inside of his wrist. "Quit it," Patrick said and moved his arm. I cheered. Peggy gloated and Patrick's mouth popped open. "Big deal," he said.

Every day I ran home from school to join in, to help out, but Patrick wouldn't let me lay a hand on him. I peered over Peggy's shoulder, dodged under her elbow to watch, but all I was was a fifth wheel. I needed an ally. "I'm going to invite Donald over to visit."

Patrick glared at me.

"What's wrong with that?"

After a long while he said, "My old life is dead, I know that. So ... I want to be dead to my old friends. Don't bring them here to see me like this. I'm such a nothing."

I wanted to yell at him, to shake him. I couldn't. I couldn't even think of anything to say.

I tried luring him out of his despondency with tales of the new neighbours on what had been Laurence Saunders' property. The people who were to run the Veterans' Home were Mr. and Mrs. Hodge. They had a daughter, Charlotte, a dimpled and fluffy-blonde girl about my age, and a ten-year-old son, Hartley. Hartley had the face of an angel and the habits of a gangster. He picked cigarette butts out of the gutter and smoked them. He lay on the cold, damp sidewalk so he could look up girls' skirts. I took the opportunity to kick him in the head one day, which made him scramble. He vowed to be my lifelong enemy. Fine with me, I told him.

Patrick was not intrigued. I told him about the renovations for the veterans, the ramps, the boardwalks, the extensions, but he was unmoved. I told him about Charlotte with her ruffles and bows and dimples. Patrick said dimples were kind of nice. "So's a bowl of rice pudding," I growled. I was envious. Secretly I poked my cheeks in, but no dimples formed. I told him about the horses. They were still there, bossy Lola (she'd lost her Lightning status) and old Bill. I had caught up with Laurence Saunders one day as he was coming out of the bakery and asked him about them. I hadn't seen them since midwinter.

"Sold 'em along with the farm," he said. "The Hodges are hiring a young lad to keep an eye on them. Surprised you haven't seen him. Hodge put an ad in the paper and this lad answered it. He's about your age, maybe a little older. Goes to the high school. He has a horse of his own he wants to board there."

"He has a horse of his own?" The boy began to grow in importance. What kind of boy would own a horse, I wondered. A prince, possibly. Or someone very princelike. A prince in disguise. "If you see this guy," I said to Laurence, "tell him I'd give anything to ride his horse. I'd even take another whack at Lola, as far as that goes."

"Sure, I'll tell him. It's young Alex Dalby I'm talkin' about. Lost his dad overseas. His mother sold the farm and moved to town. Young lad wouldn't part with his horse, I guess. He's to work weekends and in the holidays, helping out with the vets. It's a lucky break for Mrs. Dalby. The money, I mean. Their farm didn't fetch much. I was lucky." He smiled and tipped his hat. A businessman now, he no longer wore a tweed cap. "Give my regards to your brother," he said. "A harsh blow. Such a harsh blow." He shook his head sympathetically.

All the way home I thought about Alex Dalby with a horse of his own, a horse he kept right behind our backyard. No reason I couldn't do the same. Anybody could get a horse. Probably. You didn't have to be a prince. I had seventeen dollars in a box in the back of the second drawer of my desk. Maybe not enough for a horse, at least not a very good horse, but it was a start. I could save my allowance, my birthday money, give up a few things like the show on Saturdays. Unless they were playing movies about horses.

I told Patrick about the boy with the horse and about my plans to buy one of my own. He closed his eyes and frowned. He made it pretty clear that he wasn't interested.

Peggy seemed to have better luck breaking through Patrick's barrier. In the late afternoon she lit the lamp in his room. She sat in a rocking-chair which she had begged from the living-room and which Mother was glad to see the end of, knitting endless sleeves and backs of sweaters and talking about the war. She had spent a year overseas in a London hospital looking after amputees. Now, after the four o'clock bell, I rushed away from the schoolyard din to be a part of the atmosphere she was creating. I always looked up at the glow in Patrick's window as I came rushing along the street. It made me feel . . . homesick. I endured school. I only came to life in Patrick's room.

Inside, I raced upstairs, kicked off my shoes and huddled on the end of Patrick's bed. At first he didn't seem to notice. As he began to listen to Peggy's stories, though, he became aware of me. "Off," he ordered. "You're unbalancing me." I had to drag a small wicker chair into Patrick's room from mine. His room was beginning to look like a used-furniture dealer's storeroom.

I had given up resenting Peggy. It's hard to be curious about someone's real-life stories and jealous at the same time. Even though he rarely responded, I knew Patrick was listening. He would shift his gaze from time to time, instead of staring vacantly at an invisible spot on the wall. I had to interrupt Peggy and ask questions for both of us.

"Weren't you afraid of the bombs?"

"Yes, terrified."

"What made you decide to go over there?"

"Oh, well, I. . . ." For the first time since we had known her, Peggy seemed unnerved, at a loss for words. She took a breath and went on. "I went over to look for my fiancé." She looked at her watch and started to get out of the rocking-chair. "Nearly dinnertime," she said.

"No, wait!" I pressed her back down. I had drawn up my chair as close as possible to hers so as not to miss a word. "What do you mean, to look for your fiancé? Did you already have one who was lost, or were you trying to find one?"

Peggy hesitated. "Lost," she said.

I inched closer, looking intently into Peggy's face. I sensed something here. A true story, a true romance. I specialized in making discoveries about people, mysterious romantic discoveries. Then I made up what-if stories about them and told them to myself at night when I couldn't get to sleep. Sometimes I couldn't get to sleep because my stories were too exciting—especially when I starred in them, solving the mysteries and saving everybody from the jaws of death.

I begged Peggy to go on with her story.

She sighed as though she might as well get it over with. "We were engaged to be married," she began, "just before he went overseas. About six months later I received a telegram saying he was missing and presumed dead." She stopped.

"Oh, no!" I said. Peggy was busy counting stitches. If I'd been making up the story I might have said missing, but not dead. I wouldn't have brought dead into it at all. I looked at Patrick. He looked upset too. We waited for the story to go on. It didn't.

I tried to get my face between Peggy's and her knitting. "And so you wept," I prompted.

"Well yes, of course." She started counting her stitches out loud. "Thirty-two, thirty-three. . . ."

"You were stricken with grief." I needed details.

"Well, I. . . ."

"You vowed then and there to leave not a stone unturned as you searched the world for your lover!"

Patrick spoke. "Keely, for Pete's sake!"

"You certainly lead a rich and satisfying fantasy life, Keely, my dear," said Peggy.

"Well, somebody has to!"

"Yes," Peggy continued, "I went over to look, not expecting to find him, really, but not exactly believing he was dead. I didn't have the right sense of loss. It was only a hunch, a feeling, mind you."

Patrick and I exchanged a glance. "Yes, that's it," I said. "Because of your . . . sixth sense . . . you knew."

"No, it was just a hunch."

"And then what?"

"I didn't find a trace of him. The war ended and I came home." She got up at that point and squeezed past my wicker chair. Lines creased her forehead.

"But what's his name? What does he look like?"

"End of story," Peggy said crossly and went downstairs.

"Holy!"

"Now look what you did!" Patrick sounded disappointed. "You shouldn't have pumped her. You made her cross."

I ignored him. I had something to think about. "Obviously we have to find her dead soldier. This is our mission.

"For Pete's sake, Keely! He's dead."

"He's not dead. If Peggy believed he's alive, he's alive. If anyone would know, Peggy would, wouldn't she?"

"She said it was only a hunch."

"Yes, but for Peggy I think a hunch is a sure bet."

"She was pretty worked up," Patrick reflected. "If it was really 'end of story,' why would she get so huffy with us?"

"Because," I said, "she probably has a hunch about us, too." I looked Patrick in the eye. His gaze didn't waver from mine. "We are the ones!"

"You mean, she thinks we're going to find him." It wasn't a question. Slowly, and with significance, I nodded.

Something of Patrick's old intensity hovered. He seemed trapped in a dream. "Can you imagine a paralysed hero?"

"Yes," I said. "I can. If anyone can bring Peggy's dead soldier back to life, a paralysed hero can."

"I would say," said Patrick, "it's symbolic." He seemed lost in a dream tinged with hope.

"Definitely."

I still looked forward to Patrick's surprise package every day, and every day nothing continued to show up. Hopeful buds began to appear on the trees, encouraged by the sun's first warmth. Lola mooched about now, on the slope of the high pasture, and occasionally Bill. I had yet to glimpse the horse belonging to Alex Dalby, the prince in disguise. What sort of horse would he have? An ivory and black piebald or a mighty black stallion? I hoped the former. Velvet Brown was my kind of person. I reread both

National Velvet and *The Black Stallion* and memorized bits of each to get in shape for flying over the high pasture. I knew exactly how to do it. It was all so easy. Just a question of having a horse. Every week I deposited most of my allowance into the box in the second drawer of my desk.

Charlotte Hodge, whose parents ran the Veterans' Home, had taken to walking home from school with Ginny and me. Although she was the same age, she was a grade behind. We were both in the entrance class, looking longingly towards first-form high school next year.

"They'll probably skip me pretty soon," Charlotte told us. "School's really simple here, compared to Ottawa." Ginny and I exchanged glances. We scuffed along the street, not saying much. Charlotte looked down at my shoes. "Do you still have to wear Oxfords with toe-caps? In Ottawa only little kids wear those." I watch her trip along, daintily pointing the toe of her brand-spanking-new white sandal with a heel that was ever so slightly high. Even if I had white sandals, even if I *wanted* white sandals, my mother would never have let me wear them before the twenty-fourth of May—for reasons, I imagine, best known to my mother. I gave Charlotte a sidelong look and thought, what if we had an earthquake right now and Charlotte fell in?

I came in from school to find Mrs. Fisk of the Hospital Auxiliary having tea with Mother. "Hi," I said from the doorway of the living-room. Mother squinted the corners of her eyes at me and I added, "Hi, Mrs. Fisk." Mother always has these rules. . . .

Mrs. Fisk said, "My soul-and-body, how you've grown! Quite the young lady."

I gave her a lips-only smile, about to back out, but she patted the couch cushion beside her. Mother squinted sweetly at me again so I was forced to sit. I refused tea. Politely.

"Well, as I say, we were all simply flabbergasted." Mrs. Fisk seemed to have lost interest in me and my height and my young ladyness. She went on talking to my mother. "Just through an ad in the paper. Anyone knowing the whereabouts of Lance Corporal James Fisk . . . that sort of thing. And not two months later who should arrive on my brother-in-law's doorstep but the young lad himself."

I was probably staring at Mrs. Fisk with my mouth open, because she said to me, "Missing in action, you know."

I said, "Gosh!"

"He was altered, mind you, quite altered."

"How come?"

"Keely. . . ." Mother was squinting warningly at me now.

Mrs. Fisk continued. "Shell-shock, they say. But still, can you imagine? Through an ad in the paper!"

"Some people are just plain lucky, I guess," Mother said.

"Yes indeed." Mrs. Fisk looked at my mother and looked down at her teacup. "We could all use a bit of luck, couldn't we?"

"Keely," Mother interrupted, "perhaps you should get at your homework." I jumped up, relieved of my social duty, and started upstairs, thinking that the words "shell-shock" had an interesting ring to them.

"With any luck at all," I heard Mrs. Fisk say, "things will start looking up for your poor lad." I stopped at the bottom of the stairs.

"I hope you're right. What you're doing is wonderful, Anita," Mother said. "We're very appreciative."

"We all agreed it was a worthy project," Mrs. Fisk replied. "Of course, we'll need specific measurements."

Mother paused. "That may be difficult to arrange and still keep it a secret, but we'll manage somehow."

"Keep what a secret?" I asked, after Mrs. Fisk had gone.

"It wouldn't be a secret if I told you, would it?" She was being maddening.

I pounded up to Patrick's room. Patrick was reading, his book attached to his special holder. Peggy sat in the rocker knitting. I dropped my book bag on the floor, making them both jump. "What's this about a secret?" I demanded.

Patrick continued to read. Peggy looked up sharply from her knitting. She glanced at Patrick and gave me a glaring head-shaking look I didn't understand.

"What's going on, Peggy?"

Peggy rolled her eyes to the ceiling and shook her head again. "Haven't the foggiest," she said.

I watched her suspiciously. Peggy pulled a long strand of wool from the yellow ball which, inch by inch, was being devoured by the clicking jaws of her knitting needles. Inch by inch it appeared reincarnated as the sleeve of a sweater. She said she had knit all through the war and couldn't get out of the habit. I hunched down in my wicker chair. "Why am I always the outcast in this family? No one ever tells me anything."

"I'm sure all will be revealed in good time," said Peggy. "Don't destroy the chair, Keely dear."

I was picking off loose bits of wicker. "No one trusts me." I got up and paced the floor. I rubbed my nose and thought, what if the floor gave way right under Peggy?

"Get a handkerchief, Keely," Peggy said.

"I don't need one. My nose is itchy."

"Oh-oh. That means you're going to kiss a fool."

"Does it?" I asked. Patrick looked up from his book. I smooched out my lips and leaned threateningly over him.

"Help! Get her away from me. She's making me throw up."

"Keely!"

"Can't anyone take a joke around here? Am I that repulsive?"

"Yes," said Patrick, closing his eyes.

I slouched against the window-sill. "Everyone hates me, obviously."

"Nearly thirteen," said Peggy, "is a difficult age." She pulled another long strand of wool free. "You've got the tail-end of childhood dragging behind you and the tough end of young womanhood stretched out in front of you. Straighten up, Keely. Don't slouch like that or they'll be putting you in a back brace."

I stood up straight, hunching up my shoulders, thrusting out my chin. I was tall for my age. My dream was to look older and more dramatic. I said, "I left childhood behind ages ago." I was thinking of the day I had fallen off Lola and Patrick had saved me from having my head kicked in. The day Patrick got sick was the last day of my childhood, as far as I was concerned.

"You should practise walking with a book on your head, child, for your figure."

"Child! Why does everyone treat me like a kid? No one tells me anything, they keep secrets from me, they act like I'm a moron...."

"Maybe it's just that you're a little impetuous," she suggested.

"What's that got to do with anything?" I wasn't about to ask what impetuous meant. I glared at her. "You're as bad as everyone else. I ask a few simple questions about your fiancé and you walk out as if I've insulted you."

"Now, Keely." Peggy put her knitting down. "I know what you're like. If I even so much as told you he was tall you'd be out looking for him, scouring streets, questioning everyone in uniform over six feet. I wouldn't put it past you to go to Ottawa and check at National Defence Headquarters."

"Hey, that's an idea." I was cheering up. "Have you done that?"

"Keely! See what I mean? You're impetuous."

"No, I'm not. I just like to get to the middle of things fast. If you'd only trust us with some details, Patrick and I could find him."

Patrick groaned. "You're spoiling it, Keely. Can't you just grow up?"

"Grow up!" I was angry now.

"You heard me. You don't solve mysteries by putting your head down and ramming at them. And anyway, it wasn't for real. It was supposed to be . . . symbolic." His voiced dropped and he glanced quickly at Peggy and away, embarrassed. He frowned at me.

"I don't understand," Peggy said.

"I understand perfectly," I said. "Patrick thinks I'm a jerk and he hates me. Fine then. See if I ever darken your doorstep again." I gathered up my book bag and slammed out of Patrick's room. Peggy called after me, but I didn't answer. I had declared war. On the whole world. I put my head down and rammed my way into my room.

The next day, Saturday, nothing changed. The sky was leaden, as was my heart. Mother and Peggy were quietly planning something in the kitchen but changed the subject when I came in. I went out. I phoned Ginny, but she sounded funny. She was being evasive. I never beat around the bush. "What's up?" I asked her.

"Nothing much," Ginny hedged.

"Gin-n-ny!"

Ginny sighed. "Carol Katski asked me over, and Buddy Dolan, and I said I'd go."

I didn't say anything.

"It's a free country," she added.

"Fine then."

"I'll get Carol to ask you too."

"Don't bother. I hate Buddy Dolan and anyway, I'm busy." I hung up a little more firmly than was necessary.

I got out my roller-skates and clanged them together to knock off the dust. I didn't really want to roller-skate, but I didn't want to hang around the house either, being a friendless, untrusted, childish outcast. When I was eleven I asked for boxing gloves for Christmas and got roller-skates instead. They were good skates, the best, but they weren't boxing gloves. How could my parents think they were interchangeable? Sometimes I just felt like punching something, but instead I roller-skated, came home, took off my skates—and still felt like punching something.

I skated down the street towards the new Veterans' Home and toyed with a what-if story. What if, just at the corner, a Russian spy in a big, black limousine stopped, yanked me inside and held me hostage? But little did he know I had unusual powers. With superstrength I ploughed him one with my skates, grabbed the steering wheel and raced the car downtown to the police station, right beside the court-house where my father just happened to be coming out and my mother, by chance, was shopping nearby and....

A boy (it had to be the horse boy) stood at the end of the lane to the Veterans' Home, nailing a sign to the maple near the road. He whacked in the last nail and stood back from his handiwork. I was close enough to see that the sign read Sunny View Acres. He heard me rattling along, looked at me and sort of nodded before starting up the lane. I was left with my mouth hanging ready to say something like "Great day for a horseback ride." It didn't actually look like a great day for anything. It was about to pour down rain. "Hi!" I called hopefully to his back.

"G'day," he called back over his shoulder. He didn't stop to chat about horses.

G'day, I mimicked silently. What a drip!

This section of Fairly Street had been freshly black-topped not long ago. You could still catch a whiff of the hot, sharp smell of tar. It was almost as smooth as skating on the kitchen linoleum, which I used to do sometimes when Mother was out. Charlotte's brother, Hartley, came skulking down the lane now, smirking at me with his pink choir-boy mouth and glancing around, probably checking to see if I had any bodyguards with me. I didn't. Didn't need any. He slithered down and squatted under the sign on the tree, without taking his eyes off me. His hair was brushed into a kewpie-doll wave over his forehead.

I decided to ignore him.

"Hey, kid," he yelled as I wheeled close, "get off my road."

"You don't own it." I sped past.

"Do so."

"Do not." I skated back to the corner, let a car pass and skated down the middle, where it was smoothest of all. I stuck my leg out behind and, with arms spread, pretended I was Barbara Ann Scott, Canada's own darling on figure-skates. I felt a few drops of rain but I didn't care.

"Hey, beanpole, get your carcass off my road!"

"Make me, snake-face," I yelled, with both feet back under me. Hartley lunged, but I swerved and skated on. Back I came again, taunting him, daring him. Again he missed. I watched him steal away up the lane towards his house and thought he must have given up. What a disappointment! There had been something bracing in this skirmish. I didn't want to win the battle by default. I was after blood. And besides, he'd started it. I skated up to the end of the fresh paving again, turned in front of an oncoming car and, when the driver honked his horn, made a face. What a vicious place the world was! It began to rain in earnest now.

I didn't see Harley behind the parked car. The wind rushing past my face made my eyes water and deafened me. At that moment I knew I was *faster than a speeding bullet, more powerful than a locomotive, able to leap tall. . . .* Then Hartley Hodge leaped up from behind the parked car and spilled a juice can of gravel in my path.

There was blood, all right, but it was from my own torn knees and the palms of my hands. One of my skates came off; the strap had broken. I grabbed the skate and leaped to my feet faster than a speeding bullet, surprising Hartley. He was backed up against the parked car, which allowed him no escape. He ducked and dodged, but I was both taller and quicker. I grabbed him by the shirt-front with one hand, twisting it into his neck, and raised the skate over his head. A tortured, gurgling snort came from his blocked windpipe. The rain stood out in beads on his greased-up kewpie-doll wave. There was a low, threatening roll of thunder. "I could bust in your stupid, baby-doll face, you know," I panted. His eyes, alert to the threat, were little black circles of fear. He was waiting for the blow. I raised the skate higher for greater impact and suddenly a what-if scene came over me, unasked for. What if this CCM

Sunshine steel roller-skate, more dangerous at the moment than boxing gloves, flattened the kid. What if he lay on the road helpless as a baby. For ever. I couldn't wish that on even my avowed, lifelong enemy. Almost too fast for thought, I saw Patrick's dark defeat in this boy's eyes. I loosened my grip on the neck of his shirt and watched his eyes ice over as he realized he was home free. I gave him a shove and he scuttled away to the safety of his lane.

I pushed off on my one skate towards home, rain streaming down my face. Maybe I should have, I kept thinking, maybe I should have. On the other hand, what if his mother was fond of him?

from

Clever-Lazy

by
Joan Bodger

The baker and the baker's husband long for a child. The baker's husband prays for a baby as "pretty and plump and clever" as his wife. The baker hopes for a daughter who is "clever enough to be lazy, and lazy enough to be clever." When their wish comes true and they are blessed with a baby girl they name her "Clever-Lazy." This description of her childhood gives us a taste of her life to come, a life of adventure, invention and the unexpected. Where does this tale happen? Joan Bodger says it all takes place, "far away and on the other side of time."

When Clever-Lazy was a tiny baby, she rode sometimes on her father's back, sometimes on her mother's. While her parents busied themselves about the shop, she peered over one or the other's shoulder with wise eyes that seemed to notice everything. When she was a little older, they spread a mat on the bakery floor so she could crawl. They gave her pot lids to play with, and made a rattle for her by putting beans and peppercorns into a stoppered jar. When she could toddle, they let her play about their feet, opening and closing doors, dragging out cooking pots, crawling into chests and boxes.

"But won't she hurt herself?" asked the neighbors. "Won't she get in the way? Isn't she a nuisance?"

Baker and her husband only laughed or shrugged their shoulders. As soon as Clever-Lazy was able to walk, they took her to the great oven and held her hand on a part that was very warm, but not warm enough to burn her. "Hot," they said, and Clever-Lazy learned to say and know the meaning. She knew, too, by the respect her parents paid to the fire, that what was useful and beautiful could also be dangerous. Long years afterward, she would have occasion to remember that.

In the meantime, she observed that a dancing orange flame would make a kettle sing, that a dull red glow was needed for roasting and baking, that a blue flame was the hottest (although it looks cold), and that great heat could change the color and shape of metals. These things she learned because she was allowed to see.

As for being a nuisance, I suppose Clever-Lazy was often that. But her parents were willing to forgive her because she brought to them such joy and amusement. The first time she pulled a bag of flour down all over herself, they merely laughed and dusted her off. The next time they gave her a pan of flour of her own, and lent her their cups and bowls and spoons so she could pour and measure to her heart's content.

Clever-Lazy amused herself by the hour comparing and sorting little piles of rice and millet, almonds and pistachios, poppy seeds and sesame. She loved to let their names slide over her tongue almost as much as she liked to let their shapes and colors and textures slide through her fingers. She even made patterns and pictures by sticking nuts and seeds, beans and beads, to panels of wood, which her proud parents hung on the wall of their shop.

Quite early Clever-Lazy learned to count. She arranged and rearranged rows of beads so that her fingers fairly flew as she ordered the numbers. When she was older, she evolved a pattern that enabled her to help her parents calculate how many pounds of flour they would need for the months ahead, what the loss or profit would be if they enriched a recipe or how many days it was before the equinox, when the farmers would plant a new crop. Because the beads rolled away under her flying fingers, she asked her father to make a little rack. Heeding her directions, he helped her thread seven beads onto thirteen spindles, then enclosed them in a frame. Of course neither of them knew that Clever-Lazy had invented the abacus! "Click-click-click," went the beads as Clever-Lazy moved them swiftly up and down.

When the Imperial Tax Collector came to the village, he watched in amazement as Clever-Lazy, sitting companionably beside him, clicked out how much each villager owed the Emperor, far faster and more accurately than he could by adding up a long row of figures with brush and paper, or even by moving counters in a box.

The villagers were not much pleased, but the Emperor's man asked if he could have a similar bead rack of his own. He wanted to show his wife, who long ago had lived in the Province of the Dancing Mountains. Clever-Lazy gave him hers willingly. Her father said he would make her another, but somehow or other he never did. But what happened to that first abacus would one day be important to Clever-Lazy.

Clever-Lazy didn't spend all her time with grown-ups, of course. She ran and played with the other village children as often as they could get away from their chores. She played hopscotch and skipped rope and flew kites and played tag and threw balls and spun tops and ran races and played hide-and-seek. She told stories while the other children worked in their gardens or tended the cattle, and she helped them catch fish in the canals. She even devised a prawn trap for them.

The prawn trap looked something like a kite, but it was made of rice sacking stretched tight over a certain kind of root. The children would set their traps in the morning (each child had his own dark and secret little current that he thought best), then at noon they would go back and haul up the traps, cook the prawns and have a feast. It was not long before the adults copied the children, and soon the local market was renowned not only for its prawns, but for its prawn traps. The village was richer for having Clever-Lazy in its midst, but I am not prepared to tell you whether the villagers were grateful. They complained about her laziness and muttered that she was a bad influence on their children.

Clever-Lazy liked to mix things together that had never been mixed together before. She stirred, tasted and tested her recipes on top of the brazier or in the big oven. Sometimes they tasted good, and sometimes they tasted so bitter all one could do was to pull a face. Once or twice they made the whole family ill, and several times her concoctions actually exploded in the oven. Once, when that happened, Clever-Lazy noticed that the inside of the oven had lost all its crust of old soot and grease, and looked as clean as new. By remembering what she had put into her recipe (a little soda, a little lemon juice, a pinch of lye and other things), she was able to make a sort of paste with which her parents could paint the oven. They left the paste on overnight, and the next morning her father washed down the walls and found that the oven was clean again, this time without the bother and danger of an explosion.

"So you see," said her mother to the neighbors, "Clever-Lazy is more help to us than if she spent all of her time learning to do housework."

There were other benefits as well. Who invented poppy seed rolls? Who invented sesame seed bread? Why, Clever-Lazy, of course. And it was Clever-Lazy who made a sort of tea out of the stamens of spring crocus, and persuaded Baker to add it to the dough so that the whole village, and several villages beyond, learned to enjoy yellow saffron buns. Oh yes, and she taught her parents to bury the great long pod of a vanilla bean in the sugar jar so as to flavor all the cakes. And, speaking of cakes, Clever-Lazy it was who first thought to beat egg whites, and thought of adding them to cakes to make them rise in the oven. And it was Clever-Lazy who taught her parents to sift flour through a series of baskets so that the breath of air was added to exceedingly fine flour along with the egg whites. No wonder that Baker's confections were compared to the clouds that could be seen floating over the Dancing Mountains.

Clever-Lazy liked to hear her parents tell the story of how they had made a dumpling dough doll and had gone to the Goddess to ask for a baby. She made dolls of flour and eggs and sugar, too, and found that by adding corn starch, she could make stiffer figures that lasted indefinitely. She painted faces on them and fashioned clothes and armor. In the evenings, she delighted her parents by telling stories and acting them out with the aid of her puppets made from dough.

Clever-Lazy kept her ever-growing collection of story figures in a box her father made for her, which her mother lined with gold and red paper. The inside of the box was designed to hold three square trays fitted one on top of the other. Each tray was divided into sections to keep her story figures separate and safe. Only the soldiers, dozens of them, were dumped together in a jumble on the bottom. There was a latch on the box and a curved brass handle that made it easy to pick up and carry about. Clever-Lazy painted the box bright red.

Sometimes neighbors came to hear the stories too. And a certain young tinker who came by every few months to mend and sell pots and pans made it his business to spend the night in that particular village just to hear and watch Clever-Lazy tell her stories. He was a lonely young man who traveled the roads most of the year and who had no family of his own. I dare say if you had asked him his dearest wish, he would have replied that what he really longed for was a home and a family as much like the bakers' as possible. And, if you had asked him why, he would not have been able to answer.

One night when he knocked on the door, he was invited into the household and given a good supper, along with a welcome order for pots and pans. Clever-Lazy had just finished a new play and had cut out and painted a new cast of characters, so she made him especially welcome. She knew that, except for her parents, no one was as entranced by her stories as was young Tinker. He, in return, found it delightful to watch her fuss about, setting up the stage while her mother and father finished the dishes and completed their chores for the morning. If he wondered why she did not help her parents, he might also have noticed that they offered no reprimand or reproof. He soon allowed himself to forget Clever-Lazy's laziness, and to give himself over to enjoying the new play when the rest of the small audience settled down with him.

The new play was far more complicated than Clever-Lazy had ever produced before. There were an Emperor and an Empress, an easily-frightened princess, a dragon, an army (a rather small one), Daunted Knight and Proud Maiden. At first, Tinker thought that Proud Maiden was another knight, or perhaps a soldier, because she was dressed in armor and because she fought and ousted the dragon after Daunted Knight had failed. When he discovered she was a girl, he was quite sure that the knight would marry her if only she would become as docile and grateful as the princess. But that's not the way the story turned out at all. Proud Maiden sent Daunted Knight away and decided to go on to other adventures by herself.

Tinker was unsettled. True, even he had never laughed so much nor followed a plot so breathlessly, but he was left with the uneasy feeling that he would wish some other fate for the knight and the maiden. When Clever-Lazy announced that of all the characters she had ever created, she loved Proud Maiden best by far, Tinker felt an unaccountable pang. "How could a nice girl like you admire a girl like that?" he asked, puzzled. "I don't think she's really respectable."

"What does respectable mean?" asked Clever-Lazy. Tinker would have been scandalized by her ignorance if he had not realized that her not knowing was final proof of respectability. *He* worried about that question most of the time.

"Someone who is respectable does what is expected of her," he replied.

"But that's why I like Proud Maiden best. She does the *un*expected."

Next day, Tinker hoisted his pack to his back, shook the village dust from his feet and turned his face to the open road. He had never felt so lonely.

from

The Belonging Place

by
Jean Little

Elspet, an orphan, is adopted by her aunt and uncle and travels with them in 1847 from their home in Scotland to Upper Canada where they are to settle. It is a strange wild place they come to and Elspet thinks she will never feel at home. Her kitten Purrkin helps with the homesickness, but what Elspet really needs is a friend.

When we had finished moving everything indoors, the little log house was crammed to the rafters with people and their belongings. I was to sleep in the trundle bed beside Mother and Father's big bed. The boys would sleep on straw ticks in the loft. Uncle Thomas and Cousin Malcolm already had theirs up there. Charlie and Hamish jumped on the bulging straw-stuffed sacks which had been made ready for their coming, flattening them a little and filling the loft with choking dust.

"It's … making … me … sneeze!" yelled Charlie, suiting the action to the word.

"It will soon settle down and you won't notice," Malcolm said. "I'll sleep nearest the ladder so I can protect you from Hugh when he swarms up it and attacks us at dawn."

"You won't stay idling in your beds at dawn," Uncle Thomas said. "You'll pull on your shirts and britches and go milk Margaret."

I felt left out and lonely for a moment but I soon learned that there were plenty of jobs for girls. I often wished it were otherwise. Mother and I worked our fingers raw keeping our clothes and the cabin clean. We would just get the floor swept when one or other of the men or boys would tramp in with mud or even manure on his boots. Then it was all to do over. And we could not blame them. There seemed to be nowhere free of dirt. We washed clothes in the creek using homemade soap Father bought at market in Fergus.

"We'll make our own this fall," Mother said, eyeing the pig Uncle Thomas had brought home. He had built a shanty for another family and been given a piglet in payment.

"Do not become fond of that pig, Elspet," my father warned. "He's going to help feed us next winter. Do not give him a name or spend precious time scratching his back for him the way I saw you doing this morning."

After that, I avoided the pig pen whenever possible.

The cow Father had been so pleased to have waiting for us made plenty of work too. Not only did she have to be milked daily but we had to turn that milk into butter, buttermilk and cream. We set the milk to separate in big pans, skimmed off the cream when it rose and churned it to make butter and buttermilk.

We got meals ready for the men and boys, all of whom had stomachs like bottomless pits. We would make candles and soap after the pig was slaughtered. In the meantime, we used bought ones sparingly and went to bed early, so tired we were apt to be asleep before we had pulled our quilts up to our chins.

At first, Mother wished we had our own sheep so she could spin the wool and set up her loom but soon she admitted she was glad to let the making of cloth wait a year.

"I do not see how we could manage it," she said wearily.

We picked berries, crabapples, pin cherries and the plants she needed to make dye and medicine. We baked cornbread in an iron baking kettle. The bread was not the same as we had eaten in Scotland but it tasted good. All food tasted good when you worked as hard as we Gordons.

Most of these chores had had to be done in Scotland also but there Mother had had Granny to help her and, if the jobs were especially heavy, one of the village girls or her older sisters would lend a hand. In those days, with lots of hands making light work, I had been coddled, expected to help but never depended upon the way Mother did now. Now I was, of necessity, her right-hand girl and we both disliked it.

"I want some time to waste," I whispered. But I did not speak the thought aloud. When the boys or I complained about never having time to spend on our own pastimes, Mother reminded us how much better everything was than when we had been on shipboard and Father delivered his lecture on how good it was to own our own land and work for ourselves. We soon stopped grousing if either of them was within earshot. But I could tell I had Mother's secret sympathy as we looked at the filth trekked in on our scrubbed floor.

Finally my gentle mother grew short-tempered under the load of work. She never rested or ran out of chores for me to do. Father was bone-weary too. We could tell by the way he groaned getting to his feet after every meal. Uncle Thomas took to disappearing at odd times, claiming he was looking for a wife. We knew he was stretched out in the hay mow but did not tell. Even Malcolm's good humour wore thin as he did the work of a grown man.

In Glen Buchan, our parents had read aloud to us in the evening and had read to themselves too. Father still read the Bible aloud at mealtimes, of course, but now there was no time for any other reading. Although Father had unpacked the box of books first of all, they sat on the shelf and gathered dust for weeks. We had no time or energy now for *Pilgrim's Progress, The Poetry of Robert Burns* or the plays of William Shakespeare. All we still read regularly were the Old and New Testaments. I was glad there were good stories in there because I was hungry for tales of valour and romance.

"Mr. Dickens has written a new book," Father did say once. He had been to market and come home with news. "We can borrow it perhaps and read it this winter when we're snowbound."

In spite of chilblains and nowhere to go to get away from too many brothers, I could hardly wait for the luxury of being snowbound.

There was not a big crop that first summer but there was some wheat and lots of Indian corn. The land Father had bought had two apple trees close to the trail, which would become a road. One was a russet and one a yellow transparent. There was also a pear tree filled with bees and birds that liked the fruit as well as we did.

"How did those fruit trees get planted?" Mother wondered.

Father said that someone had tried homesteading here several years before but had lost heart and returned to the Old Country. They planted a few trees but left before there was any fruit. The wind helped some and so did animals, dropping apple and pear cores without eating every seed.

"We will not give up, William," Mother said grimly. "I could not face the ocean voyage again. Neither could Elspet."

I thought about Granny Ross so far away and Furkin on her knee. But I knew Mother was right. Gordons were never quitters.

"I need a girl to help with the work," my mother said one night. "There are five of you, not counting Hugh, to do the men's work here. But there are only Elspet and me to do all the jobs that are considered women's part. It is far too much for one woman and one nine-year-old, however hard we work. I had my mother and sisters to give me a hand in Glen Buchan and we could always get one of the MacTavishes in to lend a hand. But none of you men is of the least use."

My father looked ashamed of himself. He also looked worried.

"I ought to be shot not to have thought of it," he said. "I'll find you someone, Ailsa. She'll have to work for her bed and board and not much else, though. We haven't any money to spare."

"I know. Just do your best, Will," Mother said, giving him a smile.

"I still want neighbours," I muttered. "There are far too many boys and men. I need at least one girl."

Father laughed more happily at that.

"I'll see what I can do for you too," he said. "We want our women contented. Other settlers will come soon, I promise. Bide a wee while and you will see."

I longed to snap that I was sick and tired of biding a wee while but I heard Granny's voice inside my head saying, "Save your breath to cool your broth, my lass, and show respect for your elders and betters."

Father came home from Fergus two days later with a freckle-faced fourteen-year-old girl named Bridget. She talked a blue streak but she worked like a Trojan. I had a little more time to play but still no girl to play with me.

Then, after I had waited over a month, my invitation to meet the neighbours came at last. It happened in a way I would never have expected. Early that morning, Uncle

Thomas and the boys went off to the nearest grist mill, leaving Father to get on with clearing some more of the land. Even Hugh went, promising faithfully to walk all the way home without whining if Uncle Thomas or Malcolm would let him ride on his shoulders on the way there. Mother and Bridget and I were busy when, suddenly, Father came rushing into the cabin.

Mother looked up from the churn. Bridget, on her way to fetch another bucket of water, stopped to stare. I quit peeling apples for sauce. We all waited to hear what had him so excited.

"Elspet, we have neighbours at last," he shouted at us as though we were a mile away. "Come on."

I sprang up, leaving the apples without a backward glance. Mother snorted and stayed where she was. The dasher went on thumping up and down inside the churn.

"Let Bridget past, Will," she said above the noise of the churning. "I didna hear anyone. I'll have butter in ten minutes if I don't stop. You go along, child. It's probably a doe and fawn or some such creatures. If there's need for me to come, run back and fetch me. But recollect that Bridget and I have no spare time this morning. She's leaving after we finish the chores to go see her mother."

"But, Ailsa . . . ," Father started.

She did not let him finish.

"I've seen enough fascinating Canadian wildlife to last me a fortnight. Now I have work to do. Bridget, if you want to visit your mother, you'd better not stand about with your mouth open."

My father gave Mother a wry look. He stood back and let Bridget sidle past. Then he led me out the door. Sure enough, when I stood on the step and looked about, nobody was in the clearing. I didn't even see a deer browsing or another kind of woodpecker.

Father could get very excited about a new kind of bird. He had made us stand for ages watching a tall blue heron fishing in Cox's Creek and a chipmunk stuffing his cheeks with nuts. Mother usually was interested too, but she had lost some of her curiosity lately. She said her back ached.

"Where are the neighbours?" I demanded suspiciously.

"Hark and you'll hear," my father said.

I was delighted that I was sharing these moments with my father without a brother shoving his oar in. I trotted after him ready for anything but not too hopeful.

"I don't hear . . . ," I started to say.

Then I did hear it. A rooster was crowing!

"Nobody within earshot has hens. These must be new people and they can't be that far away," Father said, looking mightily pleased with himself. "Wait right there. I'll get some bread and cheese. We can stay out of your mother's hair without worrying about our dinner getting cold."

He was back in a moment with a packet of food shoved into his wide pocket. He also had my boots. He grinned at me like a boy playing truant from school.

"Put these on or you'll stub your tender toes," he said.

I pulled them on as fast as I could.

"Come on," he said, picking up an axe and striding toward a gap in the trees. "There's a deer trail we can follow on the other side of this fallen log. Give me your hand, lassie. Now jump. When the trees grow too close, I'll blaze a trail so we won't get lost coming back."

His plan sounded simple. It was not simple to put into action, though. The deer trail might have been easy for a deer. It was terribly difficult for a girl in a long, full skirt. Yet, even though branches swung back and slapped me in the face and flies nipped and nibbled at our ears and foreheads, we made steady headway. Every time we did grow discouraged, the helpful rooster sang out again as though he knew we were coming and he was determined to guide us all the way.

I was too excited to mind a few scratches. I tore a leafy switch from a sapling we passed and swung it back and forth around my head and shoulders. I was glad I had snatched up my sunbonnet from the hook by the door. It kept some of the insects off.

I had rarely been alone with my father for such a long time. We had had few chances to share in expeditions like this. Hamish was usually the chosen one. Yet here Father and I were, making a voyage of discovery together. I felt like Balboa or Sir Francis Drake.

After an hour, we stumbled into a natural clearing with a big shelving rock. It looked like a flattish limestone couch. A few feet from it, Father uncovered a spring almost hidden by grass and leaves. The two of us cleaned it out and drank thirstily. Then Father pulled out the package of bread and cheese.

"We need fortifying, wouldn't you say?" he said with a grin.

We sat, side by side, and ate every last crumb. Afterwards, we finished off with another long drink of spring water.

"Your mother will be sorry she missed this," my father told me, "but she can come later. When we visit back and forth, this spring and rock seat will make a perfect resting spot. You and I will find these people with a rooster all by ourselves, this first time, but we'll probably do lots of travelling to and fro."

I did not care about the future. The rooster crowed more lustily than ever.

"Lead on, Macduff," I said, quoting one of his favourite sayings.

He laughed and set out ahead of me. We speeded up a little. We found the second part of the journey harder because the deer trail branched off, leading away from the rooster's inviting crow. We hacked a path through prickly bushes and clambered over more fallen logs. I put my foot on one and my boot sank into a rotten bit and made me slip. Father caught my flailing arm, though, and we kept going. I stumbled again and fell but I scrambled up before he had to come to my rescue. I wanted him to see that I was every bit as tough as Hamish or Charlie. I was thankful we had stopped to eat. I could tell by the sunlight sifting down through the leaves that our usual dinner hour was long past.

Father cut blazes in the trees as we went. Then, all of a sudden, to our astonishment, we broke through one last clump of trees and stepped into a fair-sized clearing surrounded by stumps. Getting rid of the stumps was backbreaking work. They stood about everywhere like rotting wooden teeth.

But I had no attention to spare for tree stumps. As I staggered into the sunny space, the first person I saw was a girl my own age sitting on the step of a log shanty, smaller and more rickety than our own. She had black braids that curled at the ends. She was barefoot. She wore a faded pink sunbonnet and a dull brown homespun dress very like my own. She was watching the bush a little nervously and, on her lap, was a skinny calico cat.

I usually can't think what to say when I meet someone new. But this time, I did not wait for Father to speak first. Words burst out of me like water gushing from a fountain.

"We heard your rooster," I babbled, my cheeks flushing with delight. "We came to find you. I'm Elspet Mary Gordon. What's your name? When did you come here? And what do you call your cat?"

The girl stood up. The calico cat sprang to the ground and stalked off in a huff. But it did not go far.

"We've been here two weeks but Pa just brought the rooster yesterday. My cat's called Motley. I'm Jeanie Mackay," the girl said. "Mother!"

The door behind her opened while she was turning to push it wide. A roundish woman, with hair as glossy black as the girl's, stepped out. She stared at Father and me as though we were ghosts. Her eyes were wide with surprise. Then she remembered her manners and came forward.

"Good day," she said a little stiffly. "I'm Mrs. Robert Mackay. You are the first people I've laid eyes on since we arrived in this wilderness. My daughter and I have just been here ten days."

The cat watched from a nearby stump, her tail twitching. Jeanie smiled at me. She was shy too, I could tell, but her smile was friendly. Maybe she, also, had been longing for another girl to talk to.

"We're two of the Gordon clan," Father said. He shook Mrs. Mackay's hand warmly. "I'm William and this is Elspet Mary. We call her Elspet mostly. We blazed a trail through the bush when we heard your rooster. His crow told me that at last we had near neighbours. I can't understand why we didn't hear you building your shanty. My Elspet is overjoyed. She has been longing for a girl her age ever since we arrived late in July."

Jeanie laughed aloud. Mrs. Mackay's smile grew a tiny bit warmer.

"It's always good to have neighbours," she said, "especially when you are so far from home."

It didn't take that long to get here, I thought, and then realized that, when she said "far from home," she was speaking of Scotland. Was our log cabin "home" to me then? I did not know.

"We have three boys at home but only one girl," Father went on, grinning at Jeanie. "My wife Ailsa would have come too if she hadn't been in the middle of churning."

"We have only the one child now," Jeanie's mother said. Her smile went out like a candle flame being snuffed. Her voice was low and full of pain. "We stayed at an inn in Montreal, never guessing cholera had already broken out there.

Our Alastair was sickly after the voyage and, when he caught the foul disease in Montreal, he had no' the strength to fight it off. He was just a wee bairn ..."

At this, her voice broke and her eyes filled with tears. I looked away. Jeanie squeezed her mother's hand.

"Don't forget Jamie," she said softly. "We have Jamie, Mam."

"No, I'm not forgetting him," her mother said. Her words grated harshly and sounded lifeless. "But he's none of mine."

"He is ours now!" the little girl insisted, her eyes fierce and her chin high. "I'll get him. He's waking up. They'll want to meet him."

Her mother shot her an annoyed glance but Jeanie vanished into the cabin. I stood mutely listening to Father and Mrs. Mackay talking. They sounded like people in church. She was explaining something about Mr. Mackay's having come to Upper Canada first and bought the land while she and the children waited in Montreal. He had found this place with a shanty already erected. The people who had built it had no title to the land and had been glad to be bought off with a few pounds.

"My husband is no builder," she said in a cold voice.

That's why we did not hear the axe chopping or the hammer driving in nails, I thought.

I looked over at Father for permission to go after Jeanie. When he nodded, I followed her inside. She was bending over a cot. In it lay the homeliest baby I had ever seen. His hair stood up in a bush of bouncy red curls. His eyes were brilliant blue. His little ears stuck out like cup handles. He had a wide mouth and a nub of a nose.

Just looking at his funny face made me laugh aloud. Jeanie scowled at me.

"He's beautiful, isn't he?" she said defiantly.

"Beautiful," I said quickly, doing my best not to laugh again. I knew how I would feel if Jeanie Mackay made fun of our Hugh. But did Jeanie really believe Jamie was beautiful? How could she? She must be just saying so because she loved him.

Jeanie picked the grinning baby up and held him tight.

"When we were waiting for Pa, Jamie's family was staying in the same inn. The cholera killed all of them except Jamie," she muttered, her eyes on the door. "Our Alastair sickened too and, in just a few hours, he was gone."

I gasped and stared at her white face as she went doggedly on.

"When my Pa came, I was looking after wee Jamie and Ma was sore grieving. So my father said God must mean us to take the poor orphan with us, since he needed us and we needed him. I was glad. But Mam still thinks only of Alastair. She says we must find Jamie's folks. Pa did ask about them. Nobody knew who they were. We could keep him if she'd a mind to do so. But she wants him gone."

I looked at the cheerful little boy and felt a tightness inside my chest. He was an orphan like me. He was laughing. He did not seem to mind being an orphan. But he was too little to understand that Mrs. Mackay did not want him.

My family had wanted me. I was sure of that. They had never once said, "She's none of ours."

Or had they? Grandfather Gordon had said just that.

The rooster crowed again. Jeanie looked up from Jamie's funny face. She smiled at me. The smile made her eyes light up.

"I'm so glad our rooster found you," she said. "Mam is so sad. I needed a friend."

from

The Breadwinner

by

Deborah Ellis

Parvana lives in Afghanistan. In her country, under the rule of the Taliban, women are not allowed to leave the house without a man. They must wear clothes that cover every part of their bodies, including their faces. When soldiers break into Parvana's home and arrest her father the family is left trapped. Who will earn a living and buy food? Parvana's mother and older sister Nooria cannot go out. Her older brother Hossain was killed by a land mine. Her little brother and sister are too small to help. Only Parvana, not yet a woman, has any freedom. And then one day that freedom is snatched away. What will the family do?

It was strange to be in the marketplace without Father. Parvana almost expected to see him in their usual place, sitting on the blanket, reading and writing his customer's letters.

Women were not allowed to go into the shops. Men were supposed to do all the shopping, but if women did it, they had to stand outside and call in for what they needed. Parvana had seen shopkeepers beaten for serving women inside their shops.

Parvana wasn't sure if she would be considered a woman. On the one hand, if she behaved like one and stood outside the shop and called in her order, she could get in trouble for not wearing a burqa. On the other hand, if she went into a shop, she could get in trouble for not acting like a woman!

She put off her decision by buying the nan first. The baker's stall opened onto the street.

Parvana pulled her chador more tightly around her face so that only her eyes were showing. She held up ten fingers—ten loaves of nan. A pile of nan was already baked, but she had to wait a little while for four more loaves to be flipped out of the oven. The attendant wrapped the bread in a piece of newspaper and handed it to Parvana. She paid without looking up.

The bread was still warm. It smelled so good! The wonderful smell reminded Parvana how hungry she was. She could have swallowed a whole loaf in one gulp.

The fruit and vegetable stand was next. Before she had time to make a selection, a voice behind her shouted, "What are you doing on the street dressed like that?"

Parvana whirled around to see a Talib glaring at her, anger in his eyes and a stick in his hand.

"You must be covered up! Who is your father? Who is your husband? They will be punished for letting you walk the street like that!" The soldier raised his arm and brought his stick down on Parvana's shoulder.

Parvana didn't even feel it. Punish her father, would they?

"Stop hitting me!" she yelled.

The Talib was so surprised, he held still for a moment. Parvana saw him pause, and she started to run. She knocked over a pile of turnips at the vegetable stand, and they went rolling all over the street.

Clutching the still-warm nan to her chest, Parvana kept running, her sandals slapping against the pavement. She didn't care if people were staring at her. All she wanted was to get as far away from the soldier as she could, as fast as her legs could carry her.

She was so anxious to get home, she ran right into a woman carrying a child.

"Is that Parvana?"

Parvana tried to get away, but the woman had a firm grip on her arm.

"It is Parvana! What kind of a way is that to carry bread?"

The voice behind the burqa was familiar, but Parvana couldn't remember who it belonged to.

"Speak up, girl! Don't stand there with your mouth open as though you were a fish in the market! Speak up!"

"Mrs. Weera?"

"Oh, that's right, my face is covered. I keep forgetting. Now, why are you running, and why are you crushing that perfectly good bread?"

Parvana started to cry. "The Taliban . . . one of the soldiers . . . he was chasing me."

"Dry your tears. Under such a circumstance, running was a very sensible thing to do. I always thought you had the makings of a sensible girl, and you've just proven me right. Good for you! You've outrun the Taliban. Where are you going with all that bread?"

"Home. I'm almost there."

"We'll go together. I've been meaning to call on your mother for some time. We need a magazine, and your mother is just the person to get it going for us."

"Mother doesn't write any more, and I don't think she'll want company."

"Nonsense. Let's go."

Mrs. Weera had been in the Afghan Women's Union with Mother. She was so sure Mother wouldn't mind her dropping in that Parvana obediently led the way.

"And stop squeezing that bread! It's not going to suddenly jump out of your arms!"

When they were almost at the top step, Parvana turned to Mrs. Weera. "About Mother. She's not been well."

"Then it's a good thing I'm stopping by to take care of her!"

Parvana gave up. They reached the apartment door and went inside.

Nooria saw only Parvana at first. She took the nan from her. "Is this all you bought? Where's the rice? Where's the tea? How are we supposed to manage with just this?"

"Don't be too hard on her. She was chased out of the market before she could complete her shopping." Mrs. Weera stepped into the room and took off her burqa.

"Mrs. Weera!" Nooria exclaimed. Relief washed over her face. Here was someone who could take charge, who could take some of the responsibility off her shoulders.

Mrs. Weera placed the child she'd been carrying down on the mat beside Ali. The two toddlers eyed each other warily.

Mrs. Weera was a tall woman. Her hair was white, but her body was strong. She had been a physical education teacher before the Taliban made her leave her job.

"What in the world is going on here?" she asked. In a few quick strides she was in the bathroom, searching out the source of the stench. "Why aren't those diapers washed?"

"We're out of water," Nooria explained. "We've been afraid to go out."

"You're not afraid, are you, Parvana?" She didn't wait for her answer. "Fetch the bucket, girl. Do your bit for the team. Here we go!" Mrs. Weera still talked like she was out on the hockey field, urging everyone to do their best.

"Where's Fatana?" she asked, as Parvana fetched the water bucket. Nooria motioned to the figure on the toshak, buried under a blanket. Mother moaned and tried to huddle down even further.

"She's sleeping," Nooria said.

"How long has she been like this?"

"Four days."

"Where's your father?"

"Arrested."

"Ah, I see." She caught sight of Parvana holding the empty bucket. "Are you waiting for it to rain inside so your bucket will fill itself? Off you go!"

Parvana went.

She made seven trips. Mrs. Weera met her outside the apartment at the top of the steps and took the first two full buckets from her, emptied them inside and brought back the empty bucket. "We're getting your mother cleaned up, and she doesn't need another pair of eyes on her."

After that, Parvana carried the water inside to the water tank as usual. Mrs. Weera had gotten Mother up and washed. Mother didn't seem to notice Parvana.

She kept hauling water. Her arms were sore, and the blisters on her feet started to bleed again, but she didn't think about that. She fetched water because her family needed it, because her father would have expected her to. Now that Mrs. Weera was there and her mother was up, things were going to get easier, and she would do her part.

Out the door, down the steps, down the street to the tap, then back again, stopping now and then to rest and change carrying arms.

After the seventh trip, Mrs. Weera stopped her.

"You've filled the tank and the wash basin, and there's a full bucket to spare. That's enough for now."

Parvana was dizzy from doing all that exercise with no food and nothing to drink. She wanted some water right away.

"What are you doing?" Nooria asked as Parvana filled a cup from the tank. "You know it has to be boiled first!"

Unboiled water made you sick, but Parvana was so thirsty that she didn't care. She wanted to drink, and raised the cup to her lips.

Nooria snatched it from her hands. "You are the stupidest girl! All we need now is for you to get sick! How could anyone so stupid end up as my sister!"

"That's no way to keep up team spirit," Mrs. Weera said. "Nooria, why don't you get the little ones washed for dinner. Use cold water. We'll let this first batch of boiled water be for drinking."

Parvana went out into the larger room and sat down. Mother was sitting up. She had put on clean clothes. Her hair was brushed and tied back. She looked more like Mother, although she still seemed very tired.

It felt like an eternity before Mrs. Weera handed Parvana a cup of plain boiled water.

"Be careful. It's very hot."

As soon as she could, she drank the water, got another cupful, and drank that, too.

Mrs. Weera and her granddaughter stayed the night. As Parvana drifted off to sleep, she heard her, Nooria and Mother talking quietly together. Mrs. Weera told them about Parvana's brush with the Taliban.

The last thing she heard before she fell asleep was Mrs. Weera saying, "I guess we'll have to think of something else."

They were going to turn her into a boy.

"As a boy, you'll be able to move in and out of the market, buy what we need, and no one will stop you," Mother said.

"It's a perfect solution," Mrs. Weera said.

"You'll be our cousin from Jalalabad," Nooria said, "come to stay with us while our father is away."

Parvana stared at the three of them. It was as though they were speaking a foreign language, and she didn't have a clue what they were saying.

"If anybody asks about you, we'll say that you have gone to stay with an aunt in Kunduz," Mother said.

"But no one will ask about you."

At these words, Parvana turned her head sharply to glare at her sister. If ever there was a time to say something mean, this was it, but she couldn't think of anything. After all, what Nooria said was true. None of her friends had seen her since the Taliban closed the schools. Her relatives were scattered to different parts of the country, even to different countries. There was no one to ask about her.

"You'll wear Hossain's clothes." Mother's voice caught, and for a moment it seemed as though she would cry, but she got control of herself again. "They will be a bit big for you, but we can make some adjustments if we have to." She glanced over at Mrs. Weera. "Those clothes have been idle long enough. It's time they were put to use."

Parvana guessed Mrs. Weera and her mother had been talking long and hard while she was asleep. She was glad of that. Her mother already looked better. But that didn't mean she was ready to give in.

"It won't work," she said. "I won't look like a boy. I have long hair."

Nooria opened the cupboard door, took out the sewing kit and slowly opened it up. It looked to Parvana as if Nooria was having too much fun as she lifted out the scissors and snapped them open and shut a few times.

"You're not cutting my hair!" Parvana's hands flew up to her head.

"How else will you look like a boy?" Mother asked.

"Cut Nooria's hair! She's the oldest! It's her responsibility to look after me, not my responsibility to look after her!"

"No one would believe me to be a boy," Nooria said calmly, looking down at her body. Nooria being calm just made Parvana madder.

"I'll look like that soon," Parvana said.

"You wish."

"We'll deal with that when the time comes," Mother said quickly, heading off the fight she knew was coming. "Until then, we have no choice. Someone has to be able to go outside, and you are the one most likely to look like a boy."

Parvana thought about it. Her fingers reached up her back to see how long her hair had grown.

"It has to be your decision," Mrs. Weera said. "We can force you to cut off your hair, but you're still the one who has to go outside and act the part. We know this is a big thing we're asking, but I think you can do it. How about it?"

Parvana realized Mrs. Weera was right. They could hold her down and cut off her hair, but for anything more, they needed her cooperation. In the end, it really was her decision.

Somehow, knowing that made it easier to agree.

"All right," she said. "I'll do it."

"Well done," said Mrs. Weera. "That's the spirit."

Nooria snapped the scissors again. "I'll cut your hair," she said.

"I'll cut it," Mother said, taking the scissors away. "Let's do it now, Parvana. Thinking about it won't make it any easier."

Parvana and her mother went into the washroom where the cement floor would make it easier to clean up the cut-off hair. Mother took Hossain's clothes in with them.

"Do you want to watch?" Mother asked, nodding toward the mirror.

Parvana shook her head, then changed her mind. If this was the last she would see of her hair, then she wanted to see it for as long as she could.

Mother worked quickly. First she cut off a huge chunk in a straight line at her neck. She held it up for Parvana to see.

"I have a lovely piece of ribbon packed away," she said. "We'll tie this up with it, and you can keep it."

Parvana looked at the hair in her mother's hand. While it was on her head, it had seemed important. It didn't seem important any more.

"No, thanks," said Parvana. "Throw it away."

Her mother's lips tightened. "If you're going to sulk about it," she said, and she tossed the hair down to the floor.

As more and more hair fell away, Parvana began to feel like a different person. Her whole face showed. What was left of her hair was short and shaggy. It curled in a soft fringe around her ears. There were no long parts to fall into her eyes, to become tangled on a windy day, to take forever to dry when she got caught in the rain.

Her forehead seemed bigger. Her eyes seemed bigger, too, maybe because she was opening them so wide to be able to see everything. Her ears seemed to stick out from her head.

They look a little funny, Parvana thought, but a nice sort of funny.

I have a nice face, she decided.

Mother rubbed her hands brusquely over Parvana's head to rub away any stray hairs.

"Change your clothes," she said. Then she left the washroom.

All alone, Parvana's hand crept up to the top of her head. Touching her hair gingerly at first, she soon rubbed the palm of her hand all over her head. Her new hair felt both bristly and soft. It tickled the skin on her hand.

I like it, she thought, and she smiled.

She took off her own clothes and put on her brother's. Hossain's shalwar kameez was pale green, both the loose shirt and the baggy trousers. The shirt hung down very low, and the trousers were too long, but by rolling them up at the waist, they were all right.

There was a pocket sewn into the left side of the shirt, near the chest. It was just big enough to hold money and maybe a few candies, if she ever had candies again. There was another pocket on the front. It was nice to have pockets. Her girl clothes didn't have any.

"Parvana, haven't you changed yet?"

Parvana stopped looking at herself in the mirror and joined her family.

The first face she saw was Maryam's. Her little sister looked as if she couldn't quite figure out who had walked into the room.

"It's me, Maryam," Parvana said.

"Parvana!" Maryam laughed as she recognized her.

"Hossain," her mother whispered.

"You look less ugly as a boy than you do as a girl," Nooria said quickly. If Mother started remembering Hossain, she'd just start crying again.

"You look fine," said Mrs. Weera.

"Put this on." Mother handed Parvana a cap. Parvana put it on her head. It was a white cap with beautiful embroidery all over it. Maybe she'd never wear her special red shalwar kameez again, but she had a new cap to take its place.

"Here's some money," her mother said. "Buy what you were not able to buy yesterday." She placed a pakul around Parvana's shoulder. It was her father's. "Hurry back."

Parvana tucked the money into her new pocket. She slipped her feet into her sandals, then reached for her chador.

"You won't be needing that," Nooria said.

Parvana had forgotten. Suddenly she was scared. Everyone would see her face! They would know she wasn't a boy!

She turned around to plead with her mother. "Don't make me do this!"

"You see?" Nooria said in her nastiest voice. "I told you she was too scared."

"It's easy to call someone else scared when you're safe inside your home all the time!" Parvana shot back. She spun around and went outside, slamming the door behind her.

Out on the street, she kept waiting for people to point at her and call her a fake. No one did. No one paid any attention to her at all. The more she was ignored, the more confident she felt.

When she had gone into the market with her father, she had kept silent and covered up her face as much as possible. She had tried her best to be invisible. Now, with her face open to the sunshine, she was invisible in another way. She was just one more boy on the street. She was nothing worth paying attention to.

When she came to the shop that sold tea, rice and other groceries, she hesitated for a slight moment, then walked boldly through the door. I'm a boy, she kept saying to herself. It gave her courage.

"What do you want?" the grocer asked.

"Some . . . some tea," Parvana stammered out.

"How much? What kind?" The grocer was gruff, but it was ordinary bad-mood gruff, not gruff out of anger that there was a girl in his shop.

Parvana pointed to the brand of tea they usually had at home. "Is that the cheapest?"

"This one is the cheapest." He showed her another one.

"I'll take the cheapest one. I also need five pounds of rice."

"Don't tell me. You want the cheapest kind. Big spender."

Parvana left the shop with rice and tea, feeling very proud of herself. "I can do this!" she whispered.

Onions were cheap at the vegetable stand. She bought a few.

"Look what I got!" Parvana exclaimed, as she burst through the door of her home. "I did it! I did the shopping, and nobody bothered me."

"Parvana!" Maryam ran to her and gave her a hug. Parvana hugged her back as best she could with her arms full of groceries.

Mother was back on the toshak, facing the wall, her back to the room. Ali sat beside her, patting her and saying, "Ma-ma-ma," trying to get her attention.

Nooria took the groceries from Parvana and handed her the water bucket.

"As long as you've got your sandals on," she said.

"What's wrong with Mother now?"

"Shhh! Not so loud! Do you want her to hear you? She got upset after seeing you in Hossain's clothes. Can you blame her? Also, Mrs. Weera went home, and that's made her sad. Now, please go and get water."

"I got water yesterday!"

"I had a lot of cleaning to do. Ali was almost out of diapers. Would you rather wash diapers than fetch the water?"

Parvana fetched the water.

"Keep those clothes on," Nooria said when Parvana returned. "I've been thinking about this. If you're going to be a boy outside, you should be a boy inside, too. What if someone comes by?"

That made sense to Parvana. "What about Mother? Won't it upset her to see me in Hossain's clothes all the time?"

"She'll have to get used to it."

For the first time, Parvana noticed the tired lines on Nooria's face. She looked much older than seventeen.

"I'll help you with supper," she offered.

"You? Help? All you'd do is get in my way."

Parvana fumed. It was impossible to be nice to Nooria!

Mother got up for supper and made an effort to be cheerful. She complimented Parvana on her shopping success, but seemed to have a hard time looking at her.

Later that night, when they were all stretched out for sleep, Ali fussed a little.

"Go to sleep, Hossain," Parvana heard her mother say. "Go to sleep, my son."

The Chinese Babies

by

Tim Wynne-Jones

This story is part of a collection called (wait for the awful pun) Lord of the Fries. *These are stories of meetings and encounters, of first impressions and surprises and the amazing ways that humans can, finally, get along with each other.*

"Here's what you need to know. Be open."

Molly's grandfather leaned over the chessboard, his hand hovering here, there, shaking a little. Finally she watched his waxy, yellow-tipped fingers descend on a bishop and slide him all the way over to the left side of the board. Any minute now he would tell her the name of that square.

"Queen's bishop to king's rook six."

There. She didn't know why he did this. She was twelve now. He'd been doing it since she was seven, and she *still* didn't know which square was which or why they should have numbers.

And what had he said about being open? Quickly she checked to make sure her queen wasn't trapped. She wasn't. Her regal eyes were flinty, on guard. She could move all right. Her hubby, the king, was tucked up all nice and safe behind a wall of pawns with a knight by his side. Even with all that protection, he still looked scared. What a wuss.

This was the only strategy Molly knew. Keep the wuss-king out of the way and the flinty-eyed queen loose and ready to attack.

Be open?

Molly's eyes roamed the board. Everything looked fine.

Grandfather leaned back in his La-Z-Boy rocker. "I always felt sorry for that foolish duck," he said.

Molly stared at her grandfather, looked down at the board, expecting to see a duck there. She examined the bishop he had just moved, wondering if maybe the bishop was a duck in disguise.

"You know, Molly, maybe that's why I've always loved the oboe." Grandfather's fingers were tapping lightly on the arm of his chair, to some rhythm Molly couldn't hear. Ducks? Oboes? What was he up to?

"What about the oboe, Taid?"

"Hmm?"

"Why do you love the oboe?"

"Oh," said her grandfather, as if Molly had asked him a truly challenging question. "Well, because of the duck," he said. "Getting swallowed by the wolf and all. Such a bad business that . . ."

Mum sometimes said Grandfather Gareth was losing it. She called him Taid, which was Welsh for grandfather. "Taid Gareth is getting senile, Molly. He's starting to dodder a bit." Was this what she meant?

Molly waited. Waiting was a pretty good strategy with Taid Gareth. And while she waited, she examined the chessboard. Ah-ha! Her castle was right across the board from the shaky old bishop. No wonder he was praying so hard!

She was just about to slide her castle across the board and bump the old bishop off when Grandfather piped up again. "It's funny how you can know something all your life and not ever really know how it came to be."

Molly's head was spinning. Playing chess with her grandfather was difficult enough without all this doddering. She didn't wait for him to go on. With a satisfying clink, Molly took her grandfather's bishop. She hit the chess piece so hard it bounced right off the game table and landed on the dog's nose. The dog woke up.

"Sorry, Blossom," said Molly.

Blossom nosed the bishop with his big wet nose. Licked him. Poor bishop. Molly swooped the piece up before Blossom made a lunch of him. She put him into the chess box. She called the chess box Heaven. There were three of Grandfather's pawns there already. She hardly ever won an important piece off Grandfather.

She turned the four pieces so that they were facing each other, so that they could have a little chat. Otherwise Heaven was a pretty boring place.

She turned her attention back to the board in time to see Taid Gareth lift one of his castles and move it slowly all the way from his end of the board, past the square where her castle had been, right to her end of the board, behind her defence and only three squares away from the wuss-king's backside.

"Rook to queen's rook eight," said Taid Gareth.

"Queen's *castle* eight," said Molly grumpily.

Grandfather smiled wickedly at her. "Check," he said.

Molly was just about to slide old Flinty-Eyes between Wuss-King and the marauding Black Castle when she realized that she couldn't. If she moved her queen, she would automatically be in check from Grandfather's other castle.

"And checkmate," said Grandfather with satisfaction, licking his parched lower lip. The gleam in his eye didn't look very senile.

"You got me with just your castles," she said.

"Rooks," said Grandfather, chuckling, dry as dust. "You can call them castles all you like, Molly fach, but that makes them sound inactive. Just sitting there, doing nothing."

Molly wasn't a good loser, but she had learned how to be a quiet loser. Taid Gareth had taught her all about buttoning your lip when you didn't like what was going on. She glared at him one good solid glare, then started putting her players back in the box.

"So what is a rook anyway?" she asked.

"Well," said her grandfather, "there's one kind of rook that is a bird, kind of like a raven. Did you see how silently it flew down your flank there and caught you off guard?"

Molly put Taid's players away while he loaded up his pipe. "Yeah, well, how was I supposed to notice with you talking all the time?"

Taid Gareth reached across and rebuttoned her lips. His eyes wrinkled up. "I tried to warn you," he said. "Remember? Be open."

Molly had the two black rooks in each hand. She made them caw angrily at each other.

Her grandfather laughed. "The rook in chess comes from the Persian word for warrior," he said.

Molly plopped the two victorious warriors back in the box, slid the top closed and put the chess box into the drawer under the game table.

"What about the duck?" she said.

Her grandfather was leaning back now, staring past her at the great white expanse of sloping yard and wide frozen river and distant hills that the view from this room afforded him. "From *Peter and the Wolf*," he said. "You have heard it, haven't you?"

This was a trick question. He had given her a tape of *Peter and the Wolf* last year for Christmas. She had never listened to it. "Oh, that duck," she said.

Grandfather sucked on his pipe, seemingly unaware of her fib. "My favourite instrument in the orchestra has been the oboe for as long as I can recall. But I don't like the clarinet worth a hoot. Now, that's silly, really. They're not all that much different. But I like the oboe, Molly fach."

Molly curled up on the floor so that her head was snuggled against Blossom's woolly neck.

"And it's all because of the duck?" she said, her voice muffled by Blossom fuzz.

Taid Gareth nodded. "As you'll recall, in Mr. Prokofiev's story, the duck's part is played by the oboe. Such a plaintive sound, you see. The poor old duck never did get out of the wolf."

Blossom licked Molly's ear. She nuzzled deeper into his warm, smelly pelt to escape this wet gesture.

"Not even in the sequel?" she asked.

"The sequel?"

"Isn't there a sequel?" said Molly. "*Return of the Duck* or something like that?"

Grandfather chuckled. "We didn't go in for sequels much in my day. We were lucky if we got something once."

Molly uncoiled herself from Blossom and made her way over to the official scoreboard by the study door. THE ANNUAL WIGSTEAD CHRISTMAS CHESS TOURNAMENT, the sign read. With a black Magic Marker Molly recorded her loss, Gareth's win.

"Luckily there's a sequel in the tournament," she said. "I'll get you yet, Taid."

There were eight of them at the old Wigstead farm for Christmas. Taid Gareth; Molly, her mother, Charlotte, and her father, Trick; Aunt Estelle and her boyfriend, Chet; and Uncle Don, the oldest, and his sixteen-year-old son, Keith.

After round one, Grandfather Gareth was on top with six wins and only one loss, a fluke to Chet. "He's just trying to make you feel wanted," Estelle told him. "He'll clobber you next time."

When it came to chess, Taid Gareth was merciless.

Charlotte was next with five wins. Then Chet, who was tied for third spot with Estelle.

Molly was next with three wins, tied with her dad. With one round left, she could still win. Well, maybe not against her grandfather, but then he played all the time. He played by mail with friends back in Wales and some missionary in Africa.

Trailing the pack were Uncle Don and Keith. Keith had won zero games. He had lost six in a row. After two complete rounds everyone should have played seven games, but Don and Keith's game was declared a draw. It wasn't really a draw. With one angry swipe, Uncle Don cleared the table in the middle of their game. He sent the players flying every which way. He was making a point to Keith about something. Nobody knew exactly what. Then Don went out for a while, and Molly, silently, helped Keith recover the chess pieces. One of the points on the white king's crown was broken. Trick secretly took the injured king out to Grandfather's workshop in the garage and sanded it smooth. "Poor old wuss-king," Molly said, as she watched her father working. Her mother came out to the shed to see how things were going.

She was fuming. "I can't believe this childish behaviour between those two," she said.

Molly huffed. "When someone's as old as Uncle Don, shouldn't it be called adultish behaviour?"

This was the first Christmas Keith had been there since Grandmother Maeve had died. Don got Keith for Christmas only every other year. Nain Maeve had always been able to smooth things out between Don and his son. Molly missed her.

So, while everyone else was relatively happy and enjoying a few days up at the old Wigstead homestead, Don and Keith took turns walking out along the Old Bridge Road or down to the riverside.

That's where Keith was when Molly curled up in the study after lunch the day of her defeat to Taid Gareth.

It was snowing. Keith was down at the river's edge, smoking a cigarette. The cigarettes were the cause of the first big fight of the holidays. Don was furious, blamed it all on Montreal, where Keith lived with his mother. They had moved there three years ago. Don hadn't liked the idea, and Taid Gareth had sided with him. "There's only one thing wrong with Quebec, and that's the French, Grandfather Gareth had said.

"Silly old fart," Charlotte said, making Molly laugh. Then she felt bad. She loved her grandfather, even if she didn't like all the things he said.

Molly was kneeling at the picture window. Blossom was asleep by the fireplace. He twitched, farted.

"Silly old fart," murmured Molly, but not loudly enough to wake the dog. She didn't want his sloppy attention right now. Her eyes fixed on her only cousin, Keith. He was so quiet, so moody. She watched him walk out onto the river. The ice was thick this year and covered with an eiderdown of deep snow. There was a crust so you could walk on top of the snow, although sometimes your foot went through.

Mum had taken her out on the snowmobile, all the way across to the other side. That was Quebec over there, those low hills. Before the Trans-Canada Highway had been built, the old highway that passed the Wigstead place had led to a bridge upriver a bit that hopped several islands right over to the other side. The bridge wasn't there anymore, but the road was still called the Old Bridge Road. There was a barn up the road from Grandfather's house, near the highway, that had some writing on the side. "Pont d'Entente," it read in peeled and weather-beaten letters.

Molly thought it was sad that the bridge was gone. The great square stone pylons were still there, solid as ever, but they looked kind of stupid without something to hold up.

Mum had taken Molly upriver on the snowmobile, and they drove from pylon to pylon across the ice, just as if they were crossing over on a memory.

Keith was standing way out on the ice now. There was a wind out there blowing his shirttails around. He wouldn't wear a coat. That was fight number two with Uncle Don.

"Maybe your mother lets you walk around naked in sub-zero weather, but you'll wear a coat while you're up here."

It was as if the two of them were having their own private Wigstead tournament. Except that no one was winning.

Blossom sighed, content in some fire-warmed dream. But Molly was getting worried about Keith. The ice was thick, sure, but they had always been told how dangerous it was to be out too far on the river alone. There were fast currents where the ice only set thick enough to hold the weight of snow but was too thin to hold up the weight of a child, let alone a man. Every year there were accidents. And as if that weren't enough, even as Molly watched, the snowfall was turning to a mixture of snow and freezing rain.

There had been a freezing rain warning on the radio at lunch. Molly never really paid any attention to weather reports except when she was listening to see if school was cancelled. But the adults had been talking about the freezing rain warning because Estelle and Chet had driven up to town and weren't expected back until late in the afternoon. Taid Gareth immediately got into a grumpy mood about young people never being able to sit still for two minutes, and Charlotte had had to put him to bed for his nap as if he were a four-year-old.

Freezing rain. And Molly watched as her cousin—his shirt and long hair flying—disappeared before her eyes in the downpour. She ran for her mother.

Charlotte went out for Keith on the snowmobile. Molly stood with Trick at the window watching Charlotte manhandle the old Ski-Doo over the ice drifts at the river's edge, then gun the motor until she, too, was lost in the veils of wind-driven sleet.

Trick held Molly in his arms. "What's it like having Nanook of the North for a mother?"

He was trying to make Molly feel as though everything were all right. She played along. They watched and waited.

"Why doesn't Taid like the French?" Molly asked.

Her father laughed. "Oh, he's just one of those folks who doesn't like anyone except his own kind. He didn't much like me when your mother first brought me home."

Molly pulled away, astounded, and stared at her father. "Everybody likes you," she said.

Trick laughed again. "Gareth said your mother was making a big mistake marrying an Irishman. Said we were all frivolous drunks and not to be trusted."

"Did you bop him one?" asked Molly.

Trick shook his head. "No. I just told him what my father told me: that the Welsh were only Irishmen who couldn't swim."

Just then Uncle Don came into the study. He had retired to his bedroom for a nap. "Where is everyone?" he asked.

Trick told him, and Don went through the roof. "My son out in a blizzard! Why didn't someone call me!"

"You know Charlotte," said Trick calmly. "If there's a problem, your sister would rather solve it than think about it."

But Don had thrown down his magazine on a side table and soon could be heard slamming things around in the mud room as he got into his own snowmobile gear.

Molly looked anxiously at her father. "What if he crashes into Mum?"

Trick hugged her again. "Don was born on this river, too," he said.

As it turned out, Don only got as far as the riverbank before Charlotte's headlight beam could be seen heading back to shore through the downpour. Don waited there until he was sure she had Keith with him. Then he gunned his machine back up the hill to the garage and came stomping into the house. Trick met him at the door.

"It looks like everything's going to be okay," said Trick. He and Molly had their arms full of blankets.

Don scowled at his brother-in-law and headed upstairs to his bedroom. Trick called after him, "Don, for Pete's sake, the boy's learned his lesson."

Don stopped on the stairs. "I'm just getting changed," he said. But he didn't come down again.

So it was Uncle Trick who took Keith, numb and trembling, up to his room wrapped in blankets. He sat him on his bed while he ran the boy a bath. Molly made her mother sit beside the fire in the study. She put on water for tea. Blossom did his part. He flumped down on Charlotte's feet. Then Trick came down, and while the tea was brewing, he poured his wife a brandy. He poured himself one as well. He had a frown on his face.

"Is he okay?" Charlotte asked.

"Who?" said Trick. "Keith's fine. He's up to his ears in hot water. It's his father I'm worried about. He's in his room in a deep freeze."

It was Molly's idea to take Uncle Don a brandy. He was sitting in his bedroom by the window, staring out at the icy shower that beat against the glass. The glass was loose in its frame and wobbled with each new gust. He summoned up a smile for his niece, but his eyes were sad.

Taid Gareth was up when Molly arrived back downstairs. He was shaking his head. "The boy's changed," he said. "Surely you can see that."

"He's sixteen," said Charlotte. "Of course he's changed."

Then they were at it again. Molly slipped quietly away to her room, crawled under the covers, and lost herself in *The Phantom Tollbooth*. Things were pretty crazy in

Dictionopolis, but they seemed a lot more pleasant than on Old Bridge Road.

The rain stopped. Molly heard a creaking sound through the wall and realized that Keith was in his room.

She threw back the covers and made her way over to the bookshelf. This had been her mother's room. A lot of her old books were on the shelf. That was where she had found *The Phantom Tollbooth*. She knelt and looked through the books to see if there was anything a sixteen-year-old might find interesting.

She found something that looked boyish—written by a man, anyway—and before she could change her mind, she slipped out of her room and down the hall to Keith's door. She knocked. There was no reply. She knocked again.

"Enter," he said. His voice was brusque, wary.

He was in bed. He was already reading.

"What is it?" he said.

"I thought maybe you'd like a book," said Molly. "It's called *Heartsease*." She approached the bed.

Keith put down his own book and took the one she offered him.

"I think it's sort of science fiction," said Molly. While he thumbed through it, she glanced at the book on the bed-covers. "*Le dernier des raisins*," she read out loud.

He corrected her pronunciation. "It's for school," he said. Then he showed her something. "Look." In the front of *Heartsease* Nain Maeve had written, "To Donny bach, our darling bookworm, Xmas '70."

Molly examined the inscription. "Donny bach?"

She looked at Keith, who smirked. "Oh, Donny bach, you darling little bookworm," he said. Molly broke up.

She knew that bach meant "little one," if the little one was a boy. She was Molly fach, "little girl." She could remember when Keith had been Keith bach. But he was too big for that now.

Suddenly there was the noise of a car's horn outside, and Molly ran to the window just in time to see Estelle and Chet in his shiny new candy-apple red Honda turn off the Old Bridge Road, spin completely out of control in a lazy 360—right off the driveway—across the lawn and into Taid Gareth's potting shed.

The temperature had dropped fifteen degrees in less than two hours. Everything was coated with a shiny glaze of ice. The Trans-Canada was a skating rink.

The wreck of the potting shed claimed the lion's share of attention at dinner that evening. Which was unlucky for Chet, but lucky for Keith. His own misadventure on the river earned him only one derisive comment from Taid Gareth, who referred to the episode as Keith's "defection" to the other side, as if Keith were some kind of a traitor running back home to Quebec.

"If you'd drive a *real* car, Chet," said Taid Gareth.

"Oh, come on, Dad!" said Estelle.

"The Honda's a good road handler, Gareth," said Trick.

Gareth huffed. "You think a Jap fancy can handle this climate, do you?"

"Nothing can handle weather like this."

Gareth puffed. "But some good old-fashioned North American *heft* does tend to keep a vehicle on the road."

The grown-ups groaned in unison. Taid Gareth shook his head with showy dismay. "Didn't I teach you clowns anything?"

"You taught us a lot, Dad," said Don. "For one thing, you taught us not to head off across the river on foot alone in a storm."

Charlotte growled at her brother. "And obviously, Dad, you taught us to be *knuckleheaded*," she said, giving Don a withering look.

Keith sulked. Molly threw a pea at him to get his attention. Then she mouthed the words Donny, the darling bookworm, and his sulk thawed out a bit.

Unfortunately the pea did not go unnoticed. "Do not be impudent, young lady," said her mother.

It was that kind of family meal. Everyone pushing everyone else's buttons. Because Estelle and Chet had been late getting back, the roast was dry and the veggies were overdone. And Taid Gareth insisted on having the radio on so he could hear the weather updates. Christmas good cheer was getting stretched pretty thin.

At home Molly knew what to do in this kind of a situation. Ask politely to be excused, remember to carry your plate all the way to the sink—not just to the counter—then slip away to the rec room and watch TV with the volume down low. And tune in something halfway educational—definitely not *Wheel of Fortune!*—so that if Mum or Dad wandered by, they didn't have something new to start lecturing you about.

Unfortunately, Taid Gareth didn't have a TV, which was okay if folks were in a good mood. They could always play cards or Scrabble or, of course, the Tournament.

Molly grabbed Keith just as he was heading upstairs. "You want to play chess?"

He shook his head.

"You have to finish the tournament," she whispered urgently. "There's no way out of it."

He paused on the stairs. "Why isn't there?" he said. But this was a losing battle, and he knew it.

"This is the last round," said Molly. "In two days it's Christmas Eve. It has to be over by Christmas Eve."

Keith took a deep breath. The chess tournament had been Big Argument Number Three. He hated chess. Why should he have to play a game he hated? Because it's what we do, Don told him. It's a Wigstead tradition. Then Keith made the mistake of saying something about being only half a Wigstead, and Don went ballistic.

"I'll let you off easy," said Molly.

Keith grimaced. "If I beat you, nobody'd believe it."

Molly looked horrified. "I didn't mean I'd let you win!" she said. "What I mean is I'll destroy you real quick. So you can get back to your book."

Keith still looked dubious. Molly pleaded. "Don't leave me down here when everybody's being so adultish."

So Keith let her push him back to the study.

Molly set up the players. Behind her back, she hid a white pawn and a black pawn in each hand and then presented her fists to Keith for him to choose. He didn't bother picking. "Just give me black," he said.

Blossom waddled over and plunked himself down on Keith's feet. Blossom didn't play favourites. One set of feet was as good as another.

"I'm no good at this," said Keith as he moved his first pawn.

Molly moved her pawn quickly out to meet him. "I am," said Molly. "But I'll be merciful."

Keith moved another pawn. He looked behind him to see if anyone was hanging around the door. "Taid plays head games on me."

"Like what?" said Molly.

Keith frowned. "He was going on about some duck."

Molly was surprised. "He did that to me, too. And the oboe?"

"Yeah," said Keith. "He was driving me crazy."

Molly moved a piece. "Oh, well," she said, "he's just getting old."

Keith moved a piece. "No way. He was doing it on purpose."

Molly moved her knight out from behind the wall of pawns. She made the knight buck a couple of times, neighed out loud.

Keith stared at her knight. "You're going to laugh, but I never thought of those knights as being, you know, knights."

Molly picked her knight up off the board and held it out for Keith's inspection. "He's on horseback, Keith," she said, placing the figure back on the board. "What are you using for eyes these days, boy? Currants?" It was one of Taid Gareth's phrases. Keith pulled a face. "Sorry," said Molly.

"I think he pretends he's senile just to throw us off," said Keith.

Molly considered this idea while she contemplated her next move. She didn't want to believe that her grandfather's chatter was deliberately distracting, but she was pretty sure Keith was right. "So maybe I shouldn't neigh and stuff?" she said.

"Do whatever you want."

So, with a good couple of neighs, Molly galloped her knight right over Keith's pawn.

"*Maudit*," said Keith.

"Try a little bit," said Molly. "Please."

"Okay, okay. It's just that chess was always such a big deal at home. Dad wanting Mum and me to get into the game. We actually had fights about it."

"Yuck," said Molly. "No wonder you're so bad." She picked up her castle. "Taid beat me with just two castles today. But I learned something. They just look like castles. Actually, they're rooks, and that means warrior in some language or other."

Keith had moved another pawn. Now he took Molly's white rook from her and looked it over. "So it's a warrior dressed up like a castle so he can sneak up on you."

"Now you're getting the idea," said Molly. "You've got to think of the players as real people."

She took her knight, made him neigh a couple of more times, then jumped another of Keith's pawns. She made a strangling, death-rattle sound in her throat and made the pawn crawl off the board, where she committed him to Heaven.

"*Tabernacle*," murmured Keith. Molly stared at him until he looked up self-consciously. "What?"

"Nothing," said Molly, suddenly self-conscious herself.

She looked down at the board, made her move.

"Were you really heading home this afternoon?" she asked without looking up.

Keith looked down at the board. "Don't you start."

"Okay," she said. "I just wondered."

There was a silence while Keith tried to decide where to go next. "That may be Quebec over there, but it's a long, long way from Montreal," he said. He sounded homesick.

"What's it like living there?"

"The same as anywhere."

"It's on the news so much now. We even talked about it in school. About Quebec leaving Canada. Is that going to happen?"

Keith shrugged. He reached down and scruffled Blossom's neck. "Who knows?" he said. "I mean, Montreal's pretty *anglais* anyway. But when Taid says things like 'The only thing wrong with Quebec is the French'—jeez, it's so—"

"Senile?" said Molly.

"No, bigoted," said Keith.

"Is that like stupid?" Molly asked.

Keith smiled. Then his smile faded. Molly was taking one of his bishops. "Hey," he said, "you're just like Taid. Here you are grilling me about stuff, taking my mind off the game and killing me."

Molly smirked and buffed her fingernails on her sweater. It was fun beating adults as long as you were sure they weren't giving you the game. She was pretty sure Keith was playing his best, and that made her feel good. On the other hand, it wasn't much of a challenge.

She watched him bend down close to the board, try to concentrate. He was really trying. She wondered . . . The really big challenge would be to let Keith win without him suspecting her. She had never tried to lose before. Could she do it?

It was her move. She made a big point of looking studious. She moved. She began to see a way. She had to make herself open. Let Keith get to her queen. Without her queen, he just might be able to score. But he was on his guard. How could she persuade him he'd won fair and square?

She jumped on another of his pawns. That was it. Play hard around the edges with her knights, bishops and rooks as if she were out for blood. But while she was doing it, clear a path for him to her queen. It would look as if in her greediness, she had inadvertently left herself *wide* open.

She got down on her knees so that her eyes were right at board height. This was going to be exciting.

And she almost did it. She was within a couple of moves of losing when she messed up. Instinctively she moved a player out of a dicey situation and then, realizing what she was doing, moved it back right into a trap. When she looked up, Keith was staring at her, his eyes filled with resentment.

"Thanks so much," he said. "Now I really feel like one of the clan." Then he heaved himself out of his chair.

"Don't go!" said Molly. "I can still beat you if you want."

Keith rolled his eyes and headed for the door, where Taid Gareth appeared, drawn by Molly's cry.

"Leaving us again?" he said.

Keith shook his head in disgust, hurried by his grandfather, and stomped up the stairs.

Molly pouted.

Taid Gareth came and stared at the board through the smoke blooming out of his pipe. He raised a bushy grey eyebrow. "Such a hothead," he said. "And here he was winning!"

Now it was Molly's turn to leave, not in disgust but in despair and remorse for what she had done.

"What is happening to this family?" said Taid Gareth.

Molly slipped off to the kitchen to cut herself a slice of cake.

She turned off the lights in the kitchen and sat in the dark at the breakfast table in the little nook. The night was as black as the woodstove after Taid had put a fresh coat of polish on it. Steely black but pricked with holes where you could see the light of the fiery stars.

The moon was just a crescent, but it shone down on the hillsides, and there the light seemed to lose its balance on the slippery slopes and slide down onto the river. She looked out at the few blinking lights she could see on the Quebec side. What were those folks doing tonight? Playing chess? Arguing? Watching *Wheel of Fortune* in French?

With the moonlight throwing crumb shadows on her plate, Molly found herself thinking about Nain. Nain Maeve used to make angel food cake as light as moon dust.

When she was dying, the doctors gave her morphine to increase her tolerance to the pain. That struck Molly at the time. Because everyone always talked about how tolerant

Nain was just naturally, and Molly had thought that tolerance must be another word for full of life.

What they meant about Nain, Molly had come to learn, was that she put up with Taid Gareth's moodiness and narrow-mindedness.

She really wished Nain were around now.

Molly made her way upstairs. The lights were on in Keith's room. She thought of knocking but changed her mind. She went to her own room. At least she had *The Phantom Tollbooth* to keep her company.

But she didn't turn her light on right away. At home they lived in a suburb, and it was never really dark. She put on her nightgown by the thin, slippery moonlight. It was cool in the old house, but she took her time enjoying a moon-bath by the window. There were no other houses around, no one to see her.

Molly was the kind of person who spent a lot of time at windows. And that's why she was the only one in the Wigstead household who saw the second car accident of the day on the Old Bridge Road. A van inched its way down the long, slow-curving hill that passed the house. Suddenly it started wavering around and then, like Chet's car, lost control completely and ploughed deep into the snowbank. Molly watched as the driver tried to free himself, but his front tires spun hopelessly. His back end was in too deep.

The passenger door opened only a fraction, for the snow was up over the bottom of the door. The passenger heaved himself against the door but was unable to open it farther. Then the side door slid open and another man climbed out of the back and jumped down to the ground. The snow was up over his knees. Meanwhile, the front passenger clambered into the back so that he could climb out the sliding door as well. Molly could vaguely make out other figures in the van. The two men dug with their hands and then pushed for all they were worth, but they only managed to get the van stuck more deeply than before.

Molly watched as the driver joined the other two. Three shadowy men talked together, throwing their arms around, slip-sliding on the road. She watched them take notice of the Wigstead house, the only house for miles.

Molly searched for her bathrobe and slippers. Then she ran downstairs.

Already one of the men from the van was at the front door talking to Taid Gareth, or trying to. But nobody understood him. He was speaking French.

Charlotte invited the man to step inside. He was pointing up the road, but from the front door they could not see the van. Taid had thrown up his hands in despair, given up, and slipped to the back of the family crowding around the front door.

"Can't understand a damn word," he said.

That's when Molly stepped in. "Their van's stuck in the snowbank," she said.

The man may not have understood her, but he regarded her as if she had understood him. "*Pouvez-vous nous aider?*" He directed his question only to Molly. But she did not understand what he was saying.

"*Il nous faut aller tellement loin,*" he said. "*On a des nouveaux-nés dans l'auto—trois. Trois bébés. S'il vous plaît, si on pouvait avoir juste un coup de main.*"

He sounded so urgent. Molly's mind was racing. She saw her grandfather shake his head. He had an annoyed look on his face.

"Damn frogs. Always after something," he muttered.

Molly felt her face get hot all over. She stamped her foot. "Don't say that!" she said to her grandfather so sharply that he actually jumped.

"*Un moment!*" she said to the stranger. Then she raced upstairs to Keith's room. She burst through the door without knocking. He was propped up in bed, writing.

Keith looked frightened. "What's wrong?"

Molly tried to catch her breath. "There's a man at the door. He's had an accident. He's French. He can't speak a word of English."

"So?"

"So none of us can speak any French. Only you."

"I can't speak French," he said.

"Yes, you can. You were speaking French when we were playing chess."

"Just swear words."

"And the book," she said. "The one with raisins in the title. Please, Keith. I think there's something really wrong."

Keith looked down. By then Molly had come to his bedside, and—too late—he tried to hide what he had been writing. She grabbed it before he could stop her.

"Hey!" he said.

It was a letter to someone named Annette. *Chère Annette*.

"This is *written* in French!" cried Molly triumphantly. She waved the letter in Keith's face. She took his hand. "Oh, please, Keith," she said. "Try, at least. Taid is being a complete crumb-bum fart."

By the time they reached the door, the man had left. So had Trick, Don and Chet, with flashlights and shovels. Molly was disappointed, but then Charlotte told her that as far as she could make out, there were others in the car— children, maybe—and the men had gone to bring them to the house while they dug out the van.

Molly watched the men helping three women cross the treacherous expanse of shining roadway. Each of the women held an infant tightly in her arms.

"Oh, my God," said Charlotte as she helped them enter the front door. "*Entrez*," she said, smiling at the women. "*Entrez*."

How tired the women looked. There was a weariness etched deeply into their faces, as if they hadn't slept for days. Estelle and Charlotte led them into the front room. Two of the babies were crying. Taid Gareth took himself off to his study and closed the door after him.

The mothers sat and immediately attended to their children. Newborns they were. Molly got as close as she could. The babies were Chinese-looking. The mothers weren't, but all the babies—one, two, three—were Chinese. And if the clothes were anything to go by, they were all girls.

She looked quizzically at her mother and Estelle, and finally at Keith, who had not yet said a word. He was staring at the three babies.

The women talked very quietly among themselves. Perhaps they'd already been told that there was no one here who could talk to them. Every now and then one of them would look up and smile wearily and say, "*Merci. Merci bien.*"

Despite the cold, the front door had been left open. Everyone had been too busy shepherding in the mothers to bother with it. Now Molly was sent to close it. Walking out onto the porch, she could see the men working, making men noises as they each directed who was to do what, where, when and for how long. She heard them all, French and English, and from where she stood, the words were mostly indistinct: the sound of six men digging a van out of a snowbank. She reentered the house shivering and closed the door.

When she joined the women and Keith in the front room, one of the women was changing her tiny Chinese baby on the floor. She was digging out diapers, Vaseline and Baby Wipes from a fat pink change bag. She looked up suddenly and without thinking spoke.

"*Est-ce que j'pourrais avoir de l'eau chaude, s'il vous plaît,*" she said. Then she said, "Oh," as she realized they could not understand. "*Excusez-moi.*"

Molly poked Keith in the side. "Go on," she whispered.

"*De l'eau chaude?*" said Keith. "*Bien sûr. Avez-vous besoin d'autre chose?*"

All the women in the room stared at Keith with happy amazement. Molly glowed with pride.

"They need some hot water," Keith said to Estelle.

"Ask them why the babies are Chinese," whispered Molly.

"Shush," he said to her. "Mind your own business."

Then he perched on the edge of a chair and talked to the three mothers. Haltingly sometimes. Sometimes he had to worry the meaning out of a phrase in order to grasp what they were saying. Or they did not quite understand him. Yet they managed. It was obvious there was a lot to say.

At one point Molly noticed that Keith seemed worried. He said *non* a lot and shook his head. He pointed down the road and then back towards the highway, the direction from which they had come. The women grew more and more unhappy.

"What's going on?" Molly asked.

Keith combed his fingers through his long hair. "They think they can cross the river at the Pont d'Entente."

"It's not there anymore!" said Molly.

"That's what I told them," said Keith.

Molly looked at one of the women. Her face appeared to crumble, as if she'd been holding it together for too long and the news about the bridge had been too much. She wept, and the other women comforted her.

Then the men came back. They all were smiling and laughing. They had dug out the van, and Don had even found a couple of concrete blocks to put in the back for extra traction.

"I'm just going to brew up some coffee for them," said Trick, red-cheeked from a good workout in the cold. Then they noticed the looks of desolation on the faces of the women.

"*Quoi?*" said one of the men.

Keith explained. "*L'enseigne sur le bâtiment, c'est pas correct. 'Y a plus de pont là-bas. Pas depuis qu'ils ont construit le Trans-Canada.*"

He spoke nervously, glancing up at his father from time to time. Don looked at him with frank amazement.

Charlotte put her arm around her brother's shoulder. "Pretty impressive, eh?"

Hesitantly, Don nodded.

Keith continued then, with more assurance. Bit by bit things were sorted out. Keith translated back and forth.

Trick brought everybody coffee and leftover cake from dinner. Then, when it was determined that the three families could not possibly get back on the road that night, Trick went and got the brandy, and those who wanted had a dram together.

Finally, Taid put in an appearance, looking every bit the master of the house. Blossom was with him. He barked at the excitement, and that made all the babies cry. Molly shushed Blossom up and stroked his fluffy head.

Charlotte took her father aside, led him into the hallway, where the others couldn't hear. But Molly sidled nearby.

"They have to stay," said Charlotte.

"Absolutely not," she heard her grandfather say. "I thought these people wanted their own country. So why should they expect hospitality in mine?"

Molly watched Charlotte with fear and wonder. Her mother did not speak loudly, but she spoke very plainly. "This may be your house, Father. It is also my house, the house I grew up in. There has been a major collision on the Trans-Canada. The police have blocked it off indefinitely. Our guests cannot go north. If they turn around and go south, there isn't a place to stay for miles, assuming they could make it on these roads. I hate to put it this way, but they are leaving this house over my dead body."

Taid Gareth looked daggers at Charlotte, as if maybe her dead body were a possibility. He seemed just about to bluster at her when Molly jumped between them. "I wonder what Nain would have done, Taid," she said. Her grandfather closed his parched old lips tightly. He looked from Molly to her mother and back. There was a betrayed look in his eye.

Then one of the new fathers—Christian, his name was—entered the hall. He seemed to understand what was going on. "*Si ça vous dérange, on peut trouver quelqu'un d'autre. Vous avez déjà fait beaucoup.*"

Keith appeared behind him in the hallway. He looked squarely at his grandfather. "Christian here says if it's, like, a hassle, they'll go. He says you've been really helpful."

Molly watched Taid Gareth's gizzardy throat swallow a couple of times. Then the old man left them there and returned to his study. As he passed her by, Molly could not believe how frail he looked.

Christian, meanwhile, had begun to collect the others together to leave. Keith stopped them. "*Non! Non! Ça va. Vous êtes bienvenue.*

"*Vraiment?*"

"*Oui, vraiment. Le vieux, y'est juste un peu . . . b'en, vous savez les vieux . . .*"

Christian smiled, a weary smile. "*Oui, oui.*"

Then Molly saw a smirk spread across Keith's face. "*Le problème du Canada, c'est les Canadiens.*"

All of the guests laughed, and Christian slapped Keith happily on the back. The travellers agreed to stay the night.

"What did you tell them just now?" said Don to Keith. "What made them laugh so much?"

Keith looked around at his family and took a deep breath. "I told them that the only thing wrong with Canada was the Canadians."

Beds were found for everyone. Cradles were improvised in a chest of drawers, an old radio battery chest, and a dog basket that Blossom had refused ever to sleep in. The grown-ups gave up their rooms to their guests. The Wigsteads decided to camp in the living room.

The guests were exhausted and, with many thanks, retired as soon as they could. The babies would need feeding in the night. Although Molly still had a room to go to, she wasn't going to miss the camp-out for anything. So they all ended up lounging on sleeping bags and lumpy extra pillows and ragged old army blankets. Keith tried to escape to the privacy of his own room but could not go until he had told the story of the Chinese babies.

"Wait," said Don. "I want to hear this, we all want to hear this! But first, tell us about you."

"What's to know?" said Keith. He looked tired, as if he sensed a trap.

"You haven't been in Montreal all that long," said Don, "and you're bilingual. It's . . . I don't know . . . great."

Seeing Keith's face up close, Molly saw the blush even if no one else did.

"Annette!" she said. The secret was out before she could check herself.

Keith gave Molly a pinch for having such a big mouth.

"I have a girlfriend." He shrugged.

"Say no more," said Trick. And everybody laughed.

Then Don said, "Will you introduce me to her if I can get up there sometime?" After only a moment's hesitation, Keith said he would.

He proceeded to tell his family about the Chinese babies. There had been thirty couples from Quebec who had adopted newborn Chinese babies, all girls. Girls were the only thing going. The Quebeckers had flown to China to pick up their children. Christian and his friends had been on the last flight back. They had been flying for more than twenty-four hours.

"Wow!" said Charlotte. "That's a longer delivery than I had with you, Molly."

The couples had to land in Ottawa because of icy conditions in Montreal. Their flight to Rouyn would not be taking off until the following day. Christian and his friends were desperate to get home for Christmas. So they rented the van, thinking they could beat the storm. When the police blocked the Trans-Canada, they drove back to where one of them had noticed the old highway. They saw the sign saying Pont d'Entente and thought they may have found a quick way over to Quebec. They had no idea that the Old Bridge Road went nowhere anymore.

"They would have been stranded," said Trick.

"If it hadn't been for Keith," said Molly. Keith pinched her again. Finally the remaining campers rolled over and tried to get snug. There was a lot of groaning and giggles and shoving. Molly lay in the dark, thinking how amazing it was that adults still knew how to have a sleep-over.

Things eventually quieted down as people drifted off to sleep. And Molly's thoughts drifted to the Chinese babies. She even heard one of them wake up for her bottle. How far they had come to find a home.

There were a few odd stuffed toys in her bedroom. She wondered if her mum would let her give one to each of them. Their first-ever Christmas presents.

She slept, and then she woke up. It was still night. She had heard something, a slip, slip, slip sound. It was Taid making his way to the kitchen.

Molly climbed out of her sleeping bag and tiptoed after him. From the kitchen doorway she saw him at the sink getting himself a glass of water. He was taking one of his pills.

"Are you all right, Taid?" she asked.

"Molly fach," he whispered. "What are you doing up?"

She followed him back to the study. There were embers in the fireplace. Taid sat in his La-Z-Boy. Molly sat, too, and they stared sleepily at the dying fire. Taid had a blanket. She didn't think he had gone to bed yet.

"Now you're mad at Keith," she said sadly.

"What makes you say that?"

"Because he can speak French. If he hadn't been able to speak French, the people would have left. You must hate him."

There was a long silence. Molly watched her grandfather's face for a sign. Was he angry at her now? Only the embers of the fire lit up his expression.

"You must think me a very wicked man," he said.

"No," said Molly. "Well, maybe at chess."

There. He smiled.

"I've never hated Keith, child," he said. "But I don't like to see Donald unhappy. He was a moody boy himself. Nain and I worried about him so. Well, I still do. He is still my boy, you see."

"Your Donny bach."

"Yes. My Donny bach."

They sat in silence again. Molly had curled up tight, but she felt cold. She longed for her bed, not the hard floor of the living room. The party was over in there. She found herself thinking how deliciously cool her sheets would be and how she would have to shiver herself warm. She shivered now. Then she slid out of her armchair and gave her grandfather a kiss on his stubbly cheek.

"I think Don is pretty proud of Keith," she said.

"Yes?" said Taid. "Well, that's good then."

Molly was the last to wake up. The sun was blasting through her bedroom window. She made her way downstairs to where family and guests were congregated in the huge dining room. A very big breakfast lay in waste there, and Keith was busy translating the many questions everyone seemed to have. The Wigsteads were practising their school French. It was coming back to them with comical results. The guests practised their English. There was some laughter and some teasing, and everyone took a turn holding the babies.

It was still freezing outside, but according to the radio, the Trans-Canada was clear and sanded. It looked as if the Chinese babies would make it home to Rouyn in time for their very first Christmas after all.

Taid was missing from the gathering in the dining room. Molly went looking for him. She was surprised to find him in the study sitting across the game table from Christian.

They were playing chess. Blossom thumped his tail hard on the floor when he saw Molly enter the room. He was sprawled over Christian's feet. Christian hardly seemed to notice. He was intent upon his game.

Taid seemed a bit flustered. It was soon obvious to Molly why. Christian was good.

"You should tell him about the duck, Taid Gareth," said Molly, pulling up a stool. "And why you like oboes so much." She giggled. That did not please her grandfather.

"You know the rules about audience members in the study."

"But this isn't the tournament," said Molly. Taid harrumphed, then leaned back, tapping the arm of his chair in a bothered kind of way.

Despite his inability to distract his opponent, he was playing a good game. He had a confident look on his face. Molly checked the board. Taid Gareth's bishop was poised for a lethal attack. Two moves, and he would have Christian cornered.

Last night it had been too difficult for Molly to remember any of what little French she had learned yet in school. But now she could remember some. She had a plan. She would touch Gareth's bishop on the head and ask Christian what the French word was for it. Once he looked at the piece, maybe he would see the danger he was in. She rehearsed the words in her mind. *"Comment appelez-vous cela?"* Her hand stretched out across the board, but before she was even near the bishop, Christian gently brushed her hand out of the way.

"Non, non!" he said.

Obediently Molly put her hands in her lap. She glanced at Taid, whose furry eyebrows were low over his eyes.

"Whatever were you thinking, Molly fach?" he said. But there was a glimmer in his eyes that was far from senile.

"Le—how you say?—game," said Christian, "must be fair, *non?"*

He looked from Molly to her grandfather. They both nodded.

Christian folded his hands in front of his face as if in prayer, and he looked hard at the board. Then he looked at Molly again with a playful glint in his eye and wagged his finger, mock scolding her.

Molly looked at her grandfather. He was smiling. "She's a little vixen, Monsieur Christian," he said.

"Ah!" said Christian, though it did not seem that he had understood what a vixen might be. For that matter, Molly didn't know herself.

He returned his gaze to the board and made a good move. The bishop—for the moment—was stalled.

Taid Gareth cursed under his breath in Welsh, but there was no force behind it. He pretended to bop Molly on the top of her head with his pipe.

Christian laughed, pointing at her but directing his question at her grandfather. "*Vous devez être bien fier d'elle?*"

"Oh, God," muttered Taid. "What's he going on about now?"

Christian searched his mind. "Uh, pride? *Elle est bien, non?*"

"Ah," said Taid Gareth, comprehension flowering on his face. "Am I proud of you, Molly?"

She nodded and moved beside him, where he could slip his arm around her.

"You were going to give me away, weren't you, you little traitor?" he mumbled in a gruff voice that didn't scare her one bit.

She very carefully buttoned up his lip.

The game was declared a draw. It was too close, the competitors too equally matched. Besides, the new parents were anxious to get back on the road.

There were many hugs and handshakes and promises at the door. Gareth stood well back from the commotion, but Christian came to him and shook his hand solemnly. He spoke to him at length, urging Keith to translate for him.

"He said, if your car should break down on some cold winter night in Rouyn, you will always be welcome in his home, where he will gladly beat the pants off you in chess."

Gareth had to laugh.

"What do you think?" said Molly.

Gareth thought a moment. Then he said, "*Dyna Beth sydd iti wybod: bydd yn agored.*"

No one knew what he meant. Don, who was the oldest, said, "It's Welsh, but I couldn't make it out."

"Molly will tell you," said Taid Gareth.

Molly looked wide-eyed at him.

"It's what I warned you about the other day, when we were playing," said her grandfather.

She whispered it in Keith's ear, and Keith translated it into French for the departing guests. They smiled and clapped. One of the mothers kissed Gareth on both cheeks, French style.

"What does it mean?" Don asked his son when the guests had driven off and the Wigsteads were alone again.

But Keith was tired of translating, so he left it up to Molly to explain.

"Here's what we need to know," she said. "Be open."

Sisters

by

Sarah Ellis

This story about two missing sisters is one in a collection called Back of Beyond, *stories that investigate what lies behind the ordinary events of our lives—secrets, history, ghosts and the stories we invent to console ourselves.*

Mrs. Fenner's funeral was on the first day of spring. It was windy. The sky was a map of islands, grey and white, on a sea of washed-out blue. The islands dissolved and merged, continental drift in fast forward.

At the cemetery I stared hard at the clouds. I looked up to keep from looking at the ground, into the ground. Most of the words the minister said were cloud-words. Mercy, hope, peace—thin words whipped away by the wind. And a few earth-words. Ashes, blood, bread, grass. The grass at the cemetery was still yellow-dry from winter. The grave was a bright green box lined with Astroturf. Mrs. Fenner was the first person I knew who died. I think.

Afterwards I went home with Miss Poole and helped pass sandwiches. The guests were the minister, Mrs. Fenner's businessman son Robert, who flew in from Toronto, and some friends who live in Mrs. Fenner and Miss Poole's building. The sandwiches were ham or egg salad. Then there were butter tarts and ginger cookies. Mrs. Sutherland from 604 brought a pan of fudge squares. There was tea and sherry.

Robert Fenner poured out the sherry from a decanter shaped like a Scotsman with bow legs and a bright yellow and red kilt. His tartan tam was the stopper. Mrs. Fenner had made the decanter when she took up ceramics. She had also made frogs to hold hand soap and ceramic potatoes to hold sour cream. People talked a lot about all the things she had made. The things she had left behind. Then they all went away.

I should explain about Mrs. Fenner and Miss Poole. They are my foster grandmothers. I got them the year my sister Sophie ran away the first time. Mum and Dad thought I should have foster grandparents because my real ones live in Florida and France. They thought we needed more people in our family.

The foster-grandparent organizers sent us to meet three regular grandfather/grandmother pairs. One pair had a dog who liked me. One had a cottage in the mountains.

"We could take you there in the summer if you'd like that, Charlotte." One had a lot of computer games. But I didn't want any of them to be my grandparents. When Mum asked me why, I said, "They look at me too hard." I was only nine. I didn't know how to say that they had a kind of hungry look, that they made me feel like a rent-a-kid.

And then we met Mrs. Fenner and Miss Poole, two sisters. The first time we visited them we all sat at the kitchen table with old magazines, scissors, glue and cardboard ice-cream buckets. Mrs. Fenner was into decoupage that year. The sisters talked to each other and to Mum. The words floated over my head as I cut and pasted. "I think young Charlotte has remarkable colour sense," Miss Poole said to Mrs. Fenner. Their fat cat Ditto jumped onto the table and overturned the glue. Miss Poole held him close to her face and growled at him. Mrs. Fenner showed me how to pick up tiny bits of paper by licking the end of my finger. We had tea and the afternoon disappeared.

On the way home, hugging my decorated wastepaper basket, I told Mum that Mrs. Fenner and Miss Poole were my choice.

From then on I went over to their apartment lots of days after school. Sometimes the grans took me out. Fridays we went to early-bird bingo at the Catholic hall. Mrs. Fenner played eight cards at once and was calm even when she won. Miss Poole sat on the edge of her chair, talked to the numbers on her card and made mistakes.

The lady who gave out the bingo prizes was young and pretty, with red hair like Sophie. Sometimes I used to pretend she *was* Sophie and that one day she would peer down from the stage through the smoke and recognize me, her little sister. "Charlotte! Is that you?" Then she would come home with us for good, bringing all the bingo prizes. We would get on the bus carrying lamps and cookware sets and embroidered pillow cases and we would all laugh. I had strange ideas when I was nine and ten.

We stopped going to bingo when Mrs. Fenner's leg got bad. Mostly we just stayed in. I would sit at the kitchen table and make sand-cast candles or macramé belts and listen to them talk. The grans came from a village in England and they remembered all the people there. I got to know them, too. Addie's Harold, who was a right terror until they gave him a ferret to care for. "Mind you, it did take one aback when that little ferret face would peek out of his shirt." Stanley who ran in the Empire Games. "It was a miracle. To think of him being that poor weak baby. Ada had to carry him around on a pillow with his little legs dangling over." And Jeannie who went off to London to become a dancer. "Aunt Effie went to see her, a surprise like, and they put her at a table right near the front and when Jeannie came out she didn't have a stitch on, just a few of them feathers. Well, Eff just didn't know where to look. Mind, she never told Jean's mum, it would have killed her."

When I got older Mum thought I went to visit the grans because I was being good. "It's so kind of you to go and see them," she said.

Kind had nothing to do with it. I went there to escape the silence that was our house. I went there for the words. And for the people.

I went there for Addie's Harold and Stanley and feath-
ered Jeannie. I went there for mild Alf Minkin, who wouldn't
say boo to a goose and then one day upped and pelted the
grocer's van with two dozen eggs. For beautiful Emily,
known as Pigeon, who fell in love five times in one year and
threw herself down the well for the sixth. For Jack, who
revealed his true nature that night in the badger blind and
had to emigrate. For Alice, the grans' older sister, who went a
bit wild and ran off when she was a teenager. "And she
landed on her feet, didn't she, Ida? I expect young Sophie
will be just the same."

The grans talked about Sophie, even though they had
never met her. I couldn't talk about her. Her name stuck
in my throat.

But I didn't have to talk at the grans'. It was a place for
listening. Best of all was listening to Miss Poole's stories
of dead people. Car-accident victims who haunt certain
highways, dead husbands who leave messages in the
melting snow, indelible stains—"And they scrubbed and
scrubbed but the kitchen floor would never come clean.
Then one day they found an old scrapbook in the attic,
filled with yellowing newspaper clippings. And there was
the story, the grisly murder that had taken place years
before, in that very house, in that very kitchen."

"Hush up, Ida, you're just flapping your tongue," Mrs.
Fenner would sometimes say when she remembered that I
was a child and might be scared. Miss Poole never thought
of that. I knew that she didn't think of me as a child. Just
the way she didn't think of Ditto as a cat. She just talked.

To people, animals, the radio, the kettle and the bunions on her feet. Anyway, I wasn't scared. Those were my favourite stories.

I continued to visit the grans because their apartment was full of people. They crowded onto the sofa, hung around the doorways, leaned against the fridge, sat on the floor hugging their knees to fit. There were babies on the bed with the coats, and little kids hiding under the table. People jostling, elbowing, stepping on the cat by mistake and talking, talking, talking. Noisy ghosts.

We have a ghost in our house, too. A silent ghost. The ghost of Sophie who came home once, twice, and never again, who last phoned five years ago. She floats around the house like a piece of empty air. They used to talk about her. They used to argue. Once I heard Dad yelling, "She's gone, Trish. Accept it." But now the Sophie-ghost has silenced even my parents, who never mention her.

Last Christmas, when I was helping Dad unpack the tree ornaments, he pulled out Sophie's stocking. He stared at it for a minute. I wanted to say something, something like, "I expect she landed on her feet." But the words couldn't push through the silence. Dad just packed the stocking back into the box and went outside to put up the lights. I think he forgot I was there. Sophie settles like fog on Christmas and birthdays and memories.

No, I'm not a citizen-of-the-week teenager visiting the elderly. I go to the grans to keep from dissolving into a ghost myself.

· · ·

After everyone left I stayed to help Miss Poole tidy up. We took a few dirty dishes into the kitchen and then Miss Poole said, "Leave this for a minute. Come sit down." I was surprised. Miss Poole likes to get jobs over and done with. And sitting is not her style. She is always jumping up to make tea or adjust the radio or water the African violets.

She perched on the edge of her chair. Ditto did a figure-of-eight around her feet. I glanced sideways quickly at Mrs. Fenner's armchair, the big one, hoping to catch someone in it. Mrs. Fenner or someone else.

It was empty.

Miss Poole beat a little drum roll on her knees, reached into a patchwork pocket that hung over the arm of the chair and pulled out an envelope.

"Muriel left me a letter. I haven't told anyone about it yet, except Ditto. Didn't fancy discussing it with Robert, some-how. He's not much of a one for talk about the old days."

There was a large waiting feeling in the air.

"She wasn't my sister."

What?

"She was my aunt."

"Your aunt?" I couldn't figure it out. I've never been good at all that relative stuff, cousins once removed and all that.

Miss Poole gave the letter a sharp slap with the back of her hand.

"It's all there. Alice was my mother."

Alice. The other sister. Alice who was no better than she should be. Twice-divorced Alice who finally took off for

America with a weedy little man who told her he was rich and, surprise of surprises, was. Alice who lived out her final days "eaten up with the cancer she was" in New Mexico on a hacienda or some such thing.

"You mean Alice who ran away?"

"The very one. Old toffee-nosed Alice." Miss Poole snorted. "She had me when she was fifteen. So the whole family upped and moved and when they got to the next place they just let on I was the new baby in the family. Mum took me on, just like she took on Uncle Harry when he started having his turns. And then Muriel and Mr. Fenner took me on when they came here to Canada. Isn't that a turn-up for the books?"

I was still having trouble with the generations. "So who was your mum?"

"Alice."

"No, I mean the one you call Mum."

"Well, she was really my grandmother. Look, come here." Miss Poole scribbled a diagram on the envelope. "Here's Mum. Two little lines down, that's Muriel and Alice, and from Alice one little line down to me."

"They never told you this?"

"It was the shame of it. With Dad being a church warden and all. And perhaps they thought it would give me a bad feeling about myself. One of those traumas they discuss on those television talk shows."

"And you never knew till now?"

Miss Poole leaned back in her chair a little and Ditto jumped into her lap. "Is there another cup in that pot?"

I poured out some thick-looking tea and handed it to her. "It's not very hot."

"But nice and strong. Just the way I like it." Miss Poole stared out the window for a minute. "The thing of it is, I did know. Not to say anything. And not the real truth. But I knew that I didn't match. All those Pooles. They were so big and calm. They kind of just set where you put them. But I was little and I couldn't sit still."

"Hyperactive?"

"Is that what they call it now? They wouldn't have me in school. I wouldn't stay in the desk. And meals. Father couldn't stand the fidgeting. Mostly I ate my dinner sitting on the step. The other thing was I was the wrong colour. Too brown. All those pink blond people. Neighbours would comment on it and Mum used to say, 'That Ida, she does take the sun so.' Come to think of it now, I suppose I took after my father. Whoever he was when he was at home."

Miss Poole took a gulp of tea and looked at the letter again.

"I'm not denying that it is a bit of a shock, though. Perhaps not quite in the way that Muriel expected. The biggest thing is . . ." Miss Poole looked at me and grinned, "You'll be thinking I'm a dafty."

"No, I won't. What?"

"I always thought I was a fairy."

"What, with wings?"

"No, not that kind. A changeling. You don't know about them? You with all your algebra and computers?" Miss Poole leaned over and punched me on the arm.

"Fairies want human children, so they steal them away and leave their own babies, changelings, in their place. It made perfect sense to me. Changelings are dark. I was dark. Changelings cry a lot. Mother told me what a difficult baby I had been, crying and grizzling and never sleeping through the night. I just tucked these things away in my head."

I thought of a little girl sitting on the stairs eating her dinner and thinking she was some weird kind of fairy. It made me want to hug Miss Poole. But she's not a hugger.

"Did you think you were a fairy even when you grew up?"

"Well, I did and I didn't. Things got very busy when we emigrated, what with keeping the house going and taking care of Robert while Muriel and Mr. Fenner went out to work. I didn't think about it that much, to tell you the truth. But I had it all tucked away. And sometimes . . . like, one time we had this boarder. We were having a hard time making ends meet and we took in boarders. And there was this one called Merv Butt and he was a great one for making beer. He tried to make beer out of everything. He even boiled down our Christmas tree that year to try to make spruce beer. And here I was, a great grown-up girl, as old as you, and I still thought that was proof."

"Proof. I don't get it?"

"Because of trying to fool the changeling. Sometimes people could get their own babies back by tricking the changeling into revealing herself. They would act silly to try to get the changeling to speak. Like in one story the people boil water in an eggshell and the changeling baby sits up in the cradle and says, 'I never in all my life saw water boiled in an eggshell.' And then the changeling has to leave. So I thought that making beer out of a Christmas tree was the same thing. I was very careful never to act surprised."

"It sounds a bit lonely."

Miss Poole shook her head. "It wasn't that way. It made me feel strong. Magic, immortal, all those good fairy things. And it explained things. Anyway, people do that all the time. Make themselves up. I mean, look at those movie stars. They take them out to Hollywood and glam them up and give them new names and make them famous. But I did it all by myself."

Miss Poole looked over at Mrs. Fenner's chair. "She was very good to me, was Muriel. Very good."

She absently pulled Ditto's ears. He broke into a loud, rasping purr. "Who's my favourite boy?"

Then she suddenly sat forward, dumping Ditto. "Did we ever tell you about the time Muriel bought that goat at the fall fair? Well, you know how Muriel was not what you'd call a small woman? It seems that this goat . . ."

The phone rang. "Bother, that will be Olivia. I'll get it in the bedroom."

Olivia was Robert's wife. According to the grans if you put your drink next to her it would stay cold all evening.

I picked up some dirty dishes, took them into the kitchen and piled them by the sink. I looked out the window. The clouds parted and the sun angled into the room, throwing a shadow of the frog soap-dish onto the fridge.

I sent my mind out to the cemetery where Mrs. Fenner was. The trees and the tombstones would be making long shadows. I held up two fingers and gave the frog antennae. Ditto leaned against my leg and I thought about the different kinds of gone. I wondered about Mrs. Fenner and the goat. I thought about remembering, naming and telling.

Miss Poole bustled into the kitchen and made a horrible face. "She wants me to come and visit for Christmas. Very kind and all but I can't imagine anything more dismal. I'm thinking that I had better make some plans to protect myself. There's a seniors' bus trip to Edmonton before Christmas. The West Edmonton Mall, now that's something I'd like to see before I turn up my toes."

I held my hands in the sunlight and made a butterfly flutter across the fridge.

Miss Poole smiled. "That's lovely."

My sister. I wanted to say her name, to have it exist in the room, in the light and the shadows.

"Sophie taught me. She was really good at shadows because she was sort of double-jointed. She could bend her thumbs right back and gross people out."

"Oh, I know that feeling. There was a boy in the village, the youngest Crank boy, Sid. He could practically turn himself inside out. Made you sick to look at him, but you *did* look, all the same."

I suddenly remembered Sophie and me in a tent at night. I was holding the flashlight and Sophie was making huge looming shadows on the canvas walls. The terror was delicious.

I stuck my fingers out at odd angles and created another shadow. "Do you know what this is?"

"Haven't a clue."

"It's Blob-Dog, Guardian of the Underworld. He was one of Sophie's best ones. The other good one was Angel-Lips, High School Queen."

Miss Fenner grinned. "That Sophie sounds a right caution."

A right caution. I wasn't really sure what it meant, but it had a Sophie-feeling about it. Did I ever tell you about my sister? She was a *right caution.*

Miss Poole picked up a pink rosebud teacup. It was smeared with chocolate where the fudge square had melted against it. "That always happens when you have chocolate things at a tea. Seems like such a waste. I'll tell you a secret. After Muriel got beyond helping in the kitchen, I invented my own method of clean-up. Very sensible it is, too."

Miss Poole held the cup up to her mouth, stuck out her tongue and licked it clean. She handed me a cup. "Try it. This is likely the way fairies wash up."

My cup was forest green with a thin gold band. The chocolate was rich and the china was cool and both were smooth, smooth under smooth. We licked the cups clean like a pair of cats, and from the living room came a quiet hum of stories, cloud-words and earth-words, the voices of the not-gone.

from

Julie

by

Cora Taylor

"Julie had been different from the beginning." What is this difference? She sees things that other people do not see—sailing ships on prairie wheatfields, dancers in the falling leaves and events long past or still to come. Julie's family is mystified. Only their neighbour, Granny Goderich, seems to understand Julie's gift.

The geraniums stood two deep on the window sills. They crowded the stands in front of the windows, spilled onto the sewing machine, and covered an old trunk in the front hall of Granny Goderich's house. Their musty, dusty odour filled the room. The smell caught in Julie's nose just as the dust caught in the fuzzy geranium leaves.

Julie sat very still watching the winter sun glint off
Granny Goderich's glasses making her look as if she had
large, shining eyes. Even Granny Goderich smelled of geraniums. She wore a fuzzy green flannel dress the colour of
geranium leaves.

"So this is your sweet wee changeling child, Alice."

Alice Morgan set her teacup down with a clatter. She visited the old Goderich home only once a year—the old lady
made her nervous. If there was trouble at home, money
problems or even a tiff with Will, Granny Goderich always
seemed to sense it and ask a question Alice didn't want to
answer. She'd chosen to come today because things were
going well and she'd felt . . . well . . . safe. Not that Granny
Goderich was unkind or a gossip—she kept the things she
learned to herself—it was just that Alice didn't like talking
about problems too much. It made them grow, she thought.

"How old are you now, Julie?"

"Four," said Julie looking straight at the shining eyes.
"Almost five."

"The last one at home," Alice broke in. "It seems strange
not having a flock of them around. Of course the minute
the school bus comes it's bedlam." She laughed, wishing her
voice didn't sound so shrill, her laugh so nervous.

Granny Goderich sighed. "It's always special with the last
little bird that leaves the nest. I remember my George . . ."
The old woman's voice trailed off and she stirred her tea in
sad silence.

Julie moved over to stand in front of the old sideboard.
It was cluttered with interesting old dishes and ornaments.

A pink china lady whose china skirt whipped daringly about her ankles, blown by some invisible wind, stood on the bracket right by Julie's nose but she stared instead at a squat purple jar on the topmost shelf of the sideboard. On either side of the jar were pottery dogs: scotties, cocker spaniels, a Saint Bernard with a cask around its neck, a liver-coloured retriever with Souvenir of Saskatoon written on it in white letters, a dalmatian with one leg missing; and a poorly carved wooden puppy; but Julie looked only at the jar.

Alice felt uncomfortable. The loss of George Goderich had been the one sorrow the old lady had never been able to overcome. George was nine years old when he had been killed in a train accident while visiting hls grandparents in eastern Canada.

"I didn't want him to go, you know. I told my husband not to take him on that trip." Her voice was almost keening. "I knew he shouldn't go, but I didn't insist. I was too weak. I let him go."

The silence hung awkwardly in the room. More to break it than as a remonstrance, for Julie was a well-behaved child, Alice said, "Don't touch anything, dear."

Julie was still standing staring at the purple jar. Her hands were behind her back, not touching anything. Her mother noticed with a start that Julie's face was wet with tears.

"Why, Julie, whatever is wrong?"

Julie didn't answer, instead Granny Goderich answered for her. "She sees George's ashes, don't you dear?" The grey head turned slowly. "Alice, did you know Julie was a sensitive child?"

It was one of those questions Alice did not want to answer. She knew what Granny Goderich meant by "sensitive." It was not what most people meant. Her mind was still coping with the fact that here, in this living room, amongst the bric-a-brac on the sideboard, this lonely old woman kept the ashes of a son who had died over fifty years ago. And nobody knew about it. Alice was sure of that. It would have been district gossip if they had. So how did Julie know? It wasn't an urn, not the kind crematoriums use, and Julie wouldn't recognize one anyway. It looked very much like an old ginger jar. Alice wanted to get up and run out. She realized that Granny Goderich was no longer waiting for an answer to her question but had gone to Julie, dried her eyes, and given her a biscuit from a tin cookie box with a picture of the Queen at Balmoral on the top.

"Would you like more tea, Alice?"

"No ... no, thank you. It's getting on. We really can't stay too long."

"Well then," Granny Goderich's voice was brisk, normal again, "I'll read your teacup before you go." She reached out for it.

"Not today ... please." Alice wished she didn't seem so nervous. She shouldn't have blurted her refusal so sharply; Granny read everyone's teacup. She had a reputation for accuracy. Alice had always thought it was just the result of all the shrewd questioning that went with the drinking of

the tea. Reading tea leaves was just Granny Goderich's way
of giving advice. Good advice too because she was a wise
old woman. Some people came every week for tea with
Granny. "She's better than a psychiatrist and the tea is free,"
Will said. Still, Alice didn't want her teacup read. Not today.
Not with the sight of Julie's tear-streaked face so fresh in
her mind. Julie, standing before an old ginger jar and a
young boy's dog collection, weeping for that boy. Alice
wanted to go home. Quickly.

"No," she repeated, "not today, Granny. Thank you." She
stood up, hoping she had not been too abrupt.

"You may read my glass of milk." Julie quickly finished
it and solemnly held the glass out to the old woman.

Alice laughed, grateful for this break in tension. "Oh
Julie! Granny Goderich can't do that! Come and get your
coat on. Don't move, Granny, I'll get them. They're on the
bed, aren't they?" She left, glad to be released.

Granny Goderich took Julie's glass, its sides still opaque
from the creamy milk. She shook her head sadly, looking
into the eager little face.

"You're very young, Julie. You'll have to learn so much.
People would think it strange if they knew we could tell
things from a glass of milk or if they knew we didn't need
glasses of milk or teacups at all. They can believe in
teacups—teacups don't frighten them." She cupped Julie's
small solemn face in her hands. "You'll learn."

Alice bustled in with the coats.

"Perhaps you should let the car warm up a little, Alice.
It's a bitter day."

Alice wanted to be home. Now. Wanted to get Julie away. "No, we'll be fine. Julie can hold her fur muff up if her nose gets cold. Can't you, dear? And the car warms up very quickly. We'll be fine."

Julie sat huddled in the cold car, her head scrunched down in the soft fur collar of her coat. She did not hold her muff to her face at first—she puffed out clouds of white breath and watched them disappear. When, at last, she did press the muff to her reddening nose it held the musty odour of geraniums and she fell asleep.

Although Julie spent most of her time alone by choice, she wanted company. She remembered Granny Goderich and the feeling she had when the old lady talked to her.

Sometimes when her mother announced, "Dress up pretty today, Julie, we're going visiting," Julie would rush around breathlessly finding good shoes and getting her coat and be standing waiting at the door long before it was time to go.

"Are we going to tea with Granny Goderich?" she'd ask when, at last, they were seated in the car.

The answer was always no and it seemed to Julie that her mother was upset by the question so that finally she dressed quietly and went to the car never asking where they were going or if they'd see anyone she knew.

But she remembered.

Once in the spring she even tried to see Granny Goderich by herself. Joe said the school bus went by the Goderichs' every day, so one morning Julie waited in the bush by the road until the others got on the bus and then ran after it. Joe said the bus moved "like a snail. I can run faster!" But Julie couldn't. Couldn't even keep it in sight although she ran her fastest. Still, she went quite a way and she was still going, walking along in the ditch by the barbed wire fence to keep away from the dust the speeding cars threw at her, when her father drove up. He opened the door, rushed over to her, and caught her up, frightening a meadowlark from the long grass as he did so.

At first he didn't speak, just held her tight. Then asked, "Julie, where are you going? You're more than a mile from home!" Julie felt sick. She couldn't tell him, didn't want to upset him as she had her mother but it was so hard to lie. She'd never lied to him, not even "wiggled the truth so it fit" as Jane called it. She said nothing, just watched the meadowlark as it flew a few yards, then dropped one wing and began to flop across the ground. Will saw it too.

"Oh Julie, were you following meadowlarks looking for nests?"

Again Julie couldn't answer. She had never had to look for nests. She knew where they were. She had known ever since she could remember. Song sparrow nests tight in the branches of little spruce trees; killdeer nests that weren't really nests at all just hollows; the crowded nests of mallards and pintails in the long grass by the slough; nests like the one belonging to this flopping, floundering meadowlark. That nest was right beside the fence post less than a foot from the toe of Will's work boot. It had seven eggs.

Will smiled at her. "Those birds are just trying to fool you. They'll keep flopping ahead of you, pretending to be hurt, making you think you can catch them, until they've led you a long way from their nest and then they'll just fly away. No more wounded bird. They can fly just fine then." Will moved toward the bird. "See, Julie?" The bird fluttered away on cue.

Julie knew all about that. She'd watched Billy spend hours following "wounded birds." Billy never found nests and he looked so hard. Sometimes Julie would show him one of hers after he promised not to touch the eggs or the baby birds. She never showed any to the others. Joe and Jimmy took birds' eggs to school for the science corner.

He turned and strode through the ditch to the truck. "You must promise me," he said as he gave her a boost up to the high truck seat, "that you'll never wander off like that again."

Julie knew she hadn't been wandering. Even without the school bus she was sure she could find the Goderich place. She'd know when she got near it.

"Promise, Punkin," he repeated.

"I promise I won't go away like that again," said Julie carefully.

When they got to the corner by the sheep pasture, Will let her out so she could run home as he drove in the yard. Her mother had not noticed she was missing.

Julie didn't try to visit Granny Goderich again. She did not even think about her. Until she smelled the geraniums.

It was summertime and she was five. Her mother had never mentioned their visit again and Julie talked less and less. She sat at the kitchen table after supper drawing a fly that was stuck on the toffee-coloured sticky paper spiral that hung in the kitchen window. Her mother wouldn't let her pull the flies off and let them go anymore so she drew them. Flying. Mary was helping their mother with the dishes. Everything was normal.

Then Julie smelled them. Geraniums. Musty, heavy geranium smell blocked her nose, pressed against her face, crushed her. For a moment she couldn't move. She knew there were no geraniums in the house. That year they had no geraniums anywhere. She dropped her pencil, leaving the fly eternally one-winged, and ran out into the fresh evening air. But it wasn't. Not fresh at all. The summer evening that should have mixed a hundred smells and held the freshness of the breeze, pulsed with the smell of geranium.

Julie was afraid but she knew she had to do something. She couldn't stand the pressure building inside. The smell of a million geraniums.

Her father was in his workshop when she found him. She wanted to throw herself at him, cling to his greasy overall leg, and pull him to the truck but she held back.

"Daddy, if I asked you to do something very important, would you do it? For me? Now?" She rubbed her hand against her nose—hard—but the geraniums pressed in anyway.

"Sure, Punkin, I guess so." He smiled at her, amused at her eagerness. "You want me to make you something?"

"No. I want to go visiting. I have to see Granny Goderich."

He smiled and ruffled her hair. "I didn't know you and the old girl were such friends. Your mother didn't mention taking you there again. Come to think of it, she never mentioned what happened the time she did take you last winter." He looked thoughtfully at Julie as if expecting an explanation.

Julie said nothing. It was so important that he understand or that he, like Julie, go without having to understand.

He smiled again, shaking his head. "Why not? I don't mind doing a favour for a friend once in a while."

Then Julie threw herself. Buried her face in his overalls that should have smelled of barn and machinery but only held the suffocating scent of geraniums.

Will held her hand as they walked to the truck, detouring past the kitchen door to call to Alice, "Julie and I are going to return that welding torch to Behan's." And privately to Julie on the way to the truck, "Your mother would wonder and we'd have to explain things. We'll drop the torch off on the way back."

Julie sat very close to him on the seat. The truck cab still held the day's heat and it churned with geraniums but the smell was almost bearable now.

The Goderich house was dark and still in the dusk half-light. "Some of these old-timers never turn on a light until they have to. I remember when I was a boy my dad was always trying to save coal oil, now it's electricity." His voice was easy but Julie noticed that he was walking faster than usual and she had to run to keep up.

There was no answer to the knock. He knocked again, louder. Behind him Julie felt the geraniums grow stronger. The odour circled her like a whirlwind then pressed against her back so hard she nearly toppled. She slipped under his arm, opened the door, and darted in. Inside it was dark and writhing with the smell of geraniums but Julie did not stop.

Granny Goderich was lying in the parlour on the floor in front of the sideboard. The dark plants loomed and murmured against the window. She was very still but when Julie knelt beside her she caught Julie's hand and held it. Tight.

"Julie . . . ," her voice was trembling, faint, "I knew you'd come."

Then her father was bending over them, lifting Granny onto the couch. "Quickly, Julie, find the kitchen and get a glass of water."

Julie didn't want to go, couldn't go until he pried her hand free of the old, blue-veined one that clung to hers.

"Julie . . . ," the faint voice trailed after her to the kitchen. She could hear her father's voice.

"It's all right, Granny. What happened? Did you fall? When did it happen?"

Julie did not bother to turn on the kitchen light. Faster not to. She grabbed a glass, filled it, and was standing beside her father and Granny again.

Will had found the light switch and Julie could see now: the queue of dogs on the sideboard, the purple jar, the huddled geraniums everywhere—quiet now.

"Wednesday." Granny's voice was just a whisper as Will held the glass to her lips.

It's Friday now, Friday night, Julie thought. She slipped her hand back inside Granny's and felt the old hand tighten, squeeze, and hold on.

" . . . forgot about Julie . . . couldn't move . . . couldn't call anyone . . . forgot about Julie."

"Try to drink something, Granny. Julie, get a blanket. We've got to cover her, she's cold." Will held Granny's head but some of the water dribbled on her chin.

" . . . not thirsty . . . could reach the watering can . . . forgot about Julie . . . all that time . . ."

"Julie, find a blanket."

Julie couldn't move from Granny's side—the hand held her too tight. She reached up on the back of the puff-backed couch and pulled down an afghan with her free hand. It was bright and warm, made of pieces her mother called "granny squares." She realized that Granny's dress was wet and that a smell stronger than geraniums was making her eyes water.

"Where's the phone, Granny? I'll call Doc Barnes."

"Julie . . . I forgot." Granny's voice was far away.

"The phone's in the hall above the geraniums, Daddy," Julie answered carefully, not looking at him. In a moment she could hear him dialing.

"You're a good girl, Julie . . . you came as soon as I remembered you . . . . I forgot . . . memory's bad . . . too late . . ."

Julie touched Granny's cheek. Her skin was soft and tissue thin; it hung in tender folds on her neck. "I didn't know what to do, Granny. I was afraid."

"But you came, Julie. I should have called you sooner ... all my fault. . . . I forgot. . . . You came. . . ." Granny's hand gripped hers.

It's so strong, Julie thought. The other hand lay on the couch, limp and unmoving, like a dead thing.

"There's an ambulance coming to take you to Red Deer, Granny. Doc will see you in Emergency." Will had found some old coats in the hall and he spread them over Granny. "I called Mrs. Behan—figured she could get here faster'n Alice—to get you some clean clothes ...," his voice trailed off.

"She's resting," said Julie. Granny's eyes were shut, her breathing soft.

"Maybe, if I can find a can of soup, I could heat some broth for her." Will came and stood by Julie, his hand gentle on her shoulder. "You don't mind staying in here, Punkin? I shouldn't leave you alone, your mother—"

"I'm fine, Daddy," Julie interrupted quickly. "I don't mind and I think Granny wants me." She did not look up.

Will ruffled her curls and left. Soon Julie could hear him opening and closing the cupboard doors. Granny opened her eyes.

"Don't be afraid. It's a gift. You did the right thing." Granny's voice was clear and firm. "Times are different but you'll learn. You did the right thing."

"I didn't know what it meant, Granny. I never know and so I don't know what to do."

"That's how it is with us, Julie. We're not sure what to do . . . we're afraid. We don't know what to do and so we do nothing, nothing at all. Sometimes that's right, there's nothing we can do, sometimes . . ." Granny Goderich paused and Julie knew she was looking toward the old sideboard where the purple jar sat. When she spoke again it was with a sob.

"There comes a time when we have to act, like you did tonight. You have to decide and that's when the gift can be terrible. Wonderful and terrible. . . ." The voice trailed off, tired. "You have to learn when . . . you have to be strong. . . ." Slowly Granny closed her eyes.

Julie wanted to ask, How? How do I learn? But she couldn't now. She sat very still holding Granny Goderich's hand. She heard the door slam, voices in the hall, then her father and Mrs. Behan bustling busy and Julie was shooed out, to wait in the truck and watch for the ambulance, they said.

It seemed to take a long time and then they were there, attendants rushing in with a stretcher and her father at the door of the truck, lifting her down.

"Granny wants you, Julie. She won't let them take her. She keeps asking for you. 'Bring Julie,' she says."

Julie hurried into the house. Granny was still on the couch, wearing a clean nightgown, wrapped in a blanket. Her dead hand still lay unmoving but with the other, the strong one, she flailed at the two young men standing by the stretcher, "Bring Julie. . . . I want Julie."

She was still as soon as she saw Julie, held her hand, and allowed Will and the men to put her on the stretcher and wrap her warmly. "You'll be all right, Julie."

Julie nodded, holding the hard-boned hand tight.

"I won't be coming back here," Granny whispered, looking right into Julie's eyes. "Do you understand, Julie?"

Julie nodded and let go.

As soon as the ambulance men, Will, and Mrs. Behan had left the room with Granny quiet on the stretcher, Julie pushed a chair over to the sideboard and climbed up. She had to hurry but there were so many dishes and ornaments and she didn't want to break them or make a noise.

Close up, the jar was really a plum colour, not purple, and the swirls were parts of willow trees. Weeping willows. Julie picked it up carefully from among the dogs.

It was lighter than she'd thought it would be and the top was sealed on with a yellow, waxy stuff. She was relieved for it meant she could travel faster. She held the jar tight to her chest and climbed down. They were out in the yard now. She knew by the slam of the doors.

She ran out, glad to see that the men had stopped to talk to Will and had not shut the ambulance doors. Mrs. Behan was climbing into the front.

Julie slipped past the men and climbed into the back. She tucked the jar in beside Granny, felt her hand close on it, touched her cheek, and slipped back out before the ambulance men had turned around.

She was sure her father had seen her—he was facing the men and the back of the ambulance—but he didn't say anything until they were in the truck.

"What did you take to her, Julie?" His voice broke the comfortable motor-hum silence.

"Her Treasure, Daddy." Julie knew he would understand that. Julie had a box of Treasures at home: a baby tooth the tooth fairy missed, a tiny tinkling bell Will had brought her from Calgary, a locket with some of her baby hair in it, a crackerjack prize ring; and her piggy bank.

"Are you sleepy, Punkin?" was all he said.

Julie wriggled over, snuggled up to him, breathing the normal smells of father and truck; and fell asleep.

from

The Daring Game

by

Kit Pearson

Eliza, from Edmonton, is delighted to be at boarding school in Vancouver. She likes the rituals and traditions of Ashdown Academy and she is determined to do well. Things get a little complicated, however, when she starts to be friends with Helen. Helen is a girl with lots of ideas.

Sunday, September 13

Dear Mum and Dad,

It was wonderful to talk to you last night, but too short! Now I'll tell you all about Ashdown.

I'm in the Yellow Dorm and I have four dorm-mates. I like Carrie the best. She's from Seattle and she has five older

125

brothers and sisters. Jean's from Chilliwack, and she goes home every Saturday. Pam's from Vancouver, and she's our dorm head. She's very bossy. Helen's from Prince George. She's always getting into trouble.

Our matron is Miss Bixley. We're lucky because she's the nicest one.

We get up every day at 7. There is a very loud bell. We have breakfast at 8, and school starts at 9 and ends at 3. Then we have games or go for a walk with the matron. We have to walk two by two in a long line! At 4:30 we change for dinner, and then we have prep for an hour (that's what the time when we do our homework is called). After dinner there's prayers, then more prep, then we go to bed at 9 o'clock.

On Saturdays we have prep in the morning, and then we can go out until 8 and don't have to go to bed until 9:30. Carrie came out with me this Saturday and Uncle Adrian took us to Stanley Park.

The food isn't bad, except for Tuesdays. It is going to be the same every week.

Monday—Shepherd's Pie
Tuesday—Liver and Onions (yuck!)
Wednesday—Chicken
Thursday—Stew
Friday—Fish
Sunday—a roast at noon (but it's called Sunday
    dinner) and eggs at night

My homeroom teacher is Miss Clark, and she also teaches us English. She's very pretty. I am in 7A and so is

Pam. Carrie, Helen, and Jean are in 7B. It's not too hard, except for French. They start it earlier here.

My piano teacher, Mrs Fraser, is really good—she makes me work harder than the one in Edmonton though. I get to miss part of prep to practise, and I also practise before breakfast every day.

Miss Tavistock is strict, but I like her. She calls me Elizabeth. So do all the teachers, but the matrons call me Eliza.

Next Saturday all the boarders are going on a picnic to Saltspring Island.

Please make sure Jessie gets brushed every day. I'm so glad she's not trying to run away. Give the Demons a kiss for me. Please send me some of those cookies with the nuts and raisins in them. Would a cake crumble in the mail? We're allowed to keep our own food downstairs.

I miss you very much, but I'm happy here. It's just like I thought it would be.

> With heaps of love,
> Eliza
> XOXOXOXOXO

P.S. Please send me a flashlight.

There! Eliza shook out her aching hand and stretched full length on her bed. It felt good to write everything down in a letter. And her parents had sounded so worried on the phone, she had to assure them she was all right.

She *was*, although she felt more bewildered by everything than she would have admitted to them. So much had been crowded into this long first week—so many new faces and new voices and new subjects and new rules—that it was difficult to sort it out. But she liked the way the days ran so smoothly, with a slot for each activity. There were fascinating people to watch, and most of them were friendly. Already she knew the names of all the junior and intermediate boarders in the Old Residence. She *did* like it here—almost as much as she'd written.

She wrote another letter to one of her friends in Edmonton, telling her the same things. Maggie, however, would probably not be interested; she had just sent a long epistle filled with dull details about a boy she liked. Already Eliza felt so immersed in her new life that her friend seemed like a stranger.

She glanced around the Yellow Dorm. It was Sunday rest time, and no one dared say a word: the Pouncer was on duty. Carrie and Jean were reading. Pam was winding white tape around her grass hockey stick. Eliza had played hockey twice herself this week. All she'd done was to chug up and down the field, purposely avoiding coming near the ball. A lot of the other players appeared to be doing the same, but no one noticed.

She wondered what Helen, unusually still, was up to underneath her. The only really uncomfortable part of school so far was Helen. The volatile girl both alarmed and intrigued her. She was prickly and funny at the same time, and the liveliest person in the Old Residence.

All of the Yellow Dorm liked food, but Helen ate more than any of them. She won the toast-eating contests at her table every morning. "I don't mean to be personal," Pam told her, "but you should go on a diet."

"And you should mind your own business," retorted Helen.

The two of them were always scrapping. "When I found out I had to board, I was hoping Helen would be in the other grade seven dorm," Pam confided to Eliza and Carrie. "Last year she came to a barbeque I had for the whole class, and she started everyone making water bombs in the swimming pool out of paper cups. My mother says she's a disruptive influence." Pam tried to tell them more about all the trouble Helen had caused in grade six, but Eliza and Carrie didn't like her righteous tone and changed the subject.

Helen never missed an opportunity of needling Pam, but she was fairly pleasant to the rest of them. As well as calling Pam and Eliza "P.J." and "Eliza Doolittle," she had nicknames for the others. Jean was "Scotty," and Carrie was "Turps," after a ball bouncing rhyme the juniors were always chanting:

Queen, Queen Caroline
Washed her hair in turpentine
Turpentine made it shine
Queen, Queen Caroline.

Already Helen had had to "go and speak to Miss Tavistock," a threat the matrons were always holding over them. On Tuesday evening Jean had locked herself in the bathroom when the wobbly old doorknobs had fallen off. The rest of them heard her timid knocks and cries, growing louder as she became more frightened. They crowded around the door.

"I'll go and get a matron," said Pam quickly.

"No—wait!" Helen looked overjoyed that something was happening. "They'll just make a fuss. Keep calm, Scotty," she called. "We're going to rescue you! Come on, everyone—push!"

She thrust her weight against the door and pounded it rhythmically. The flimsy panel showed a crack of light at each shove.

The others watched her doubtfully. "Wouldn't it be better to try to get the doorknobs back on?" suggested Eliza.

"*Stop* it, Helen—you're going to break it!" cried Pam.

"That's . . . the . . . idea!" puffed Helen, red in the face. The door crashed inwards with a screech of ripping wood. Helen fell in with it. Jean screamed, then laughed nervously as she realized she was free.

In an instant both Miss Bixley and Miss Monaghan were there, gazing in disbelief at the shards of wood hanging from the side of the door.

When Helen returned from seeing Miss Tavistock, she wouldn't tell them what the headmistress had said. But her ecstatic mood had disappeared. "Everyone blames me for everything around here," she growled. "I was only trying to help." Underneath the grumbling, however, she seemed secretly triumphant.

Eliza wasn't sure where she stood with Helen. When the other girl used her nickname she felt they were on friendly terms; at other times the two of them were uneasy with each other.

Her feelings were especially mixed on Thursday. In the morning Eliza and Helen were alone in the dorm; they were the last to change their sheets. Eliza found it tricky to do this on an upper bunk, especially when the bed was so close to the wall. Helen hadn't even started. Her clean sheets were folded on her chair and she sprawled across her stripped mattress, reading a Batman comic. Every so often she peered at Eliza moving around her. She looked superior, as if she, Helen, did not have to bother with such a dreary task.

It made Eliza nervous, being alone with her. Neither of them spoke. The silence made Eliza even more jittery, and she flapped her top sheet to make a noise. It knocked John off her bed—and out of the open window.

She ran to it, leaned out and spied him on the ground below. He had landed on his back and, with his paws spread out, looked as if he were appealing for help.

"What are you doing, Eliza Doolittle?" yawned Helen, throwing her comic onto the floor.

"My bear's fallen out!" Eliza started to leave the room.

Helen stopped her. "Why don't you just go down the fire escape?" The wooden structure went all the way up their side of the residence, past the window by Carrie's bed. Eliza examined it and saw that it would be a lot faster than going around the building. She opened the window wider, stepped onto the stairs, dashed down and snatched up John, then scurried up again.

But after breakfast Miss Tavistock said to her quietly, "Would you please see me in my study, Elizabeth?"

It was strictly forbidden to go on the fire escape, the headmistress told her firmly, after she had closed the door.

Mrs Renfrew had spotted Eliza from her room in the New Residence and reported her.

"I'm s-sorry, Miss Tavistock," said Eliza, standing in front of the desk and trying not to cry. How terrible to do something wrong her very first week! "I didn't know it wasn't allowed—I just went to get my bear." Admitting that she had a bear sounded so babyish that her cheeks flamed.

Miss Tavistock's voice softened. "If you didn't know, Elizabeth, then I forgive you. I know you're not the type of girl to intentionally break a rule, and it's hard to remember everything at first." The headmistress raised her eyebrows. "But goodness me, your dormitory is troublesome this week! I hope this isn't an indication of how you're all going to behave for the rest of the year!"

"I'm sorry, Eliza Doolittle," said Helen nonchalantly when Eliza confronted her later. "I thought you *knew* it wasn't allowed, and I didn't think you'd get caught."

Eliza wondered if she should believe her. Getting into trouble seemed unimportant to Helen, and she did appear genuinely amazed that Eliza was upset about it. It would be safest, however, not to trust the other girl.

But that night she changed her mind again. Eliza had quickly discovered she was the only one in the Yellow Dorm who still wore an undershirt. No one except Pam seemed to need a bra, but each person wore one as if it were a badge of membership in grade seven. Eliza had no wish to acquire something so grown-up, but she also hoped the others wouldn't comment on her difference. So far, they hadn't.

On that Thursday evening, however, Pam examined Eliza thoughtfully as they were undressing. "Don't you think you should ask Miss Bixley to get you a bra, Eliza? You can get padded ones," she added sweetly.

Eliza's face burned. She turned her back on Pam to hide both her flat chest and her sudden tears.

But now she was facing Helen, who had been standing behind her. The red-haired girl looked straight at Eliza; even behind her glasses, her sympathy was apparent. Then her eyes shifted to Pam and glinted with fury.

"You leave Eliza alone, P.J.!" she hissed. "It's none of your business if she wears a bra or not. I hate mine. My mother only got it because it was an option on the clothing list this year. In fact, I think I'll get rid of it." She picked up the white cotton garment and twirled it around her head dramatically. Then she flung it into the wastepaper basket.

Pam looked offended. "I was only trying to give Eliza some advice, Helen. Don't get so excited."

Eliza finished buttoning up her pyjama top. She blinked back her tears and smiled at Helen. "Thanks," she mouthed. Helen actually winked at her.

The next morning Miss Bixley found the bra and made Helen take it back, but Eliza couldn't forget her surprising defence.

"Time to go down to the dining room and write your letters home, girls." Mrs Renfrew's no-nonsense Scottish voice pierced the Sunday silence. She crept about so quietly, she always surprised them.

"I've done mine," said Eliza, slipping her second letter into an envelope and addressing it.

"So've I," said Helen, emerging from underneath with a small grubby envelope.

The Pouncer looked suspicious, but took the letters to mail. "Very well, you two may begin your free time, but I want you to stay inside. It's too wet to go out. The rest of you hurry up, please."

"Mrs Renfrew, I can't find my green sweater," complained Carrie, all her dresser drawers gaping.

"I found it under your bed this morning, Carrie," said the Pouncer. "It's in the Pound. You'll have to pay me a dime to get it out." She sniffed disapprovingly. "We're going to make a lot of money out of *this* dormitory, I can see that already."

Eliza shoved her writing paper quickly into a drawer. The only tidy person in the dorm was Pam. She was so extreme she made up for the rest of them, draping her pristine uniform carefully over a chair each night in readiness for the next morning.

When Carrie, Jean and Pam had left, Eliza got out a book and prepared to sink into it. One problem with boarding school so far was that there wasn't enough time to read. Settling back against her pillow, she was immediately transported into Roman Britain.

But Helen's voice underneath her broke the spell. "Listen, Eliza. It's time to make plans."

"Plans?" asked Eliza, reluctantly putting down *The Eagle of the Ninth*.

Helen moved across to Pam's bed. She fixed her glasses on Eliza as if they were a pair of binoculars.

"Yes. It's a plan for all of us, but I wanted to tell you first. You seem to be gutsier than the others. I liked the way you rescued your silly bear, even if you didn't know you were breaking a rule. Will you support me if I suggest something to everyone?"

Eliza felt flattered and frightened at the same time. She didn't want Helen to look down on her, but she didn't want to clash with Miss Tavistock again either.

"It depends what it is," she said as agreeably as she could. But Helen looked ruffled.

"Oh, don't bother if you're worried about it. I guess you are just as chicken as the rest of them."

Eliza was ashamed. After all, in her books the boarders were always planning some prank or another. Wasn't that one reason she'd wanted to come here—for excitement? She had never thought of herself as a coward, and she wondered why she felt afraid.

"I'll support you," she said quickly. "Tell me what it is."

"Eliza and I have an idea," Helen announced that night. By now they chattered fearlessly for an extended period after Lights Out—except when the Pouncer was on duty.

Eliza clutched John under the covers. She was just as curious as the others, for Helen had told her only part of the plan.

"What we propose," said Helen, getting out of bed, opening the curtains and squatting on the floor so she could see them all, "is a game. A Daring Game. This place is boring. We need to do something to liven it up."

"I don't think it's boring," protested Carrie. Eliza agreed silently; everything was too new to be boring. But she liked games. She and Maggie and some other friends in Edmonton used to play at being knights, or Robin Hood, or horses, until the others told her they were too old.

This game sounded different—not pretending, but real, which made it riskier. It had the same allure of important secrecy, however, that had been present in her other games. Helen's bravado when she described it had a lot to do with this. Eliza had never known anyone her own age who seemed so sure of herself.

Remembering her role, she made her voice sound enthusiastic: "It might be fun." She watched Carrie listen to Helen with more interest.

Pam lay on her back and stared at the ceiling. "Well, go on, Helen. But I won't play if it's dangerous or anything."

Jean, silent as usual, just watched Helen with wide eyes.

Helen grinned at Eliza, who felt relieved she'd said the right thing.

"Okay," continued Helen, "a Daring Game. What we'll do is take turns doing dares. I can think of lots, but you can make up some too, if you want. It has to be something that takes a lot of nerve."

"But what's the point?" said Pam.

"The point is to do it, of course. It'll be fun to see how much we can get away with in this dump."

That was a mistake. Pam rolled over. "Well, count me out. I don't want to get into trouble, and I'm the dorm head, so I don't think any of you should do it."

So far, thought Eliza, the job of being dorm head consisted of informing everyone of the position; its only duty seemed to be the collection of the laundry slips each week.

"You haven't even heard what the first dare is," said Helen. "You'll like it, I bet. It's for all of us." Pam refused to answer, but the others begged her to continue.

"A dorm feast. I dare us all to bring food up here this Saturday and have a huge feast after Lights Out."

Eliza stretched out her legs with relief. She'd imagined all sorts of dreadful things Helen might have proposed. Dorm feasts, however, seemed a requirement of boarding school. She was surprised at the tameness of the first dare, but she decided that Helen probably wanted to test them with an easy one.

"Come on, Pam, how about it?" said Helen, in an unusually wheedling tone. "Everyone has feasts. The Red Dorm had one last week. We had three when I was in the Nursery, and we never got caught."

"I have some chocolate bars in my tuck box," said Carrie.

"Maybe my aunt would make us a cake," said Eliza.

"I think I could bring something from home," said Jean softly. They waited for Pam to reply.

"Oh, all right," she said finally. "If everyone else does it I suppose it's okay. As long as you're sure we won't get caught. I'm going out with Deb this Saturday—I'll get some buns or something."

"Let's make a list!" Carrie jumped out of bed to find a paper and pencil.

By nine-thirty on Saturday night, the food that had been concealed beneath coats, hurried up the stairs and stashed under beds, in drawers and in the closet far exceeded the items on the list.

"Goodnight, girls," said Miss Bixley, turning out the light. They waited fifteen minutes, then arranged all the food in the middle of the floor on Pam's large bath towel. Drawing back the curtains, they sat crosslegged in a circle around the feast, gazing at its beauty with relish.

A glistening pile of red licorice sticks
A box of Stoned Wheat Thins
A jar of peanut butter
Three American chocolate bars
A giant bottle of Coke
Half a dozen Bismarck doughnuts, oozing with jam
One slightly squashed chocolate cake
Six pieces of fried chicken

"Who bought all the licorice?" asked Carrie.

"I did," said Helen. "When Bix took us for our walk yesterday I persuaded her to let us stop at Crabby Crump's."

They all preferred the twisting red licorice sticks from Crump's Groceries across the street to any other kind. Mrs Crump disliked the noisy Ashdown girls who crowded her tiny store, but they gave her so much business she had to put up with them.

"I thought you said you had to spend all your pocket money on buying a new math scribbler," said Pam nastily. They all knew Helen had dropped her old scribbler in a mud puddle on purpose because she hadn't done her homework.

Helen shrugged. "Oh, I had some left over." The two dollars they collected in small brown envelopes from the office every Friday never went very far. Much of the food for the feast was donated from the downstairs tuck boxes that were kept full with "care packages" from parents. Helen, however, was never sent anything from home.

Pam looked as if she didn't believe Helen, but she became distracted by the chocolate bars Carrie was cutting into five pieces each with her nail file. "Yum," munched Pam, biting into part of an Almond Joy. "I've always wanted to know what these taste like."

Carrie dipped her piece into some peanut butter. "Try it this way—it's tremendous."

"They should feed us like this all the time instead of starving us," said Helen, holding a piece of chicken in one hand and a doughnut in the other, taking alternate bites of each. She hummed the song they had learned on the picnic last week, and they started singing it softly, the words muffled by food and laughter.

There is a boarding school
Far, far away
Where they get onion soup
Three times a day.
Oh, how those boarders yell
When they hear the dinner bell!
Oh, how those onions smell
Three times a day!

Jean chewed licorice cheerfully; bits of it stuck to the wires in her mouth and she picked them off. "I hate braces," she whispered to Eliza beside her. Jean had stopped crying at night, but she still looked like a scared rabbit most of the time. Tonight, however, she was a little more relaxed.

Pam was spreading the crackers evenly with peanut butter, using the round end of her toothbrush. She paused. "Do you hear something?" They listened hard, but there wasn't a sound; the whole house of boarders was asleep.

"It's just your imagination, P.J.," said Helen. "Bix won't come up for ages."

The lights from the parking lot created eerie squares of light across the wall and ceiling. Eliza shuffled closer into the circle. For the first time she felt as if they were a real group instead of five separate personalities. Almost like a family of five sisters, even though sisters wouldn't be so different from one another. It was more like a pyjama party that never ended, with no parents to tell you to go to sleep. For a second this thought made Eliza lonely. Then it made her feel curiously free.

Eliza raised her toothbrush glass full of Coke. "Here's to the Yellow Dorm," she whispered. The others joined her in a silent toast.

Ten minutes later none of them could get down another morsel, but there was still a lot of food piled on the towel.

Helen thrust a drumstick at Eliza. "Have another piece of chicken."

"Ohhh, I can't," groaned Eliza, who had already had a large dinner at her aunt and uncle's.

"We'll have to put it away and sneak it into our tuck boxes tomorrow," said Pam. They gathered the food up quickly into a paper bag and stowed it in the closet. Then they staggered back to bed.

"That was the best feast I've ever had," sighed Helen. "I think you all performed our first dare very well. I am extremely proud of you, girls," she added, imitating Miss Tavistock.

She had barely finished her sentence when the lights flashed on, and a voice said crisply, "What is going on in here?"

It wasn't Miss Bixley. It was Miss Tavistock.

"N-nothing, Miss Tavistock," stammered Pam.

"I can smell chicken. Do you have food in the dormitory? You know that is forbidden."

There was no use concealing it. No one ever dared hide anything from Miss Tavistock. Morosely, Helen pulled the paper bag out of the closet.

The headmistress peered into its greasy depths, wrinkling her nose with distaste. "Very well. Put on your dressing-gowns and slippers and come downstairs. Bring the food with you."

Eliza climbed down and nervously jerked her dressing-gown sleeve over the flannelette sleeve of her pyjamas. Her knees shook with an almost pleasant kind of fear. What was going to happen to them? This was probably a greater crime than going onto the fire escape by accident, but she was more curious than frightened. And this time they were all in trouble together.

Carrie seemed to feel the same. All the way down the stairs she squeezed Eliza's arm. "Oooh, I'm so scared," she breathed, but she sounded as if she were going to laugh.

"Silence, please," said Miss Tavistock. She led them along the dark hall into the dining room and made them sit on both sides of one of the long tables.

"Put everything on the table, Helen," she ordered. "Pamela, fetch some plates from the kitchen. Since you seem to be so hungry for extra food, you can finish your meal down here."

They looked at one another with horror. Finish it! Eliza's stomach lurched in protest as she stared at the mess Helen was spreading out on the table. The remains of the chocolate bars were stuck to the chicken. Squashed dough-nuts leaked their fillings onto broken crackers. The empty Coke bottle was smeared with chocolate icing, and the cake had disintegrated into soggy crumbs. Pam's toothbrush, encrusted with dried peanut butter, lay ludicrously on top of it all.

"Oh, please, Miss Tavistock, I can't eat any more!" begged Carrie.

"We won't do it again, Miss Tavistock. I'll be sick if I have another bite!" said Pam.

"No arguing. Eat it up, every crumb. Come along, Elizabeth, have another piece of chicken. Helen, you're the one who's starving—have some licorice."

The only sound was the low ticking of the clock down the hall and five mouths chewing hesitantly. No one, not even Helen, could force down more than a few mouthfuls, and Jean looked pale.

"All right, girls," said Miss Tavistock finally. "I think you've learned your lesson. Throw it all away and then you can sit in the hall for fifteen minutes. I hope I will never catch you with food in the dormitory again."

Sitting in the hall without speaking was a common punishment. The headmistress arranged them on chairs down its length, then went into her study. Eliza was sitting under the clock. Its steady voice was reassuring in the darkness.

Miss Bixley came out of the matrons' sitting room, noticed her five charges and stopped in astonishment, then wagged her finger at them and continued up the stairs.

Despite never wanting to eat again, Eliza felt peaceful for the first time since she'd come to Ashdown. This was what boarding school was supposed to be like, getting into trouble with your dorm-mates and feeling a bond of companionship with them because of it. She glanced over her shoulder cautiously and grinned at Carrie.

When they were all back in bed, Pam risked a whisper. "I don't like your game, Helen. I'm not going to play it ever again."

But Eliza burrowed contentedly into her pillow. At least we've proved to Helen we're not cowards, she thought as she fell asleep.

from

The Moons of Madeleine

by

Joan Clark

Madeleine is eager to get to Calgary to visit Selena, her cousin and best friend. She hasn't seen her in three years. But when she arrives she has a shock. Selena has changed. Who is this angry, scornful, bored person with purple lips? How is Mad going to survive a whole month of holidays in her company?

In the morning Mad heard Aunt Louise in the kitchen. Still sleepy but very hungry, Mad got up, put on her bathrobe and went down the hall. She wanted to get to the kitchen before her aunt left for work. At home she was used to helping herself to meals, but she hadn't been here long enough to do that.

Aunt Louise was wearing a pale, rose-coloured dress with a pink scarf, rose-coloured lipstick and earrings. She was sitting at the glass and chrome table making out a list and drinking coffee.

"Why, Mad, you're up early," she said. "I thought you'd sleep in." The tone of her voice suggested she wasn't too pleased with the interruption.

Already Mad could see her aunt was the sort of person who liked things to go exactly as planned. And she had planned that Mad would sleep in.

Perhaps Mad had this wrong and her aunt was simply surprised to see her up this early because she went on, "Selena seldom gets up before noon except for acting class."

"I didn't know Selena took acting," Mad said. "I thought she was into rowing." She felt there were large areas inside Selena she didn't know anything about, countries she had never visited.

"Rowing was *last* summer. *This* summer it's acting. Selena's always in one phase or the other. We don't take it too seriously," her aunt said dryly. "Actually, it's in art that she shows the most talent. I signed her up for a drawing class this summer. Figure drawing. I thought she would like it. She absolutely *refused* to take it. Everything I suggest, she vetoes." Aunt Louise sighed. The corners of her lipsticked mouth turned down. She drank some of the coffee and sighed again. "How do you get along with your mother?" she said suddenly.

"We get along all right," Mad said.

"Do you help her?"

"I work in the shop," Mad said, "but I get paid for that."

"But you're busy," her aunt prodded, "doing other things."

Mad squirmed. This interrogation was making her uncomfortable.

"There's always lots to do on the lake," she admitted. "It's a full-time job cleaning up the litter people throw into the water."

Her aunt pounced on this eagerly. "That's the key," she said, "keeping *busy*. Frankly, that's Selena's main problem. She and her friends don't have nearly enough to do. They spend *far* too much time on the phone and hanging around the downtown mall." Her aunt stood up and brushed a wrinkle out of her skirt. "I think your being here will be a good thing for Selena. Which reminds me," she picked up the slip of paper and gave it to Mad, "I've been making a list of things you and Selena can do together. I asked Selena to make up a list, but she said she couldn't think of anything."

Mad read the list:

Museum
Planetarium
Stampede
Picnic
Calgary Zoo
Heritage Park
Swimming

Mad didn't want to follow a list, but she was too new here to say this directly. Instead she said, "Do you mind if I help myself to your books?"

"Most of them are Gregory's," Aunt Louise said, "but you go ahead. I should warn you, though, that your Uncle Gregory is *very* fussy about his books. He doesn't like so much as a thumb-mark on them. I suggest you wash your hands before you handle them."

Her aunt taped the list to the fridge door.

"I wish Selena would read more. She used to read a great deal but seems to have given it up," Aunt Louise said. "Maybe if she sees you reading, she will too."

Mad stared at the floor. It was beige with brown and copper speckles in it. She definitely did not want the job of changing Selena.

Aunt Louise opened the dishwasher door and placed her cup on a rack inside.

"What would you like for breakfast?" she asked. "There are fresh blueberry muffins I made last night. Waffles. English muffins in the freezer. Eggs. Bacon. Do you know how to use a microwave?"

"No."

Her aunt went through the steps, showed her the book of instructions, and then opened drawers, cupboards and the fridge, finishing with, "Feel free to help yourself. All I ask is that you clean up afterwards." She looked at the oven clock. "I have to go. I left egg salad sandwiches in the fridge for lunch." She started to leave the room, then stopped and said, "By the way, your mother phoned last night after you went to bed. I told her you'd arrived safe and sound." Then she was gone.

Mad looked out the window. In a few minutes she saw her aunt backing the car out of the driveway. Mad took the bacon out of the fridge so she could try the microwave; at home they cooked on a wood stove. She cooked the bacon and heated up one blueberry muffin after another so she could sample as many of her aunt's jams and jellies as possible. After she had eaten, she cleaned up the kitchen and washed her hands. Then she went into the living room which was bright and airy with the glass windows letting in light from outdoors. Mad looked at the moon mask. In the daylight its expression seemed passive, dreaming, as if it was asleep. She went to the bookshelves and began to browse through the books. Finally she selected a book entitled *Greek Goddesses* and sat down on the chesterfield to read.

It was late morning when Selena, wearing a short nightie, wandered into the living room eating a bowl of yogurt. Though she still had the green streak in her hair and the purple nailpolish, without last night's makeup on her face, she looked softer, younger. She grinned at Mad.

"Well, Coz, I see from the list on the fridge that The Oracle hath spoke. It's museum day."

"We don't have to go," Mad said.

"Oh, we'll go," Selena said firmly. "I already told someone I was going. But first I want to work on my tan."

Mad turned the corner of the page down to mark her place in the book before she remembered her aunt's warning. Hastily, she smoothed the corner flat.

"I hope Uncle Gregory won't be bothered by this crease," she said. "Your mother told me how fussy he is about his books."

"Oh, he *is*. But he's also absent-minded. He probably won't notice. He often puts things down and forgets where he's put them." She giggled. "Once, he threw his shoes in the laundry chute, thinking they were socks. Mother says one good thing about him being away is that Tittle Tattle can keep the house tidier."

"Who's Tittle Tattle?"

"Our cleaning lady. She comes once a week."

Selena got up and went into her bedroom, then called back, "Are you going to work on your tan?"

"Sure," Mad said. This was something she never did at home. Lying in the sun was a waste of time. For one thing, she couldn't read. The bright light made the letters jump off the page. And there was always something better to do. But she'd try it now in order to get along with Selena.

By the time Mad had changed into her bathing suit, which had a large mend on the behind where she had caught it on a raft nail, Selena was already outside on the deck, sitting on the chaise lounge, oiling her legs and arms. She was wearing a white bikini which accentuated her breasts and hips. Mad had no hips. So far, her breasts were small, tender points which she covered with blouses and T-shirts. Sometimes she wondered what it would be like to have the full body of a woman, but most of the time she never thought about it any more than she thought about going out with boys or getting married or having children.

Those things hung somewhere ahead of her like a hazy, undefined cloud. She was in no hurry to enter this cloud. In fact, if she had her way, she would stay on this side of it indefinitely. Periodically there was a tenderness in her breasts, an unfamiliar twinge in her belly to remind her that she was closer to the cloud than she cared to admit.

Mad stood on the deck and looked at the outdoor furniture. Besides the chaise lounge there were four chairs padded with thick cushions, and a table with an umbrella overhead. On the table was a basket of stones. Mad sat in one of the chairs. She noticed the cushions had orange flowers splashed onto a beige background.

'Why is so much of your house beige?" she burst out. She liked a place where colours were mixed up like a paint box.

"It's Mother's idea," Selena said. "Being an interior decorator she likes things co-ordinated: furniture, people, the works. All that colour-wheel stuff. She's even had her own colours done."

"What do you mean?"

Selena gave her a quizzical look.

"Don't you know? You go to a colour consultant and she tells you what colours you should be wearing to go with your hair and skin. Mother's in her rose and beige period. I hate beige." Selena yawned. "If you ask me, it's boring." She leaned back on the chaise lounge, put earphones over her head, closed her eyes and turned on her Walkman.

Mad looked around. The sun was so blindingly bright she couldn't see much. She could hear the muted roar of traffic from the other side of the Gully. She went inside for her peaked brown cap which had *Mountain High Ski Tours* stitched on it in white. It was Louie's favourite cap, but he had given it to her before she left as an advance birthday present. She came back outside with the cap jammed low on her head, sat down again and stretched out her skinny legs to the sun.

It was so hot that she soon got up and wandered aimlessly around the deck, bored and disgruntled. What was the point of being out here with Selena when her cousin ignored her? Mad went to the table and picked up a stone from the basket. She saw that it was no ordinary stone. It was a marble egg, caramel-coloured, with streaks of white running through it. Mad picked up another stone. It, too, was egg-shaped, though slightly smaller. This stone was of highly polished jade, green as a mountain lake. Mad looked at the other stones in the basket. All of them were egg-shaped and roughly the same size. One was a deep sea blue with whorls of lighter blue inside as if whirlpools of water had solidified beneath the earth's crust. There was a pink egg with raspberry-coloured veins running through it, a coarse, rough stone with flakes of green embedded in its surface like lichen. Circling one end of the stone was a smooth furrow. It looked like a narrow strip of material; possibly a leather thong had been wrapped around it so that it could be used as a tool of some sort. There was a polished, milky stone, white as the moon except for a small black mark near the top, almond-shaped like an eye. Mad picked up one stone after the other and held it in the palm of her hand. Automatically her fingers closed around the shape. Each stone felt cool against her skin. She flattened her hand and allowed the stone to roll back and forth across her palm. It was a relaxing, soothing sensation. Mad looked at Selena, wanting to ask her about these stones, wanting to know where they had come from, but her cousin was obviously lost in the music. Her eyes were closed as her foot beat out a rhythm against the plastic-covered pad. Mad returned the stones to the basket, got up and went to the edge of the deck where planters of white petunias and red geraniums were lined up in neat precision. Beside the deck a catoni aster hedge was trimmed in the shape of a long, narrow box

Mad walked down the steps and crossed the clipped lawn. It sloped gradually downward to a thick stand of aspen trees. This was where the Gully began. Mad found a path between the trees and continued walking. Soon she came to a clearing which she recognized as the place where she and Selena used to have picnics. She sat down on the cool grass and listened to the light breeze lifting the aspen leaves, spinning them like paper tops. There was a peacefulness in the glade, a green drowsiness that made her want to stay. Here trees and shrubs grew in tangled profusion, a welcome relief from the ordered landscape of the Gibsons'.

As she sat there, a deer emerged from between the trees and nibbled at the grass on the edge of the clearing. Mad took the deer's presence as an encouraging sign. Not everything from her childhood here had changed. She sat unmoving, watching the deer. The deer lifted its head and saw her. Its eyes were round, curious, its body poised for flight. For a long time girl and deer stared at each other, neither one willing to break the spell. From the house came the sound of a ringing phone. The deer turned and walked gracefully away. Mad watched until its tail disappeared among the green leaves.

She heard the door to the deck slide open. She got up and went back along the path towards the house. Selena was no longer on the deck. Mad went through the glass doors. She heard shower water running. She went into the kitchen, opened the fridge and took out the egg salad sandwiches and milk. After she had eaten, she went into the bedroom and got into her jeans and a blouse. Then she went into the living room to wait for Selena. She heard a train whistle down in the Gully. She looked out the glass windows but she couldn't see the train. In the sunlight the woods below looked green and wild, thick as a jungle. The river gleamed, a golden road. The river made her long for the lake, for a cool plunge into the cove. The Barrows kept a raft anchored partway out in the cove on a seam where the lake bottom dropped off. She and Louie liked swimming along the edge where the shallow and the deep water met. There was both safety and danger in this. If you put your foot down on the shallow side, you touched bottom. If you put your foot down in the deep, blue-black side, you felt the beginning of a vast, watery unknown.

Selena came into the living room wearing a white shirt, a black bow tie and a man's black suit with a pink rose on the jacket lapel. Her hair was slicked back and her face made up. She looked half-girl, half-boy. Mad gaped at her.

Selena appeared not to notice. Mad followed her cousin outside. Selena locked the door, slipped the key in her pocket and they walked to the bus stop. The people on the bus took no notice of Selena. They were used to seeing young people dressed up like this. Mad couldn't shake the feeling that the person beside her was someone else, not her cousin. They passed a school, a garage and shopping centre, a motel, another shopping centre, a golf course. Beyond the golf course was a park-like area in which there were several long buildings. On the gate was a wooden sign: *Two Pines Lodge*.

"That's where Grandma lives!" Mad said excitedly.

"That's right, Coz."

"Do you see Grandma much?" Mad said.

Selena shrugged. "Not that much. She has her own friends at the lodge, the ones who haven't died off, that is. Sometimes she comes to the house for dinner. Sundays, usually."

"Does she send you a dress every Christmas?" Mad asked. "And a silver spoon?"

"Well, now that I'm fourteen she's sending me forks. Imagine sending that sort of thing in this day and age," Selena said. "Sometimes I think Marie Delphine is back in the Dark Ages."

"Do you wear the dress?"

"I wouldn't be caught *dead* in the crummy dress she gives me. I mean, it's so *old-fashioned*. All that lace and frills."

Mad didn't wear her dress either. There was no place to wear it. She put the silver spoons in her top bureau drawer.

For your hope chest was what Marie Delphine always wrote
on the card accompanying the spoon. Mad didn't have a
hope chest. Her mother's hope chest was where she had
once stored china and linen in preparation for marriage.
Her mother had sold off the china. Now they used pottery
plates, woven table mats. The wooden chest was used to
store her mother's skeins of wool.

"Do you have a hope chest?" Mad said.

"Are you kidding? I'm never getting married," Selena
announced, "or having kids. I can't imagine anything more
bor-ing." Whenever Selena pronounced *boring,* the word
had a nasal ring to it. "A hope chest is another one of
Grandma's old-fashioned ideas. Girls don't have them like
they used to. But it's just like Grandma to try to get us to
start one. Daddy says Grandma's the last of the great matri-
archs. He calls her Eurynome the Second. Eurynome was
the first Greek goddess," she added knowledgeably.

"I know," Mad said. Only this morning she had read
how Eurynome, the goddess of all things, had risen naked
from Chaos and divided the sea from the sky. She had
danced on the waves while the wind moved around her.
Finally she had mated with the wind and the human race
had begun.

The bus descended a hill and the skyscrapers began
closing in on either side of the street until Mad felt she was
being squeezed into a narrow valley. They got off the bus in
front of a hotel and crossed the street to the museum.

The museum was dark and windowless inside. In the
centre of the lobby was a sculpture that towered through an

open spiral staircase to the third floor. It looked like a tree made of giant icicles. There was an explosion of colour and the icicles shimmered with red, green, blue and yellow lights. As the lights played across the surface of the icicles the sound of music could be heard: a faint, tinny sound like distant chimes. Then women's voices, high and ghostly. Mad imagined the roof of the museum had opened to the sky and women's voices were floating down from outer space. The lights shifted and the sound of horns mingled with the chimes and voices. Mad stood spellbound, looking up at the sculpture until the last notes faded away.

"It's a clock," Selena said. "It's supposed to look like the northern lights."

They drifted into the Native Canadian exhibit. Mad looked at a large teepee painted with a design of a strange animal that seemed to be half-weasel, half-skunk. There were quite a few things here that reminded her of Old Angus: carved chests and benches and the dark woodsiness of the rooms. Mad felt she was on the floor of a forest, a forest of giant cedars which soared overhead. Angus carved his masks in a cedar grove. Sometimes he carved a mask in the tree and cut it out after it had been finished. Here, there were a grave-marker mask weathered grey, a bee mask with a needlelike stinger, an open-beaked raven mask. None of them was as beautiful as Angus's sun and moon masks. Mad looked at the tools: bone knives used for cutting meat and scraping skins, stone mallets for pounding corn, spindle whorls, digging sticks. There were ladles made from horns, berry pouches of animal bladders, a wooden cradle. She looked at the spears, the bow and arrows and shields used by the warriors. She saw a bracelet of teeth and shells. A sign explained that the bracelet had belonged to one of the first people, an ancient Cree woman. The bracelet was believed to have magical powers. Selena went on ahead but Mad spent a long time looking at the bracelet. Then she went back and looked at the stone mallets. One of them was egg-shaped. It was tied to a wooden handle with a thong. It looked like one of the stones in the basket on the Gibsons' deck, only this one was larger.

Selena came back.

"Seen enough, Coz?" she said.

"I'll go if you want," Mad said, though she preferred staying. Being in this exhibit was like wandering through a wilderness.

They walked down the spiral staircase. At the bottom of the staircase, Selena said, "Let's look at the exhibit on Ancient Greece."

She led the way into a large area where there were statues of Greek gods and goddesses: Zeus and Athena, Poseidon and Aphrodite. There was a large model of the Acropolis, graceful temples with white marble columns and spacious steps built on top of a hill. On one wall was a painting of Artemis, goddess of the hunt and the moon. Dressed in a white tunic and carrying a silver horn, a silver bow and arrows, she was riding a silver chariot.

"Daddy opened this exhibit," Selena said proudly. Mad suspected the reason Selena wanted to come here was so she could brag about her father. "I came with him dressed in a white tunic." She giggled. "Someone asked me if it was a sheet. They asked Daddy to open this exhibit because he teaches Greek history at the university. He knows a lot about Greece. That's why he's conducting a boat tour of the islands this summer. He likes explaining all that stuff to tourists." She stood gazing up at a large map of Greece. "I wonder where he is now," she said. She sounded wistful, as if she would like to be on the boat with her father.

Mad stood beside her cousin. Together they studied the sprinkling of white islands on the blue sea. Mad imagined she and Selena were on this sea in her red dory, *The Explorer*. Selena was in a bikini, of course, lounging in the bow, her hand trailing in the water, while Mad rowed towards one of those islands. Mad imagined them landing on the island, just the two of them. They were the first ones there and they were exploring it. They had to stick close to each other, help each other out in order to survive. They were standing on the pebbled beach when a boatload of rough-looking seamen appeared, coming towards them. Mad pointed to a cave in the hills behind the beach. It seemed the natural place to run to for protection. She was about to tell Selena they should climb up to the cave when she felt an urgent tug on her arm.

"Come on," Selena said, "we've got to go. Someone's waiting for us."

Mad blinked. "Who?" The boatload of sailors vanished.

Selena shrugged. "You'll see."

They went through a set of glass doors opposite the entrance doors and walked towards the downtown mall where two city blocks had been made into a concrete park. On the mall there were heavy concrete tubs planted with trees and shrubs, a concrete Eskimo sculpture, concrete paving slabs, a concrete stage. On the stage, a long-haired, sad-looking man was strumming a guitar, but no one seemed to be listening. People streamed past on their way to stores, shops, offices and banks. Down the centre of the mall were several eating stands that sold pizza, hamburgers, hotdogs and French fries; clustered around them were metal tables and chairs. Selena headed for one of these and boldly sat down at a table occupied by two boys. One had red hair cut like an Iroquois warrior: two sides shaved close with a tuft of hair on top. He was wearing a black satin cowboy shirt and medallions around his neck. The other boy's head was close shaven. He wore a gold stud in one ear, leather gloves with the knuckles out and a T-shirt with *Try Me* written on the front. Mad hesitated; she didn't want to sit with these weird guys. What was the matter with Selena?

"Hi, Darcy. Hi, Joe," Selena said. "This is my cousin, Mad."

Darcy's eyes flicked briefly across Mad's face then back to Selena's. Joe didn't look at Mad at all but somewhere behind her.

"Sit down, Coz," Selena said.

Mad sat. She looked around. Most of the other tables were occupied by people in bizarre, outlandish dress. At the next table was a girl with her hair cut in wings, wearing what looked like a yellow curtain. The boy sitting opposite her wore lipstick, a gold clip on one nostril and a frilly, pink blouse. Further down the mall Mad saw a gray-bearded man in a poncho dancing with an imaginary partner, twirling around and around passersby as if he were dancing on a ballroom floor. In front of the Bay store, beneath the columned portico, a small, pinch-lipped woman was holding up copies of *Watchtower*. She kept close to one of the columns, shifting from one foot to the other as if she were balancing herself on the edge of a fiery pit.

Through the noise of the rushing crowd and the plaintive crooning of the guitarist, Mad heard Selena say, "You having anything to eat, Coz?"

Mad looked at Selena. Her cousin wasn't looking at her, but fluttering her eyelashes at Darcy.

"No, thanks," Mad said. She wasn't hungry. She wanted to get out of here quick.

"Don't mind if I do," Selena said gaily. She stole another glance at Darcy, then jumped up and went to one of the food stands. Darcy followed her. At this point, Joe came alive. He lit a cigarette, slouched forward in his chair and looked insolently at Mad.

"Cat got your tongue?"

Mad's cheeks flamed. She stared at the messy tabletop, at a Styrofoam cup with a cigarette butt inside.

"No."

"So talk. Where're you from?"

"A place near Inverary. You wouldn't know it." There was the imprint of a woman's red lips at one end of the butt.

"Why wouldn't I?"

Mad ignored this. She didn't want to talk to this creepy guy. The nerve of Selena leaving her alone with him.

"Do you come down here much?"

Mad reached out and crumpled the Styrofoam cup.

"You know," Joe drawled, "if you took that cap off, I could get a better look at you." He leaned closer as if he was going to remove the cap.

If he touched her, Mad would give him a swift kick. She wasn't ready for any of that kissy stuff yet. When Willard Soper had tried to put his arm around her one day in the school corridor, she had belted him one in the chest. After that, he'd kept his distance. Mad pulled her cap lower on her head.

Shrugging indifferently, Joe got up from the table and ambled down the mall.

Selena and Darcy returned with paper plates heaped with French fries and cheeseburgers. They were both carrying chocolate milkshakes.

"Where's Joe?" Selena asked.

"I wouldn't know," Mad said sullenly. "I think I'll go home."

"Don't be a baby," Selena said. "We just got here."

This made Mad mad, really mad. The nerve of Selena, calling her a baby just because she didn't want to sit here with a bunch of weirdos. Mad left the table and headed for the Bay store. She glanced over her shoulder to see if Selena was following. She wasn't. This made Mad even madder. The least Selena could do was come after her, especially since Mad was Selena's guest. You were supposed to put yourself out for a guest, you were supposed to be kind and helpful. Selena wasn't doing that. She had used the trip to the museum as an excuse to meet this creep, Darcy. And this Joe character, did Selena think he would be Mad's date? Mad had never felt so humiliated in her whole life. She would show Selena she couldn't be used like that. She would clear out of here fast, take a bus back to the Gibsons'.

Mad saw a blue bus on the other side of the street and realized she didn't know which bus to take. She hadn't paid any attention to the numbers when they were on their way downtown. She was too stubborn to go back and ask Selena. Besides, she didn't want Selena to know where she was going. She crossed the street but the bus pulled away before she could ask the driver. She recrossed the street, walked through the columned portico of the Bay store to a set of revolving doors. On the other side of the doors was a marble foyer and marble steps. At the bottom of the steps was a cosmetic counter. A woman in a white uniform was standing behind the counter in front of a tray of eye-shadow. The woman had a blonde pompadour, beige skin, and eyelashes that stuck out like spider legs. She stood so still, she could have been a figure in a wax museum. When Mad asked her about the bus route, the red lips repeated 101, 101, 101, like a mechanical doll's. Mad went outside and crossed the street to wait for the 101.

Hands thrust deep into her jeans pockets, her peaked cap low on her head, she kept stealing glances towards the mall, hoping Selena would show up looking for her, but there was no sign of her cousin. Selena didn't even care enough to come looking for her. People streamed past. Hardly anyone gave Mad a glance. Their eyes were unfocussed, intent on some inner landscape. Mad felt lonelier in this crowd than if she were by herself in the middle of the lake in the *Explorer*. The bus came and she got on. There were no seats left, so she hung onto the overhead rail and read the advertisements over the windows: BABIES ARE FLIPPING FOR PAMPERS. HAVE YOU HUGGED YOUR CHILD TODAY? This made her feel even lonelier. By the time she reached the Gibsons', she had made a decision: she was going to phone her parents and tell them she was coming home.

Mad crossed Gibsons' lawn, heading for the back deck. Then, thinking she might go for a walk in the park, she changed course and went to the top of the tobogganing hill. She looked down, into the Gully. At the bottom of the tobogganing hill was a rough grassy area that went all the way down to the river, which was bordered on both sides by a rocky beach. To the left of the grassy area was a parking lot, and beside that, a playing field where there was a picnic shelter, fire pits, swings, climbing bars, a slide and a wishing well. Behind the playing field was a second hill which was rockier and more pointed than the hill where she stood. Running past the grassy area, the parking lot and the playing field were train tracks that were roughly parallel to the river. Mad saw a car drive into the parking lot from the road that wound along the gully bottom. She couldn't see the road from here because it was concealed by trees and by the steep sides of the tobogganing hill. She watched the man park the car and open the back door.

Two large black dogs with pointed noses bounded out of the back seat. Even from this distance Mad knew they were Dobermans. She recognized the breed because there was a Doberman chained beside the gas station in Inverary. If you went near it, the dog growled and showed its teeth. Mad decided she wouldn't go for a walk in the park after all.

She went back to the Gibsons' deck and sat in the chaise lounge. She didn't want the embarrassment of being found on the front step like a lost child. Selena, of course, had the house key. The deck was now in shade. It was comfortable sitting here, staring into the woods.

Her heart jumped when she heard the glass door open behind her and a voice say, "Why, Madeleine, what are you doing here? I thought you'd gone to the museum."

Mad turned around and saw her aunt standing in the open doorway, an apron over her rose-coloured dress.

"I did. I was," Mad faltered. "I decided to come back here."

"Where's Selena?"

"She's still downtown."

"You came back alone?"

"Yes."

Her aunt frowned. Mad braced herself for another interrogation, but none came. Instead, Aunt Louise said, "I think it would be better if you girls stuck together when you go on these outings. In a city this size . . ." she paused, then changed course, "just to be on the safe side."

"Aunt Louise, can I phone home?" Mad said.

"Go right ahead. There's a phone in the den you can use. If you need me I'll be in the kitchen getting supper."

Mad went into the den and closed the door. She would let the phone ring a long time in case her mother was weaving in her studio. But her mother answered on the second ring, which meant she was in the kitchen getting supper like Aunt Louise.

"Mum, this is Mad."

"Why, hello, Mad!" Her mother's voice was so warm and vibrant, Mad felt a thickening in her throat. "How are you?"

"Mum, I want to come home."

"Why?"

"I don't like it here," Mad whispered. She didn't want Aunt Louise to hear. It wasn't her fault she didn't like it; well, not entirely. Mad was aware she had walked into a home that was out of kilter somehow. But she couldn't tell her mother that; she was Aunt Louise's sister.

"But you just got there!" her mother said.

"I know."

"Is it Selena?"

"Yes."

"Listen, Mad, relationships take time. It will take a while for you and Selena to get to know each other again."

"I don't know if I want to get to know her again. She's changed, Mum. She's different than she used to be. She's a witch. I want to come home."

"Well, she's older than you. You have to take that into account," her mother said.

"I want to come home," Mad repeated. "I want to be home for my birthday."

"But, Mad, the visit is your birthday present."

Mad was silent. She couldn't very well say she didn't want the present anymore. It would hurt her mother's feelings.

"Tell you what," her mother said. "Try it for a week. One week. And if you feel the same way after a week you can come home."

"Why can't I come home tomorrow?"

"I think it's better if you stayed a while longer."

Please, Mum.

"Okay?"

"Okay."

But I may come home anyway.

"Have you seen Marie Delphine?" her mother said.

"No."

"Why not?"

"She's got a virus or something. Aunt Louise said I'd better wait a few days."

"Is Louise there?"

"Yes."

"Put her on, will you? I want to speak to her about Mother."

"Okay."

"And remember what I said, Mad. Give it more time."

Mad laid the receiver on the desk and went into the kitchen. Her aunt was chopping celery.

"Mum wants to talk to you," Mad said.

Her aunt jerked back from the counter.

"Oh! You startled me." She put down the knife and wiped her hands on a paper towel. "I'll take it in here on this phone. Can you hang up the other receiver?"

Mat went into the den and hung up the phone. She sat in the swivel chair and spun it in angry circles. She didn't need her mother's permission to come home. She had a return ticket in her suitcase. She could go anytime she wanted. It was *her* present, after all. If she showed up in Inverary, her parents couldn't very well make her go back, could they? She might do that.

Abruptly, Mad stopped spinning and looked at the shelves. On the highest shelf were five puppets stuck on pop bottles. Mad recognized Red Riding Hood, Cinderella, Goldilocks, Hansel and Gretel. On the next shelf down was a chalk-white mask. It was an old woman's mask. The face looked both strong and peaceful. The peacefulness seemed to come from the closed eyes, the wrinkles pressed flat, relaxed, as if all the struggle had gone out of the face. The face looked like a statue's, the kind she had seen in pictures of kings and queens lying on tombs. The mask made Mad uneasy. It seemed oddly familiar, yet she couldn't quite place it. She shifted her attention to a pile of stones on the shelf below. Most of them weren't like the stones in the basket on the deck. They were greyish-brown and irregularly shaped. Two had gay, amusing faces painted on them. The other shelves were crammed with books and papers, crude pottery bowls, sand sculptures, handmade candles. On the walls were two children's paintings entitled *Day* and *Night*. The sun was Stephen's, the moon, Selena's. Judging from the wobbly signatures and the enormous size of the circles, they had probably painted them in kindergarten. There were also animal cutouts on the walls and crude weavings made from sticks and wool. A mobile of paper birds hung from the ceiling. The room was so cluttered Mad couldn't think of it as belonging to her aunt. It seemed her aunt was two persons, or a person with two sides: one tidy and the other not so tidy. Mad liked the untidy side better. Mad heard the door to Selena's room open. She was back. Mad got up and went down the hall to Stephen's room, leaving the door open in case Selena should decide to come into the room and apologize.

But Selena did no such thing. Mad heard her cousin go into the bathroom and close the door. After a while Selena opened the door and came out into the hall. Instead of going into her bedroom, she continued down the hall to Stephen's room where Mad was lying on the bed. Selena leaned against the doorframe in her man's suit and hissed, "Don't you ever take off on me like *that* again!"

Mad sat up.

"You were the one who took off on me, remember? With that creep, Darcy."

"Darcy isn't a creep."

"He looks like a creep."

"You don't even know him. For your information, *dear* Coz, he helped me look for you. We looked and . . ."

"Don't call me *Coz*. I hate it."

"Okay, *Madeleine*. For your information, we looked high and low for you. Joe, too. I go to the trouble of introducing you to my friends and you huff off like a little snip."

"Your friends are weird," Mad said.

"And you seem to think you're better than anyone else."

Mad got up off the bed and walked towards Selena. When she got close enough, she spat out, "Why don't you shut up, Selena? Why don't you just shut up?"

Selena flounced into her room and slammed the door. Soon Mad heard savage voices screaming from the tape deck.

Aunt Louise had made lasagne and tossed salad for supper. Selena refused to eat the lasagne.

"It's fattening," she said. Naturally she didn't say anything about stuffing herself at the mall. She refused to look at Mad.

Aunt Louise ignored the impasse and talked animatedly about her clients.

"I have a man who wants a goldfish pond installed in his living room and the entire room designed around it." She shook her head. "I'm trying to talk him out of it."

Selena broke her silence to say, "I think it's a neat idea. If someone got to be a real pain, you could push her into it." She glared at Mad.

Mad glared back.

"At least I'd float," she said.

Selena shoved back her chair and stalked out to the kitchen.

Mad couldn't eat much either. The little she had eaten sat on the bottom of her stomach like a lump of plasticine.

"Well, we'll have enough left over for your lunch tomorrow," her aunt said. "You can heat it up in the microwave." She stood up and scraped food off the dishes into the garburator. "I have to deliver some drapery samples to a client. Do you want to come with me? If you brought a book along, you could read in the car. I shouldn't be too long."

"Sure," Mad said. Anything to get away from Selena the Witch.

She and her aunt tidied up the kitchen. Mad got her uncle's book on Greek goddesses and climbed into her aunt's Datsun. They drove for about twenty minutes before her aunt stopped in front of a house as large as a barn. The houses surrounding it were equally large and close together. Boring, Mad thought, ugly, nothing to interest her here. She opened the book and began to read. She read the story of Arachne, the weaver, who challenged Athena to a weaving competition and was changed into a spider. She read about Hera, goddess of marriage and childbirth, who was so jealous of her husband's attention to other women that she set about ways of punishing the women and their sons. She read about Ceres, the goddess of growing things, whose plants wilted while she was try- ing to rescue her daughter, Persephone. Pluto had kid- napped Persephone and taken her to the underworld. Mad was surprised at how mean and spiteful some of the goddesses were. She thought there should be an ideal place where goddesses lived in harmony and did not fight with each other. It was beginning to get dark when her aunt came out of the house. Aunt Louise got into the car, started the engine, backed out of the driveway and headed for home.

"I didn't think I'd be so long," she said. "It turned out the woman not only wanted her living room and family room done over, but the bedrooms as well. There were five. Not that I'm complaining. It's a big job. My partner will be pleased. It's a very competitive business, let me tell you. You have to scramble to stay ahead." At the traffic light, she turned to Mad. "Were you bored sitting in the car?"

"No," Mad said. "I just about finished the book."

"Selena certainly would have been bored," her aunt said. She sighed. "But then, as I said, she doesn't read."

When they got home, Mad gathered up her nightgown, bathrobe and book and carried them into the bathroom where she ran water for a bath. She realized she couldn't take the book into the tub with her as she was used to doing. She might get it wet. She set the book on a towel, got into the tub, lay back and thought about home.

If she were there now, she might be swimming in the lake. She and Louie sometimes went swimming in the dark. They especially liked to do this when there was moonlight on the water, a silvery pathway that went ahead of them no matter where they swam. Maybe she'd go home the day after tomorrow. Tomorrow she'd go out and buy Louie some comic books. She might even visit Marie Delphine.

She got out of the bath, dried herself; put on her nightgown, picked up the book and went into Stephen's room. On the other side of the wall she heard Selena laughing. She was on the phone again, probably with that creep, Darcy. Mad got into bed with Monkton. She plumped up the pillows, leaned back and opened the book. Soon she had finished the last few pages. She leafed backwards through the book and reread her favourite story, which was about

Artemis, the Moon Huntress, who captured a deer, harnessed it to a chariot and then drove over the mountains. Being a goddess, she could do that.

Mad put the book on the floor. Then remembering her uncle's fastidiousness, she got up, padded into the living room and returned the book to its shelf. As she passed the sliding glass door, she looked outside. The moon, round and pearl-like, was rising in the dark night sky. It glowed softly, touching the tops of the trees in silver light. They looked like the crescents of incoming waves. When she was a little girl, Mad believed the moon disappeared early each morning and came back each night. She thought the moon went someplace else, a mysterious place on the other side of a dark curtain where there was another world. Sometimes the moon hid on the other side of the curtain for several nights, but it always came back. Only when she studied Science in school did she learn that the moon's disappearance was simply an absence of light. Even though Mad knew this, she still thought the transformations in the moon were somehow magical.

Mad went back to bed and turned out the lamp. Selena's voice had dropped to a low hum on the other side of the wall. Moonlight filtered through the curtains. Mad fell asleep imagining how glorious it would be to ride over the mountains in a silver chariot pulled by a silver deer.

When she awoke, it was the middle of the night. She opened her eyes. Moonlight silvered the room. She heard three notes. They seemed to be coming from outside. They sounded like the chime of the icicle clock she had seen in the museum. She heard a chorus, very faint, of women's voices.

Mad got up and went into the hallway. Moonlight poured into the living room through the glass windows. Mad thought she caught a movement outside on the deck, but when she looked, she saw only the chaise lounge, the table and chairs. Mad looked at the moon mask on the stone fireplace. Moonlight shone on the smooth cheeks, the smiling mouth, illuminating it with an eerie silver glow. All of the moon's light seemed focussed on that circle face. It was as if the moon and the mask were at either end of the same beam of light. Mad stared at the mask. Out of the corner of her eye, she caught another movement outside on the deck, but when she turned, the movement was gone. This happened once more before Mad reached for the mask and put it on. She looked through the eyeholes and stared through the glass door. She saw a fair-haired girl outside, looking in. The deck furniture had vanished. There was only the girl. She had a white, waxy face and was dressed in a short white tunic and sandals. She carried a silver hunting horn. She rapped urgently on the glass.

Mad saw her mouth form an O.

"Open," she seemed to be saying.

Mad unlocked the door and slid it open.

The girl thrust something through the opening and into Mad's hand. Mad saw that she was wearing a bracelet.

"It's very important that you keep this safe." She hurried to the end of the deck, then turned. "Guard it carefully!" she said. Then she climbed into a silver chariot, put the horn to her lips, blew three notes and was gone. The chariot was pulled by a silver deer.

Mad looked at the object in her hand. It was a smooth, egg-shaped stone. Mad held the stone to the moonlight. It was made of white marble with a tracery of lines running through it like fine black writing enclosed in ice. The lines looped around themselves and curved into valleys, as if they were forming words. But the words were unfamiliar, like a language from another time. Mad shivered. What was the meaning of this stone? And where did the girl come from? A shaft of cold air flowed through the open door. Mad hung the moon mask back on its spike and slid the door closed. She noticed the deck furniture was back in place. Maybe it had never been gone. Maybe she had imagined its disappearance. But she had this stone in her hand, didn't she? She hadn't imagined that. She could feel its hard smoothness on her palm. Mad shivered and rubbed her bare arms.

She went into the bedroom, got into bed and pulled the covers over her head. She lay there shivering, holding the stone. Gradually the stone felt warm in her hand and she began to relax. She felt the warmth creeping up her arms to her shoulders. She followed the warmth down to her breasts, to her hips and thighs. By the time the warmth had reached her toes, she was asleep.

from

Naomi's Road

by
Joy Kogawa

During World War Two, when Canada was at war with Japan, Canadians of Japanese origin were sent from their homes to internment camps. In this story Naomi is one such person. She and her older brother Stephen are sent from Vancouver to the interior of B.C., where they are cared for by their aunt, Obasan. Like newcomers everywhere Naomi wants to be accepted; she wants a friend.

A year has passed since we came to Slocan, and a school has been built. It's half a mile away, where everyone lives in the rows and rows of huts.

The path to school is through the forest. Every school day, Stephen and I carry our lunches and schoolbags. For lunch I have a boiled egg and dandelion greens and Obasan's onigiri rice balls with a salty red plum in the middle. Stephen takes sandwiches and an apple or an orange.

On the way home from school, Stephen and I walk by a big white house. There's a swing in the backyard. A pretty girl about my age lives there. She has light golden hair like Goldilocks. Sometimes, before we reach her yard, we can see her swinging on her swing. Higher and higher she goes, her toes pointing up to the sky.

One day we stand at the fence and watch her.

"Boy," Stephen says. "I bet she'll go right around."

Toys are all over her backyard, like a toy store. There's a doll carriage and a doll house and a doll's tea set on a doll's table. And there are two real live white bunnies hopping in a pen. I wish I could hold the bunnies. They look as fluffy and soft as cotton wool.

The golden-haired girl sees us standing at the fence. She scrapes her feet on the ground to stop her swinging. Then she jumps off.

"What are you staring at?" she asks. She sounds angry. I want to run away into the trees. She makes a face at us and stomps her feet.

"Go away," she shouts.

What a mean girl. "Come on," I say to Stephen. I start to walk down the path.

But Stephen is angry. He whacks at the grass with his lunch pail.

"Go 'way," the girl shouts again.

"Why should I?" Stephen says. "This is a free country."

"It's not your country," the girl says.

"It is so," Stephen says.

"It is not," she shouts.

A red and white checked curtain in the window behind her moves. There's a woman who also has golden hair, looking out at us. She raps on the window with her knuckles. The girl looks back. The woman is shaking her head.

"I can't play with you," the girl says in a sing-song voice. She points her chin to the sky and turns her head.

I run through the trees, taking a shortcut away from the path. The thick pine-needle floor crackles as I go. I can hear Stephen behind me hitting the trees with his lunch pail.

I don't like the horrid girl. I don't like walking by her house. I don't like school either. In the morning I don't like having my hair combed. My hair is getting long and Obasan braids it in pigtails. I don't like my pigtails.

But I like climbing the mountains. I like playing with my Mickey Mouse who can walk by itself down a slope; I like reading my grade-three reader and Stephen's grade-five reader. And I like reading the comics in the newspaper.

There are some funny roly-poly comic-strip boys called the Katzenjammer Kids. They play tricks on a mean little rich boy called Rollo. And there's a fuzzy-haired girl with empty-circle eyes called Little Orphan Annie. She is always saved from danger by her Daddy Warbucks. Sometimes I lie in my bunk bed at night pretending I'm Little Orphan Annie being rescued by my Daddy.

Stephen likes to read the comics too. But he also reads the harder parts of the newspaper. He says he has to know what's happening in the war. Uncle and Stephen talk about the war together while they chop wood.

One day Stephen comes running home with a red, white, and blue Union Jack. It's the same as the flag high up on a pole at school. He holds it high in the air and the flag flaps behind him.

"Where did you get that?" I ask.

"I won it," Stephen says. "I traded it for all my marbles." Back and forth he waves the flag. Then he nails it to a long pole and plants it in a hole at the top of Uncle's rock garden. The flag hangs quietly and peacefully high up in the air.

When Stephen jumps back down again, he stands at attention facing the flag. Then he salutes it.

"We have to sing 'God Save the King,'" Stephen says. He makes a trumpet out of his hands. After that we sing "Land of Hope and Glory" and "O Canada."

When we are singing "Hearts of Oak," I see the horrid girl walking up the path.

We stop. She stops too. She's staring at us and staring at the flag.

"That's not your flag," she says.

"It is too," Stephen says.

"You stole it," she shouts. "Give it to me."

"It's mine," Stephen shouts back.

"You're going to lose the war," she says in her sing-song voice.

"We will NOT!" Stephen yells so loud I cover my ears and run into the house.

From inside the house Obasan and I listen to Stephen pounding on the tub drum. Obasan's eyes are shut.

After a while Stephen comes in and climbs into his bunk. He lies down and takes the flute from under his pillow. All the songs he can remember, he plays and plays and plays. Even when it's time to sleep he keeps playing. Uncle joins in with the tappity-tappity sounds of spoons on his knees.

"Good music," Uncle says to Stephen.

"Good drumming, Uncle," Stephen replies.

When Nomura-obasan was with us, she used to say, "Music will heal us all." Obasan says it now, quietly, with her eyes closed. Obasan is still praying.

Three days pass. It's around noon. I'm playing at the side of the house making a little pond with rocks and flowers and a bowl of water. Obasan is washing clothes in the back with a washboard and tub. All my clothes from Vancouver are too small now and Obasan has added hems and sleeves to make them bigger.

I'm putting a buttercup in the bowl for a pretend lily pad when I hear someone saying "Hi."

The horrid girl and her mother are in the middle of the road. They are both shielding their eyes from the sun as they look up. The Union Jack flaps coolly in the mountain air.

"Hello," the mother says to me. "I can see the flag from the window."

I stand up. I feel shy and want to go to Obasan.

"I'm Mitzi," the girl says. "What's your name?"

"Naomi."

"Hello, Naomi," the mother says. She's smiling.

"Hello."

Mitzi comes up to the fence and leans on it. "Can you come and play at my house?" she asks.

I can hardly believe what she's saying. Will she let me pet her bunnies?

"Ask your mother," Mitzi's mother says.

She doesn't know Obasan is my aunt.

When I ask Obasan, she wipes her hands on her apron and nods. She goes into the house and brings out a bag of cookies.

"For Mitzi," Obasan tells me.

"Oh, thank you," Mitzi's mother says to Obasan when I give them to Mitzi. "Say 'thank you,' Mitzi."

"Can I eat one?" Mitzi asks.

Obasan smiles and Mitzi's mother smiles. It seems to me that the trees and the birds and the sun and the flag and all the creatures in the whole world are smiling right now.

Mitzi skips down the path munching the cookie.

"Come on," she calls to me. I feel too shy to skip but I walk quickly to keep up.

When we come to her yard, Mitzi breaks one cookie into little pieces. She puts them in a little doll's dish on her doll's table.

All afternoon we play together. I cuddle her bunnies. At first they make little jerky jumping movements with their back feet. But afterwards they get used to me. They eat sticks of carrots and pieces of lettuce. Their wriggly noses sniff and sniff. One is called Patsy and the other is called Gruff. Mitzi tells me that when they have babies

I can have one. I want to jump up and run home and tell Stephen.

Almost every day after this, Mitzi and I make up games and concerts. We make a playhouse out of blankets in the trees. We make mud pies and pine-needle tea and have tea parties with the dolls. One time when we're playing house, she wears my best bead necklace. She likes it so much, I let her keep it.

Mitzi has three favorite dolls. One has eyes that close with a "click" sound when you lay her on her back. She's a fancy doll in a lacy dress. She has white socks and white shoes and tiny white shoelaces. When you spank her or put her on her stomach, she makes a crying noise.

The second doll is a Raggedy Ann with long pigtails like mine. She was a Christmas present when Mitzi was four. She loves her Raggedy Ann the best.

"I want braids like yours and my dolly's," Mitzi says.

"I want curly hair like yours," I tell Mitzi.

"Let's trade," Mitzi says. We giggle because we know we can't do that.

Her third-favorite doll is the most dear baby doll I have ever seen. It has big blue eyes and chubby little arms and legs. She drinks from a bottle and wets her diaper. Her name is Baby.

When we get tired of playing with Mitzi's dolls, we play "Hide-and-go-seek" and "Mother-may-I," and "Simon says." We read Mitzi's story books and play with paper dolls. We play "Snakes-and-ladders" and jacks, and color in coloring books and make shadow plays with a sheet. We swing and eat tea biscuits that are just like the ones Mama used to make. Most of all I like making up stories about Mitzi and me. I pretend we're magic and can become invisible or tiny as Tom Thumb. Elves and fairies ride away with us into the forest at midnight.

On my ninth birthday, Mitzi brings me a present in a box so big she can barely carry it.

"What is it?" I ask.

The box is wrapped in white tissue paper and has a big pink bow.

"Guess," Mitzi says.

It's not a heavy box. I hold it and rattle it and shake it. It doesn't make a sound.

"I can't guess," I tell Mitzi. What could be so light and in such a big box?

I undo the bow carefully and open the box. All I can see are big handfuls of crumpled tissue paper. I wonder if it's a joke and Mitzi's brought me an empty box.

"Keep going," Mitzi says as I take out the paper.

I take out more crumples. And then—and then—I see her. It's Baby! It's the dearest sweetest doll in the world. I can hardly believe it. I put my hands down into the crumples and lift her up gently. She's wearing a brand-new pink knitted dress with little pink booties and a pink and white bonnet. Her bottle is around her wrist with an elastic band.

"Oh!" I hold her in my arms.

"Isn't she pretty?" Mitzi says. "Mommy made the dress."

I hardly dare to ask if I can keep her.

"It's your birthday present," Mitzi says.

I want to laugh and cry at the same time. I must be the luckiest happiest girl in the whole world. I wrap a tea towel around Baby and cradle her in my arms.

"Can I really keep her?" I ask.

"Yes," Mitzi says.

The Cousins

by

Deirdre Baker

"Perseids" is the name given to the annual meteor shower that appears in the Northern Hemisphere towards the middle of August. "Bioluminescence" is how people describe the effect of a chemical reaction that occurs among some kinds of micro-plankton with the motion of water. In this story Deirdre Baker celebrates these two natural phenomena of light through the events of one magical summer night.

Becca's cousins were coming.

"We'll pick them up at the ferry tomorrow," Gran said. "Imagine! All my granddaughters at once!"

She was pleased, and Becca was too. Becca loved Molly and Ardeth. They built the best sandcastles in the world.

They rowed the boat out and let Becca jump off in her life jacket. They played Hide and Seek, Capture the Flag and Kick the Can. They took Becca for hikes and picnics. Yes, there was always something happening when Molly and Ardeth were around.

When the cousins arrived, they were big. Becca knew that, but this summer they loomed and towered, or they bounded about with great, strapping bodies, laughing at things that puzzled Becca. They were fifteen, and twins.

"Let's swim!" they cried, hurling clothes as they dug for their bathing suits.

They ran into the water with Becca between them, swinging her over the waves.

But the next morning they slept late.

"Let's swim," Becca said, poking the lumps in sleeping bags.

"They're still asleep," said Gran, quite unnecessarily. "But there's nothing to stop you and me from going swimming."

Becca could hardly wait for them to wake up.

She and Gran swam, made and ate breakfast, washed and dried the dishes, pumped water from the well, visited the Recycling Depot and shopped at the Farmers' Market.

But Molly and Ardeth were still asleep.

"It must have been a long trip," Becca said, excusing their sleepiness.

Gran smiled. "Probably," she said. "Let's pick the lavender."

Becca loved the deep, oily scent of lavender. She picked each stem carefully and laid it in her basket, thinking of last summer, when she had played with Molly and Ardeth, and with all their friends from around the bay—Kathy and Sue, Marion from next door, Frances and Tasha—

"Last year we all went swimming in the waves before breakfast," she said. "It was the very first day after they got here. Remember?"

"I remember," said Gran.

"Why are they so sleepy?" Becca wondered.

"Sleep is like food for them," Gran said. "You'll be like that too, when you're a teenager."

"Never," said Becca.

"Actually, they're a lot nicer than many fifteen-year-olds," Gran said.

It took a long time to pick lavender, and when they returned to the cabin, Molly and Ardeth were reading.

"What are we going to do?" Becca cried, jumping onto Molly's lap.

Molly laughed and gave her a squeeze.

"Read! Now we're going to read, and then later, we'll go for a swim."

Every day it was the same. Molly and Ardeth slept, and then they read. Then they napped. They would play for a while, and then they would read again for a long, long time. Becca liked books too, but she wanted to *do* something.

"We've only got four days!" Becca wailed. "When are we going to start having fun?"

"Go on!" Gran protested. "Yesterday you swam with them, and the day before they took you out in the boat! And every night they tuck you in and read you two stories!"

But it wasn't enough, a few bursts of fun in between stretches of reading or sleep. Sometimes they even napped in the afternoon! Becca hadn't done that for years.

"There's something wrong with them," Becca insisted. "It's not fair!"

"That's enough, Becca!" Gran said. "Nobody likes hearing you moan. Go pick the beans—that will distract you."

Becca took the basket and went to complain to the bees.

That night when she went to bed, she peered over the edge of the loft, down at the heads of Molly, Ardeth and Gran, all bent over their books. Evening was the time to read, Becca thought. She could understand that. But day—day was the time to explore, to swim, to play hard and to talk.

Molly and Ardeth had no life at all.

Long after she'd fallen asleep, Becca awoke. Something smelled delicious. Even though it was far into the night, there was a light on below. Becca squirmed to the edge of the loft.

Ardeth and Molly were playing Scrabble. Molly was laughing so hard she was leaning over sideways, her face buried in her arms. It was the tiny squawks of laughter that had awoken Becca, perhaps.

"Hand over the popcorn, Molly," Ardeth whispered. "Don't be such an animal. You sound like a pig."

"What are you doing?" Becca asked in a low voice. "Can I have some?"

"Becca!"

Ardeth smiled and got up. She stood under Becca and held out her arms.

"Come down!" she invited her. "It's a midnight feast!"

Becca slipped into her arms and Ardeth carried her to the table.

"Help yourself!" she whispered. "Molly, if you don't stop laughing you'll have to go outside! You'll wake up Gran."

"There, I won," Molly announced, stuffing her mouth with popcorn. "Have some," she offered.

It wasn't just popcorn, it was caramel popcorn. Delicious was not the word for it: it was like eating clouds. Becca's mouth seemed to rain when she tasted it.

"Are you still playing Scrabble?" she asked. "Can I watch?"

"We're finished," Molly said. "But now we're going to —"

She stopped, and looked at Ardeth.

"We're going swimming," she whispered. "Do you want to come?"

"What about Gran?"

"Sh! She doesn't know," Ardeth said.

"It's our secret," Molly boasted. "Heh heh!"

She gave a great wink.

It looked awfully dark when they tiptoed onto the beach, but after a moment Becca's eyes changed, or the stars grew brighter, or perhaps the water began to glow. Something changed and Becca could see, faintly, the stones at her feet.

"We'll go down to the sand," Ardeth said, meaning that they wouldn't go off the rocks in front of the cabin. Although Gran couldn't be woken from here, Ardeth spoke quietly. It seemed, somehow, that the bay itself might be asleep, silently rocking reflections of the stars.

As they crunched over snails and dried seaweed, Becca thought she heard other movements, footsteps not their own. "Stop," she said, tugging at Molly's hand. "What's that?"

"It's only Marion," Ardeth said.

"Is Marion coming too?"

Marion joined them and panted, "I almost fell over Dad and Mum! They were sleeping on the porch and I didn't even know!"

Molly stifled her laughter, but mysteriously, Becca heard it, a chuckle from somewhere along the beach. Out from the trees stepped Tasha, almost as if she'd been waiting.

And down on the sand were Frances, and Sarah who worked at the store.

"Put your towel here," Molly said. "That way it won't get soggy. We'll go down to the water while we wait for the others."

"What others?"

The stars changed as they waited there. For one thing, there were more of them, a great swoop of sparkling, magical dust. The Big Dipper, the only constellation Becca knew, was lost in the multitude that shone there.

For another, some of the stars darted about. Becca saw them zip, dazzle and disappear. Twice, yellow fire fell out of the sky, leaving a trail of sparks that glowed, then faded almost instantly.

And it all happened in silence, without a crackle.

"What are they doing?" she asked, but nobody heard her, or even seemed to notice the stars. Perhaps they were used to them.

Instead Ardeth said, "Here come Kathy and Sue. It's time to go."

Holding the hands of Molly and Ardeth, Becca waded into the black water in a company of girls.

There was no turning back, even when the night water shrank her skin. The shapes of Kathy and Sue, Frances, Marion and the others gleamed like a pale grove about her. The only sound was that of water disturbed by arms and legs, water that carried broken reflections of stars.

"Do they fall into the water?" Becca asked, for in the darkness she could see the sparkle of a thousand stars where she walked. She thought the reflections had sunk, or the stars that had fallen before had started a new life underwater.

"Do what fall in the water?" Ardeth asked.

"The stars. There are stars all over my legs."

Becca stopped walking.

"Well, you can't see them now," she said, confused. "Where did they go?"

She walked and lights prickled in the sea. A sweep of glitter billowed in her wake.

"Wow!" Ardeth exclaimed quietly. "Look, you guys, there's tons of it!"

"Tons of what?"

"Tons of luminescence!" Ardeth said.

"What?"

"Little plants and things that light up," Ardeth said.

It hardly seemed the way to describe stars on Becca's legs.

"It's a natural wonder," Molly muttered.

That made more sense.

One by one, the girls sank into the sea, and Becca did too, holding tight to Ardeth. Sarah and Frances squeaked as they went. The others just sighed and started to swim.

"I've never seen so much," Ardeth murmured.

For it was as though they were clothed in light, trailing a glory that burned white beneath the night sea. When Becca lifted her arm glitter dripped from it, and she saw stars in Ardeth's wet hair and even on her teeth. The girls around her twinkled like heavenly bodies, waved glowing arms like angels' wings. A school of fish flashed away like fireworks, leaving trails of light that winked and faded, like the ones Becca had seen, could even see now, in the regions of the Milky Way.

"Is this falling stars too?" she asked. "Do falling stars happen in the sea?"

"Holy cow!" Ardeth said. "No, it's—falling stars! Look up, you guys, look up!"

And every one of the starry girls lifted her face and saw what Becca had already seen, could see even now—a shower of meteors flashing in the August night.

Becca slept in the next morning, but still, she woke up before Molly and Ardeth.

"Goodness me," Gran grumbled. "I don't know where all these dirty cocoa cups came from. Someone used my whole collection of mugs!"

Becca smiled at her sleepily, her vision blurred by twinkling memories of the night.

"And so," said Gran, "did you enjoy your night swim?"

"Gran!" exclaimed Becca. "You knew!"

"Sh," whispered Gran. "Don't tell Ardeth and Molly!"

She winked, just the way Molly had the night before.

"Gran," Becca whispered, "we got new skin! We were covered in light. What is that?"

"Dear child," said Gran, "go back to bed. I'll explain all about it when you've caught up on your sleep."

That morning, Gran swam alone.

A Coyote Columbus Story

by

Thomas King

This is not the story of the discovery of America that we learn from textbooks. Here Thomas King takes time and stirs it into a big stew, mixing Christopher Columbus in with computer games and sky diving. Then he adds talking turtles, Cartier and a bag of licorice jelly beans. Who better to star in this adventure than tricky Coyote, who in this story is a girl whose nose falls off when she thinks too hard and who really just wants to have fun even if she is the creator of the world.

It was Coyote who fixed up this world, you know. She is the one who did it. She made rainbows and flowers and clouds and rivers. And she made prune juice and afternoon naps and toe-nail polish and television commercials. Some of these things were pretty good, and some of these things were foolish. But what she loved to do best was to play ball.

She played ball all day and all night. She would throw the ball and she would hit the ball and she would run and catch the ball. But playing ball by herself was boring, so she sang a song and she danced a dance and she thought hard, and pretty soon along came some beavers.

Let's play ball, says Coyote.

We've got better things to do than play ball, says those beavers. We have to build a dam so we'll have a pretty pond to swim in.

That's all very nice, says Coyote, but I want to play ball.

So Coyote sang her song and she danced her dance and she thought hard, and right away along came some moose.

Let's play ball, says Coyote.

What a foolish idea, says those moose. We'd rather wade in that lovely pond over there. And they do that.

Playing ball is a lot more fun, says Coyote, but those moose don't hear her.

I better sing my song and dance my dance and think real hard again, says Coyote. And she does. And in a while, along come some turtles.

You're just in time to play ball, says Coyote.

What a sweaty idea, says those turtles. We'd much rather lie on a nice warm rock in the middle of that beautiful pond.

But who will play ball with me? cries Coyote.

Tra-la-la-la-la, sing those beavers and moose and turtles in that happy pond.

I'll get it right this time, says Coyote, and she sings her song and dances her dance and thinks so hard her nose falls off, and right away along come some human beings.

Do you want to play ball? says Coyote, and that one makes a happy mouth and wags her ears.

Sure, says those human beings. That sounds like a good idea to us.

Hooray, says Coyote, and she lets the human beings hit the ball first.

Well, Coyote and those human beings become very good friends. You sure are a good friend, says those human beings. Yes, that's true, says Coyote.

But you know, whenever Coyote and the human beings played ball, Coyote always won. She always won because she made up the rules. That sneaky one made up the rules, and she always won because she could do that.

That's not fair, says the human beings. Friends don't do that.

That's the rules, says Coyote. Let's play some more. Maybe you will win next time. But they don't.

You keep changing the rules, says those human beings.

No, no, no, no, says Coyote. You are mistaken. And then she changes the rules again.

So, after a while, those human beings find better things to do.

Some of them go shopping.

Some of them go sky diving.

Some of them go to see big-time wrestling.

Some of them go on a seven-day Caribbean cruise.

Those human beings got better things to do than play
ball with Coyote and those changing rules.

So, Coyote doesn't have anyone to play with again.

So, she has to play by herself.

So, she gets bored.

When Coyote gets bored, anything can happen. Stick
around. Big trouble is going to come along, I can tell you that.

Well. That silly one sings a song and she dances a dance
and she thinks really hard. But she's thinking about changing those rules, too, and doesn't watch what she is making
up out of her head.

When Coyote stops all that singing and dancing and
thinking and she looks around, she sees three ships and
some people in funny-looking clothes carrying flags and
boxes of junk.

Oh, happy days, says Coyote. You are just in time for the
ball game.

Hello, says one of the men in silly clothes with red hair
all over his head. I am Christopher Columbus. I am sailing
the ocean blue looking for India. Have you seen it?

Forget India, says Coyote. Let's play ball.

It must be around here somewhere, says Christopher
Columbus.

I have a map.

Forget the map, says Coyote. I'll bat first and I'll tell you
the rules as we go along.

But that Christopher Columbus and his friends don't
want to play ball. We got work to do, they says. We got to
find India. We got to find things we can sell.

Yes, says those Columbus people, where is that gold?

Yes, they says, where is that chocolate cake?

Yes, they says, where are those computer games?

Yes, they says, where are those music videos?

Boy, says Coyote, and that one scratches her head. I must have sung that song wrong. Maybe I didn't do the right dance. Maybe I thought too hard. These people I made have no manners. They act as if they've got no relations.

And she is right. Christopher Columbus and his friends start shouting and jumping up and down in their funny clothes.

Boy, what a bunch of noise, says Coyote. What bad manners. You guys got to stop jumping and shouting or my nose will fall off.

We got to find India, says Christopher Columbus. We got to become rich. We got to become famous. Do you think you can help us?

But all Coyote can think about is playing ball.

I'll let you bat first, says Coyote.

No time for games, says Christopher Columbus.

I'll let you make the rules, cries Coyote.

But those Columbus people don't listen. They are too busy running around looking for India. Looking for stuff they can sell. And pretty soon, they find that pond.

I see a four-dollar beaver, says one.

I see a fifteen-dollar moose, says another.

I see a two-dollar turtle, says a third.

Those things aren't worth poop, says Christopher Columbus. We can't sell those things in Spain. Look harder.

But all they find are beavers and moose and turtles. And when they tell Christopher Columbus, that one squeezes his ears and he chews his nose and he grinds his teeth. He grinds his teeth so hard, he gets a headache, and then he gets cranky.

And then he gets an idea.

Say, says Christopher Columbus, I'll bet this is India. And he looks at the human beings. I'll bet these are Indians. And he looks at his friends. I'll bet we can sell these Indians.

Yes, says his friends, that's a good idea. We could sell Indians. And they stop trying to catch those beavers and moose and turtles.

Whew! says those beavers and moose and turtles, that was close. And they run and hide before Columbus and his friends change their minds.

Wait a minute, says the human beings, that is not a good idea. That is a bad idea. That is a bad idea full of bad manners.

When Coyote hears this bad idea, she starts to laugh. Who would buy human beings, she says, and she laughs some more. She laughs so hard she has to hold her nose on her face with both her hands.

But while that Coyote is laughing, Christopher Columbus grabs a big bunch of men and women and children and locks them up in his ships.

When Coyote stops laughing and looks around, she sees that some of the human beings are missing. Hey, she says, where are those human beings? Where are my friends?

I'm going to sell them in Spain, says Christopher Columbus. Somebody has to pay for this trip. Sailing over the ocean blue isn't cheap, you know. Grab some more Indians!

But the rest of the human beings see Columbus coming, and they jump in the pond.

I'm a beaver, they says.

I'm a moose, they says.

I'm a turtle, they says.

Hmmmm, says Columbus, and he scratches his nose. Where did all the Indians go?

They went that way, says those beaver human beings and moose human beings and turtle human beings, and they point in all directions.

Wait a minute, says Coyote. What about my friends you have locked up in your ships? You got to let them go.

Tra-la-la-la-la, says Columbus, and that one goes back to Spain and sells the human beings to rich people like baseball players and dentists and babysitters and parents.

Another couple of trips like this, Columbus tells his friends, and I'll be able to buy a big bag of licorice jelly beans and a used Mercedes.

After Columbus and his friends leave, the beavers and the moose and the turtles come out of hiding, and the human beings come out of the pond.

You're supposed to fix up this world, cry those beavers and moose and turtles. You're supposed to make it right. But you keep messing it up, too.

Yes, says the human beings, you better watch out or this world is going to get bent.

Everything is okay, says Coyote. I made a little mistake but I'll take it back. I'll take Christopher Columbus back. You'll see, everything will be balanced again.

So Coyote sings her song and she dances her dance and she thinks really hard. She thinks so hard her nose falls off again, and, when she looks around, she see another bunch of funny-looking people.

Bonjour, says one of those funny-looking people. I'm Jacques Cartier, and I'm sailing the ocean blue.

Oh, oh, says those beavers and moose and turtles and human beings. Coyote's done it again. And they catch the first train to Penticton.

Don't panic, says Coyote. Everything is under control.

I'm looking for India, says Jacques Cartier. Have you seen it?

Coyote makes a happy mouth. And that one wags her ears. Forget India, she says. Maybe you want to play ball.

from

Round the Bend

by

Mitzi Dale

Deirdre sounds like a smart, funny kid who tells it like it is. In the second sentence of this novel she reveals, "It's a year to the day that I got out of the loony bin." But as her story progresses, and we get to know her family and her fictional self, the courageous lady rancher, we start to find out that the truth is neither plain nor simple.

We moved to the suburbs when I was six. My brother had flown the coop by then and I think the idea was that I would go to school in a "decent" place—not the city. In kindergarten I'd hung around with a tough crowd. Go on, laugh. It's true, though. It was a tough crowd and I'm a little embarrassed to say it was one of the few times I can remember having real fun. We used to do things like open our eyes during nap time and steal Plastitak. This is a ridiculous admission, but I don't think I was ever so scared as when Miss Murdoch found me with a huge wad of Plastitak in my pocket.

Miss Murdoch had white hair and had been teaching for years. You wouldn't think she'd still have the energy to terrorize little kids, but she did. Just before bathroom break one day, she took a whole bunch of new supplies out of the big closet at the back of the room. As she walked by I could see, along with new chalk and pencils, a brand-new package of Plastitak. She put these things down on the edge of her desk and refilled her chalk-holder with a fresh piece of chalk. Miss Murdoch always used a chalk-holder.

She clapped her hands and said, "Break time, people," and everyone stood up and filed out row by row. Miss Murdoch always stood at the door while we filed out, so as I walked by that desk with the white Plastitak looking so tempting in its clear wrapper and blue label, I just couldn't resist taking it and stuffing it in my pocket. As I went past I thought Miss Murdoch gave me a funny look, but I just kept going. I went to the bathroom, and I was just washing my hands at the big round sink when she came in. She had her arms crossed and was staring at me.

"Do you have something for me, Deirdre?" she asked. I shook my head.

"I think you do. Where is it, young lady?" She grabbed me and put her hand in my pocket and pulled out the evidence. All the kids were watching by this time. Her

nostrils were flaring. She held the package up for everyone to see.

"This is stealing," she said to the whole group. Then she
grabbed me by my arm and started dragging me out of the
washroom. I tried to hold onto the sink, but that made her
madder and she squeezed my arm even harder. She yanked
me out of there and dragged me to the principal's office.

My parents were called. I guess that's the first time I
realized they were so opposite. My mother actually seemed
pleased that I'd stolen something. My father kept apologiz-
ing for my behaviour, but my mother kept referring to me
as mischievous. We drove home in silence, except for my
father repeating, "This will not happen again." It didn't.

So we moved to the suburbs, and I stopped having fun.
At my new school there was a bad crowd, but I didn't
bother getting in with them. I stayed pretty much on my
own. I know this upset my mother. I think she wanted me
to go and steal something at the new school. But I didn't
do anything.

It was the year we moved that I started my ranch daydream. I had this ongoing story in my head about how I
owned a ranch. I had hired hands, but I did most things
myself, like brand cattle and round up horses. I never
stayed after school for sports or anything, but got into this
routine of coming straight home from school, flopping on
my bed and getting into the ranch thing. This wasn't an
ordinary daydream. It was almost like a movie in my head.
I'd pick up right where I left off the day before, so new stuff
happened each day. I couldn't just go over and over the

good parts. Those were the rules. This could get pretty exhausting, but it was the best part of my day.

"A lady should be dainty and refined." My father's words came back to me as I stood on a knoll that overlooked the ranch. He had always said that, and yet he was the one who had taught me to ride and handle the lasso. And now he'd left the ranch to me, his only child. Everything I could see from that knoll, I owned.

I took off my hat and wiped the sweat from my forehead. Well, I wasn't dainty and refined. But you'd think people would be used to that by now. A couple of men who'd worked for Pa most of their lives had quit the day before. I guessed what they could take from a rancher's daughter they couldn't take from the rancher. Especially a woman rancher. I wanted to find out the truth, though, so I went over to Old Joe for some straight talk.

"Joe," I said, "how long have you known me?"

"Since you cut your first teeth, ma'am."

"And have I always been straight with you?"

"Straight as an arrow. Just like your pa."

"Then you'll be straight with me."

"You bet, ma'am."

"Why did those two men leave?"

There was just a moment's hesitation in Joe's eyes, but I was looking level at him, waiting.

"They didn't like the way you talked to them," he said after a beat.

"Am I rude, Joe?"

"No, ma'am."

"Am I asking too much of the men?"

"No, ma'am."

"Have I changed since taking over, Joe?"

"No, ma'am, you always was one to give orders."

I raised my eyebrows and his lips curled into a smile. "We may be short-handed for a while around here, Joe," I said.

"I don't doubt it, ma'am," he said, "so I'd best get back to work."

I slapped my hat back on my head and trudged across the fields. Why should I take half an hour to wheedle a favour out of a man when I could just tell him what I wanted? If they expected me to be batting my eyes and saying pretty please, they had another think coming.

For the first few weeks at my new school, my mother would ask me every time I got home what had happened that day, and each day I'd say, "nothing," and head up to my room.

The strain of me not being amusing was too much for her. I didn't realize how much until I was nine. We were sitting around the dinner table and it was very quiet. I had just woken up after a long sleep following a pretty intense daydream session about my favourite mare being in foal. All of a sudden out of the silence my mother spoke. "The Irish only hit their children for one thing—not being charming." I started to smile, because I did think it was kind of cute, when my father looked up and said, "You're not Irish, dear." Now, usually over something like that she'd wrinkle her nose and call him an old silly, but this time she did a really strange thing. She started to cry.

Well, to tell you the truth, I felt a little trapped. My father clearly wasn't going to try to find out just what he'd done wrong, and I couldn't bring myself to say anything. I'd been the brunt of her joke, after all, and I didn't feel like helping her out of this situation. That was the first time I felt really stuck, kind of paralyzed. I saw the whole thing from all three points of view, and so I just sat there.

I just sat there, and my mother cried, and my father ate his dinner. Can you imagine that? Sitting through dinner when one of the three of you is bawling her eyes out? That's the way we were. Nothing came of that incident. It was never mentioned again and my mother never made the Irish comment again.

I was ten years old when my parents had the dinner party. It was my job to greet people at the door with my parents and then wander around afterward with a tray full of little mushroom and bacon things. I got a new dress for this occasion. Red velvet. The only good thing about it was I'd chopped my hair off a few weeks earlier, so at least they couldn't curl it into ringlets. I didn't do the greatest job of cutting my own hair. My mother took me to a hairdresser to straighten things out, and I have to confess I was very pleased with the results. My mother, however, was almost in tears over the fact that I no longer had long hair. She looked at me with the saddest face, but I was pleased as punch with myself.

So I greeted people and passed around the appetizers in my new red dress. Everything went very nicely. I heard people exclaiming about my cuteness, at which point my mother would moan about how much cuter I had been when I had hair.

When we all sat down to dinner, I was between my father and a man from his company I had never met before. Now, I was very quiet. Kids are supposed to keep quiet at dinner tables, right? The problem with this is that if you're not joining in the conversation, you can really notice everyone else. That was the problem. I really noticed everyone else. I noticed every time each person took a piece of bread or cleared their throat or waved a hand in a certain way. Here's what it was like.

The man to my right would carefully put down his fork, tines inverted, and his knife so that his cutlery formed a V on his plate. Then his elbows were resting on the table, and then came the nose rubbing. Hands clasped, index fingers forming a steeple, he would run each finger along each nostril in unison, forming another steeple after each rub. There were usually two or three rubs, never just one.

The woman to his right, after saying something she thought was funny, would burst into laughter and scratch her head. Her husband, instead of laughing, would bite his lower lip and smile with his head back as though he were laughing. My mother was fiddling with her earring. She often fiddled with her earring.

The couple across the table was younger than the rest and both had long hair. The woman squinted her eyes up all the time even though the lights were turned way down, and her husband was pick-pick-picking at a wart he had on one of his bony fingers. My father, of course, was biting his cheek. Even over the sound of everyone talking and laughing, I could hear the click-click of his teeth beside me.

I couldn't believe it. Rubbing, picking, scratching, chewing—did they know how hideous they looked? How dreadful they sounded? Couldn't they stop? Pick, scratch, rub, squint, fiddle, rub, click, rub. I couldn't stand it.

Then suddenly it all stopped. All at once like someone had turned off a switch. I looked up and everyone was staring at me. I didn't know why they were looking at me until my mother said something and I had to take my hands away from my ears to hear her.

"Do you have a headache?"

"Yes," I lied. "Yes, I have a headache."

"Then go lie down, and I'll come and check on you soon."

I was so relieved to be able to get out of there. I went to my room and lay down and thought how strange it was that I didn't recall putting my hands up to my ears. And yet I could remember the noise of their chewing and twitching getting louder and louder until it filled my head.

After a while my mother did come in to see how I was. She brought me half an aspirin, which I took even though I didn't really have a headache. It tasted awful and got stuck at the back of my throat. While I drank the whole glass of water to force the aspirin down, my mother fiddled with her earring.

"Why do you do that?"

"Do what, Deirdre?"

"Fiddle with your earring like that."

"Just a nervous habit, I guess. Now, why don't you get out of your dress and into your pajamas."

"Dad bites his cheek. He always bites his cheek when he's angry but doesn't want to show it." She looked at me more strangely that time.

"Yes, I know."

"Is he angry tonight? Having dinner?"

"No, Deirdre, of course not. Why would he be angry? Now, why don't you just try and sleep and never mind people's habits."

Well, I got into my pajamas but I couldn't help thinking about nervous habits. A lot of the kids at school had nervous habits. Practically all the girls bit their nails and the boys picked their noses. The teachers and principal were worse, though. They always did exactly the same things with their hands or coughed in a certain way before they said anything, or ran their hands through their hair all the time.

In grade six I had a teacher who had just a ton of habits. For one thing she was always rubbing her temples as though we were making her head hurt, except that I saw her and her husband in a store once, and she was rubbing her temples at him, too, so I know it wasn't just us. Also, she had this thing where she would go "mmm" and then cough a little before everything she said. When you figure out how many hours you sit in front of these people, it can get pretty irritating when they start every other sentence with "mmm, ahem."

I started tuning them out a lot. Teachers, I mean. It got so irritating for me to listen to them sniffing and coughing or watch them scratching and jerking that finally I just tuned them out. This meant that a lot of the time they would think I had been daydreaming, but I hadn't. I wished I was daydreaming because that would be interesting at least, but basically I was just stopping myself from hearing or seeing them. I mean, if you really stopped and looked at people, it could drive you crazy.

But I wasn't crazy. Even though just about everything going on around me was enough to drive you crazy, I stayed sane. I did it by just turning off things. It got so that I could tune out people's nervous habits and still talk to them. I mean, I could carry on a conversation and answer questions and everything, but not really be there.

Meanwhile, my mother acted like she hadn't noticed my nonbehaviour at all. She carried on as though I was still behaving a certain way when I wasn't.

Once, when I was eleven, I stopped in front of the hall mirror to comb my hair. Big deal. I was just combing and kind of daydreaming, when I saw my mother's reflection in the mirror, too. She was standing in the doorway of the kitchen with her arms folded and her head on one side giving me this goofy look.

"What?" I asked.

"Always in front of the mirror." Smile.

Now, this didn't sound like my mother to me, and besides, I was not "always" in front of the mirror. I didn't say anything. I just swore to never ever stand in front of the hall mirror again. And I didn't. But every so often, no matter what I did, even if it was just snap my gum, she'd get that goofy look on her face and I couldn't stand it. I knew, I just knew, that that goofy look was over something she had read in one of her magazines about adolescent girls. I decided to find out for sure.

Every day I snitched one magazine from the huge pile she kept in her bedroom closet and then put it back when I'd finished looking through it. Sometimes the articles I found were even more disgusting than the one I was looking for. All kinds of stuff like "How to Make Your Man More Passionate." Anyway, you can imagine that my days were kind of full what with school, the ranch, sleeping, and then looking for this article.

Well, after a couple of weeks I found it. It was called "Mothers and Daughters" and the opening line—I swear to you—was, "Remember when you used to spend all your time in front of the mirror?"

I screamed at the top of my lungs for about five minutes.

All right. Maybe I should have mentioned that screaming stuff right at the beginning, but I didn't want you to think I really was loony. I mean, it all sounds pretty dramatic, and you can bet you-know-who came running really fast, but it was just a scream, after all.

That's when they took me to the shrink. I can remember my mother and me sitting in the waiting room. As soon as we got there the secretary smiled and got up and went into the office behind her desk. She came out a few moments later and said, "Dr. Clarke would like to see Deirdre on her own, first."

So there I was, eleven years old, standing across a desk from a shrink. She reached out and shook my hand. "Hello, Deirdre," she said. "Please, have a seat." She smiled, but her mouth wasn't designed for smiling. She had these really thin lips that seemed to disappear into her face when she wasn't talking. Her hair was very blonde, parted in the middle and pulled back into a kind of roll that went the whole length of her head.

She must have noticed me looking at the pictures on her desk, because she said, "These are my children." She was pointing at one of those frames that holds three oval pictures, but there were other pictures on the walls, too. One wall was plastered with her degrees and the rest were plastered with pictures of hubby and kids. I immediately had her typed as one of those women my mother's magazines described as "Having It All" and, boy, did she ever want everyone to know it. I'm mentioning this because, after a few preliminary chatty questions about school performance and peer pressure, she started in on home life. She kept scratching lines on a pad of yellow foolscap as though she was underlining something over and over, even though I was looking her right in the eyes.

"What time do you usually get home, Deirdre?" Scratch, scratch.

"Four."

"Every night?" Scratch. "No extra-curricular activities?"

I shook my head.

"Music lessons, perhaps?" That's how she talked—in questions. "Anyone home when you get in?"

"My mother." She stopped scratching, and her lips disappeared as she looked at me for a moment. Then she said, "Mum always home when you get in?" Now, this little habit of always speaking in questions was already getting on my nerves, not to mention the pen going back and forth on the foolscap. Also, her voice, which was already pretty high, going up at the end of her sentences like that, didn't match her face, which could have been carved out of marble. Pale blonde hair, pale face, beige suit. She looked like a talking statue. I was thinking all this when she repeated the same question. "Mmm? Mum always home when you get in?" I nodded.

"Is that nice?" I just looked at her. "Nice to have Mum home when you get in?"

I shrugged. "It's okay," I said.

"Just okay?" She'd stopped scratching, so I guessed that she thought this was important stuff. I couldn't figure out what she was getting at, so I decided to ask her.

"What are you getting at?"

"Getting at?" She paused and put down the pen and linked her fingers. "Would you prefer it if Mum had outside interests? Say, volunteer work? Or, perhaps, a career of her own?"

I screwed up my eyes and said, "So who's with your kids right now?" She picked up her pen again. I could tell she wasn't thrilled with the question.

"Their nanny, whom they adore."

"Black?" I said. "Or East Indian?"

"Neither." She looked very smug.

"Oh," I said, drawing out the "oh." "An energetic young thing with a certificate in Early Childhood Education." She underlined a lot at that point. I think she actually took notes sometimes, too, because I made out the word "hostile" on the foolscap. I can read upside-down. It comes in very handy. She must have realized there was no point trying to get me to gradually open up, because after her lips disappeared again for a few moments she got right to what she referred to as "the magazine incident."

"Where did you find it?"

"My mother's room," I said.

"Mum's room?" A couple of scratches. "Bedroom?" I nodded. "Mum has her own bedroom?" Oh, God. Why had I let that slip? Ever since I could remember my parents had had separate bedrooms. This had been no big deal to me until I realized from TV shows that parents were supposed to sleep in the same room. Anyway, Dr. Clarke really made a big deal of this. From then on my parents slept in the same room. I felt very creepy that they'd know I'd mentioned such a personal thing. So I was very careful about what I said to Dr. Clarke after that.

Actually, they stopped sending me to her after a while. Just like that. A report was sent to my house, though. I was home when the mail came, so I held the envelope up to the light: It was hard to read because most of the words overlapped where the letter had been folded, but I could make out the last line. It said, "trying to reconcile her desire to remain a child with her nascent sexuality." I immediately looked up nascent. "In the act of becoming."

So the shrink thought I screamed because the magazines were too much for me. She looked for such complicated reasons for things.

My older brother came home for Christmas that year. My mother kept saying, "Isn't it nice that Donald's coming all the way from out West" so many times that I knew he was doing it just for me. He got me a Wrinkles dog, even though I was almost twelve. My mother was fluttering around working really hard, and then when it came time for Christmas dinner she hardly even ate. First she took all the skin off her turkey, and then she scraped off the gravy my father had ladled on her white meat. She thought we didn't notice because she had developed this trick of pushing her food around on the plate a lot and waving a loaded fork in our faces while she talked. But I noticed.

I also noticed that my brother couldn't wait to get out of there. Home for two whole days and he couldn't even take it. He actually did this stupid big brother thing. He sat on my bed on Christmas Eve and said if I ever wanted to visit him, he'd send me the plane ticket. I asked him what I'd want to visit him for.

"You know, to get away. Be on your own for a bit."

I couldn't understand what he was getting at, so I just kept looking at him.

"It wasn't as bad for me, Deirdre, because I got out a lot and played a lot of sports. But you know, well, Mum says you're home all the time."

I just sat and listened to this. I hated the fact that they'd talked about me behind my back with my brother. What would he know?

While he was rambling on, trying to be a big brother, the real meaning of what he was saying hit me like a ton of bricks. He was saying it had always been like this—even when he'd lived at home. I used to go through the old family albums and see the pictures from before I was born. My brother was just a baby, my mother looked absolutely gorgeous, and my father was standing very straight and proud. I had figured that everything had been just wonderful at some point and now here he was telling me it had been miserable for him, too. I just kept looking at him and occasionally squinting my eyes. Eventually he gave up and went downstairs.

So. Christmas wasn't much fun that year, either. I stuffed myself silly, but instead of pleasing them this seemed to upset them. They wouldn't give me thirds. Finally I just excused myself and went to my room, but before I closed the door I heard my mother sigh and say, "What have we done now?"

I wished she wouldn't take everything so personally.

I closed the bedroom door and flung my weary body across the bed. I couldn't even be bothered to remove my clothes, but lay atop the patchwork quilt, thinking. How would I ever raise enough money to pay this year's taxes? I could put on my fancy go-to-meetin' clothes and sweet-talk the banker, but I was too proud for that. No. There had to be another way.

Nightshade. I could sell Nightshade. As soon as the thought entered my mind I felt sick at heart, and yet I knew I would have to go through with it. A neighbouring rancher had offered me plenty for my prime stallion many times, but each time I had refused.

I forced myself out of bed. I splashed water over my face and neck and looked in the glass that hung on the back of my door. If I was going to command a good price with Burghardt, I would have to look as though I didn't need it.

I straightened up and set to work. I brushed my thick red hair a hundred times and tied it back with a blue velvet rib-bon. Then I went to my wardrobe and pulled out my smartest riding outfit. I polished my good riding boots until I could see my reflection in them.

Saddling up old Buzz, I glanced over at Nightshade standing alone in his paddock. My heart skipped a beat. What a beautiful horse he was. Strong and beautiful and black as the night.

When I arrived at Burghardt's, I swung down from old Buzz and tied her to the fence. Before I was halfway up the walkway, Burghardt appeared at the door, a big grin on his clean-shaven face. For a moment I had the urge to turn on my heel, but the thought of another meeting with the tax man forced me on.

"Well, well. To what do I owe the pleasure of your visit, ma'am?" he smiled, his thumbs hooked through the suspenders that bulged over his fat belly.

"Can't a neighbour call on a neighbour?" I said as non-chalantly as I could. He stared at me suspiciously as he waved

me into the house, turning sideways so that my arm brushed against his fat belly as I squeezed through the doorway.

"Well, neighbour, will you join me for tea?" he asked, grinning.

"I'm not overly fond of tea," I said, "but I'll join you in a whisky."

Now, I seldom drank whisky, because a woman on her own on a ranch has to have a clear head about her. But it was on my mind that if he had a couple of drinks he might be less inclined to quiz me about my sudden interest in selling Nightshade. He disappeared, chuckling to himself, and came back a few moments later with a couple of glasses and a half-full whisky bottle.

I knocked the first shot back just like that, which caused him to hoot with laughter and do the same. After that I kind of made a show of drinking, but secretly poured my whisky in his spittoon when he was up to get a cigar or another bottle. Before too long he was drunk as a skunk, and I was beginning to worry he would never get around to what he usually got around to eventually. Nightshade.

"Why don't you ever take me up on my offer for that stallion, ma'am?" he finally said through his whisky. "I'd give you a damned good price."

"I can't imagine a price worth giving up my Nightshade."

This did the trick. It was the first time in all the times he'd pestered me that I'd even picked up on the talk about money. Well, he sank back in his chair, his eyes kind of red and watery, and quoted a price. I tried not to give any reaction, but inside my heart skipped over. It was twice the amount I needed for taxes. I couldn't let him see how excited I was.

"I don't know," I said out loud. "I love that horse. Raised him myself. Even fed him myself when his mother wouldn't. I don't know."

Then he named another price, twenty-five dollars more than the last. I thought I'd better not push my luck.

"I'll have to think about it," I said prettily and then pretended to hiccup. This had the effect I had intended.

"No!" he said. "No need to think about it. It's a good deal and you know it. Now, why don't I draw something up right now, and we'll sign like gentlemen . . . uh, gentlefolk."

"Well." I hiccuped once more for effect. "All right, I suppose."

And that was that. I left his house with a fistful of cash in my hands and a pain in my heart. But I had saved my ranch. That was all that mattered.

Something Fishy

by
Linda Holeman

This story is included in a collection of ten stories entitled
Saying Good-Bye. *What are the characters saying goodbye
to? Really they are saying goodbye to being children, to the
things they believed about themselves and others. They are
trying on new selves. Sometimes, as in the case of Rebecca in
this story, the new self is not a very good fit.*

You know the fishwife, that old hag in the kids' story?
She's always griping to her husband about how rotten her
life is, about how she doesn't have what other fishermen's
wives have. A real whiner.

One day Mr. Henpecked catches this magic fish, who
says (I always figured the real magic was that he could talk)

that the fisherman can have one wish. But instead of wishing for a new boat, or at least a new net, the guy goes home and tells his wife. Even though this is long before the women's movement, the wife figures the wish should be hers—and she nabs it, saying she wants to be a high-class lady. Voilà! There she is, all dressed up and living in a big house.

But soon she wants a bigger house and more clothes and jewels, so she sends hubby back out to sea again, to have a chat with the fish. Once again he snags it—what a coincidence—and he gets another wish. Or rather, his wife gets another wish.

The story goes on and on, with the wife eventually winding up as some kind of queen of all the land. But then she makes her big mistake. She wants to have it all, rule the earth and the sky *and* the sea. Bad judgment. The fish gets all bent out of shape and—poof—the woman is back to the hut on the beach, all dressed in rags.

Seems as if what happened to that old lady, and to me, is what always happens when you get what you ask for.

You just want more.

I had a regular kind of life. So regular that it felt as though it belonged in a museum with all the other extinct things. It was like one of those old Doris Day movies, where everyone was always polite and neat and nothing serious ever went wrong. The kind of movie where the wife said things like "Happy, darling?" to her husband as they smiled at each other over the martinis they always had just before dinner.

Obviously ours is not your typical nineties family. It's not separated, step, half, blended, or unique in any noticeable way. My father has a secure administrative job with the Wheat Board; he's been there since I was a baby and has no plans to leave until retirement. My mother was always "home" for us. In the last few years, however, it has dawned on her that she's on the verge of empty-nest syndrome, as well as closing in on menopause. This causes her to cry on a regular basis and work her Thighmaster with grim determination as she scans the classifieds, hoping to find the perfect part-time job to take her mind off her age.

I have an older brother, Richard, who's working toward a science degree at university. He never allows anyone to call him Rick, doesn't believe in belonging to a fraternity, and chose home life over living in the dorm or renting a cheap apartment. Those facts alone say a great deal about Big R, as I refer to him. Having an older brother seemed to be an advantage for most girls—there was always the chance one of their friends would show an interest in a younger sister—but my brother has never brought home anyone even remotely interesting. On top of this lack of promising friends, Richard has never been in trouble with the police, has never been involved with an unsuitable partner with children from a previous marriage, and has never embraced a new religion. All of the above seem to happen to my friends' siblings fairly regularly, and their homes are alive with electrical tension and the rush of knowing there may be some sort of emotional upheaval at any given time.

It's hard to imagine any kind of raw emotion bouncing around the energy-draining beigeness of our house. Everything in the whole place matches everything else, in varying shades of browns and golds, from drapes to wall-to-wall carpets to furniture. I would love to come home one day and find a bizarre abstract painting on the wall over the couch, or an unusual, decorative object on the coffee table. A bibelot. I love that word, but it rarely comes up in conversation.

But even as I hated the drab state of my home and family, I have to admit, sadly, that I also fell into the same category. This is who I am; this is Rebecca Olchowecki:

My looks can only be described as passable. I'm not exactly short, but not tall, either. I'm neither heavy nor slender, my eyesight is good, my teeth fairly straight, and my skin just acts up for a few days a month, right before my period. I can't even take comfort in dreaming of some remarkable metamorphosis, a shining beauty emerging after one summer, sans glasses and braces and with old weight lost or new curves acquired.

While I never tripped over my own feet at track or slapped at the volleyball with open palms, I still wasn't good enough to make the second cut on any of the school teams. My grades have always been respectable, but I would never bring any honor to the school with my prowess on the debating team. I am far too inhibited to try out for the drama club, although I did joyfully raise my voice from the anonymity of the glee club's large contralto section for an operetta last spring.

I haven't been totally dateless. A few boys from school have taken me out, but they certainly never tried to convince me to do anything that was slightly thrilling and maybe just the tiniest bit wicked. I noticed, more than once in fact, that by the end of the evening they seemed more uncomfortable than I did, hurrying away with a joke or an awkward attempt at a pecking sort of kiss. It was as if they sensed the dullness that surrounded me and were afraid that if they got too close, it would seep into them by osmosis. They were always polite after those indifferent dates, making small talk in class or in the lineup in the cafeteria, but I could see their eyes drifting away from mine, searching over my shoulder or the top of my head as we discussed the unfairness of the day's homework assignment or the state of Tuesday's lasagna. I knew they were looking for greener, more interesting pastures, wanting me to realize that, while they thought I was a nice girl, I wasn't to misinterpret their friendliness.

One morning I realized, with an unpleasant jolt, that, like the tortoise, I was simply slow and steady. I'd get there, wherever it was that I was headed, but with no amazing burst of glory or accomplishments worthy of media attention. I would just plod through the rest of my teenage years, never failing, but never really succeeding. It was such a dismal thought that I swore that, by the end of the school year, I'd have changed the course of my life.

I just wanted a little bit. I thought I'd be satisfied with something small. After all, I was that kind of person, used to doing small, insignificant things, staying in the background most of the time. But then something happened, without any preconceived plan. It was just a slip of the tongue. And what followed made me realize that I wanted a whole lot more than a little bit of anything.

We were sitting on the bleachers in the gym, waiting for a basketball tournament to start. It was Lauren, Katelyn, Mara, and me. We're friends, and we hang out together, but I can't really say that any of us are best friends. Each one of us more or less depends on the others to go places with and to be a shoulder to cry on. Occasionally one of us has a date, but there are always at least three of us looking for something to do each weekend. We just try to be there for each other. I don't know if girls everywhere do it, but it works for us, this unspoken pact between the less-than-popular girls that never lets one of us feel too alone, too out of things.

Lauren was talking. "You know my cousin Alexander, the one in Sleeping Lion?"

We all groaned. How could we forget good old Alexander? Although we had never seen his group, Lauren gave us weekly updates about the great new Toronto hotspots where the Lion was appearing. Since none of us would probably ever get that far east in the next few years, there wasn't much chance of us actually catching Alexander or his spectacular drumming.

"Well," Lauren said, ignoring our expressions, "Sleeping Lion is going to be on MTV next weekend!"

"Really?" Katelyn asked, her face getting a pinched, suspicious look. I felt my features narrowing, too.

"Really. Swear. I swear it." Lauren slapped her hand to her chest, then took it off. "Well, they're *supposed* to be on. It all depends on some network timing thing. But if they are, Jessica Jann will be interviewing them on Saturday night's show. My aunt phoned my mom last night and told her."

We were all sick of Lauren's bragging about Sleeping Lion and how they were always rubbing shoulders with big name bands and were always on the verge of cutting a record deal—except every deal fell through because Sleeping Lion didn't like this or that clause in the contract. It was just getting to be too much.

I was in a particularly bad mood. Just before I left the house my mother had declared, brightly, that we could spend Saturday together reorganizing my closet and dresser drawers. Even new shelf paper. She said it the way I would imagine other mothers announcing a trip to an L.A. film studio to watch the taping of a movie starring Keanu Reeves.

I looked at Lauren, sitting there so smug and proud just because of her cousin. I wanted to make her feel as bad as I did. "Well, that can't be true," I said, "because Jessica Jann is my father's daughter from his first marriage, and I happen to know that she's going to be down in New York taping a special."

All three of the girls leaned forward and stared at me.

"Would you repeat that, please?" Mara said, her eyes bulging out in an unattractive way.

I licked my lips. I couldn't believe I'd said that about Jessica Jann. I couldn't believe I'd said anything. I wasn't a liar, I didn't even stretch the truth—at least not about anything important. I did sometimes tell little fibs to my parents, like adding a half hour on to how long I'd been doing my homework or saying I'd had a great time at a party when really I hadn't. But I was basically an honest person, the kind of person people believe. And I guess that's why I didn't know how to take the Jessica Jann lie back. When I thought about it later, I realized it would have been easy to shrug and laugh and say, "Just kidding." But I didn't.

"I said, Jessica Jann is my father's daughter from his first marriage, and—"

"But that means she's your sister!" Katelyn squealed. "Your half-sister, Rebecca. Jessica Jann is your half-sister! I can't believe it!"

They all pushed up against each other on the bleachers.

"Why didn't you say anything, Rebecca?" Lauren asked, shaking my arm. "You could have got Alexander a big break a long time ago, maybe last year."

"Shut up about Alexander, Lauren," Mara said. "We want to hear about Jessica. Have you met her, Rebecca? Does she ever . . ." Mara leaned farther forward, ". . . come to visit your dad?"

Suddenly there were loud cheers, whistles, and hoots, and we all looked down at our team as they jogged out onto the gym floor. Mara, Katelyn, and Lauren looked back at me. "Tell us, Rebecca, tell us what she's like," Katelyn shouted over the noise. A whistle blew and the crowd settled down.

"Let's get out of here," Lauren said. "Come on, Rebecca. Let's go somewhere where we can talk."

Nobody said anything on the way to the fast-food place near the school, but I practically had to run to keep up. It was as if they couldn't wait to hear everything, but didn't want me to start until we were seated. As if it were too important to discuss on the street. That gave me time to think something up.

When we finally had our food, Katelyn took a long slurp from her straw and said, "Now. Tell us everything."

No one had ever demanded that I tell them a thing. I was usually the listener, hearing everyone else's stories and making appropriate sounds of delight, horror, or envy. I wanted to prolong this moment.

I wiggled a french fry in the little white container of ketchup. "Well, my dad had this really brief marriage, ages ago," I started. "He was working in Toronto, and he met this woman and they got married. They had a baby, had . . . Jessica . . . but the marriage didn't work out. So my dad split and came here, and a few years later he met my mom. That's it. That's all there is." I took a deep breath. It was a logical enough story. It happened all the time.

"But why didn't you ever say anything before?" Lauren asked.

I noticed no one was eating except me. "It just never came up," I said, trying to sound casual.

"It never came *up*?!" Mara shrieked. "It never came up that you're related, very closely, to the queen of the rock shows? To the person who talks to every hot group in Canada, not only backstage, but also in the dressing rooms? Rebecca! Jessica Jann is, like, an idol to a lot of people. How could you never mention it?"

I had a scary, excited feeling, as if I were standing at the edge of a frozen river that had a sign that said Thin Ice, and I knew I was going to try to cross it anyway. My teeth kept mechanically grinding the cardboard fries. I crossed my arms on the table and leaned over them. I kept my voice low. "Look. It's like this. My dad doesn't really want people to know. He was kind of a jerk about it all, I guess. Left Jessica's mother, didn't send child support, that kind of thing.

"So he only confided it to me recently, you know, when he figured I was old enough to handle it. He told me right after we watched this TV show about people who need a lot of attention, glamor, adoration—sort of like Jessica— because something was lacking in their childhood, something important, like a parent."

Everyone nodded. It sounded as though I knew what I was talking about. And the TV show part was the truth. I had (alone) watched a talk show about attention-seeking adults one afternoon when I was home from school with strep throat.

"It comes down to the fact that he doesn't really want anyone to know how irresponsible he was. He told me in the *strictest confidence*." I added that last part for security. Stories seem to sprout faster when they start as dark secrets. "So don't say anything, okay?"

Of course, three heads nodded.

Of course, by Monday, half the school knew.

• • •

The school corridor was busier than usual, with kids leaning up against the lockers and sitting cross-legged on the floor. I saw the small crowd as I turned the corner. "Here she comes," I heard someone say.

There was a sudden silence. I raised my chin and tried to look natural, even though my lips were trembling by the time I got to my locker. I could hear a rustling, restless moving, as if everyone was waiting for something to happen. I got my locker open, grabbed my books, took a deep breath, and turned around.

"Hey, Rebecca," Victor Muñoz called. "So what's she like? Is she as cool as she looks on TV?"

Victor Muñoz, the school's top jock, had never even acknowledged my existence before.

"Yeah, she's pretty cool," I said, as I slammed my locker shut. He was right beside me. I could smell him, hair gel with a tiny undercurrent of socks. I inhaled deeply.

Small murmurs ran through the crowd. "Did she ever take you backstage with her, Rebecca?" "How many times have you been to the set?" "Does she give you free tickets to concerts?" I glanced at my watch, as if I had somewhere to go, then smiled and started down the hall. It was hard to walk away, especially from Victor, but I wanted to take my time with my answers.

The quiet street my family lived on got busy over the next few days. Cars filled with kids from school drove up and down for hours, slowing as they passed the house.

"Seems to be a lot of traffic," my dad said when he came in from work. "I had to wait for three cars to go by before I could even turn in to the driveway." He shook his head. "I hope our street isn't getting to be some kind of thoroughfare."

"Oh, I'm sure it's nothing, Mel," my mom said, moving between the stove and the table with a platter of Shake 'n' Bake chicken. "Probably just some minor detour somewhere, diverting the cars down our street for a day or two."

"I hope you're right," Dad said, taking the platter from her and handing it to me. "Take a drumstick, Rebecca," he said. "I know what my little girl likes best."

As I took the drumstick, there was a passing blast of music from outside. I gave the platter to my mother.

"You know, I noticed that most of those cars were filled with teenagers," Dad remarked. I looked up, and he smiled at me. "I'm so glad you're not that kind of girl, Rebecca, joyriding in the streets, music blaring. Isn't this much nicer, sitting down to supper together? Those kids out there don't know what a real family is all about."

A few evenings later, as I came out of my room to get a snack, I passed the living room and saw my mother. She was in her powder blue sweatsuit, a towel draped around her neck and a pink sweatband holding her short dark curls away from her forehead, puffing away on her Nordic-Track. As her arms and legs slid back and forth, she read the paper, which she folded on a little stand that was attached to the base of the skier.

"Anything, Mom?" I asked, stopping.

My mother gripped the ski poles and swung her arms more vigorously, her face an unflattering burgundy. "Not today," she said, gasping slightly. Even with the gasp, I recognized the slight tremor in her voice.

"Come on, Mom, you'll find something. But you really should take a computer course. It would definitely make you more marketable."

Mom's jaw jutted forward. "I'm too old to learn all that stuff. I have enough trouble figuring out Celsius and kilometers."

"You're not that old." Then, as Mom's face swung toward me, her eyes puffy and owlish behind the magnified lenses of her glasses, I changed it. "You're not old, Mom." I walked across the room to look out the front picture window. "I bet you could learn—" I quickly stepped back behind the drapes. A group of girls was standing across the street, taking pictures of our house. The swishing of the skis stopped. "What are you looking at, dear?" Mom came up behind me. She stepped in front of the window, mopping her forehead with the towel. "Oh. Do you know those girls?"

I peeked around the edge of the curtain. "I think they go to my school."

"Now why would they be taking pictures of our house?"

I pulled my head back, ran my fingers up and down the edge of the drape, and raised one shoulder in half a shrug.

Mom put her hands on her hips. "Seems strange." Suddenly she threw her arm over her head and started waving to them, a big, back-and-forth wave, as if she were signaling a ship.

"Mom! Stop! What are you doing?" I peeked again. The girls were talking to each other and pointing at the house. One started to cross the street.

"Just being friendly. Maybe they want to come over. You're not doing anything, are you, Rebecca? You could—"

I fumbled for the drapery cord and yanked on it, so the drapes swung shut, catching part of Mom's head. She clawed at the heavy brown material, stepping backward.

"Rebecca! Don't be so rude. They looked friendly."

"No. I have a lot of homework. And I don't even really know them." I edged away from her, out of the room. "Please, Mom. Leave the drapes shut."

"Well, all right," she said, her brow furrowed. She started to disassemble the skier. "But when you see them at school, ask why they were taking pictures of our house."

"Right," I said, heading off toward my bedroom.

By Friday I had invitations to three parties for Saturday night. The crowded hallways at school opened as I passed through. There was a moment of reverent silence as I entered a classroom.

On Saturday afternoon I spent all the money I had on a long black velvet jacket, the kind Jessica often wore with jeans and a bustier on her Saturday night program. I *almost* got a hat like hers, but didn't want to overdo it. With my birthday money I planned to get some boots, black lizard, just like Jessica's. I had already seen them in the window of Buck's Saddlery.

On Saturday night I chose the party that sounded the most promising and got ready to go.

"I still don't know why you spent all your money on that one jacket," Mom said. "You could have got a couple of outfits from Valu-Mart with what you paid for that."

"I like it, Mom. It's cool."

Mom sniffed. "Since when is cool so important? Being neat, neat and clean, is what I've always stressed."

"Yes, Mom." It came out as a sigh. "See you later."

"Hold on, now. Your brother was kind enough to offer you a lift there, but how are you getting home?"

I smiled. "Don't worry. I'm sure I'll get a ride."

Michael Reznick from my chemistry class took me home. He parked outside my house and seemed really interested in what I had to say. Then, right in the middle of a sentence, he leaned over and kissed me, long and hard, as if he really meant it. It was my first real kiss, the first one with feeling. I liked it, but it made me think about what it would be like to kiss other guys. I knew I didn't have to limit myself to Michael, even though a week ago I would have given my right arm for a date with him. He asked me out for the next Saturday, but I had already promised another boy from the party, a cute guy called Serge, that I would go over to Mary Louise Mafee's place with him.

"Thanks anyway, Michael, but I'm busy," I said. I saw his face fall. I actually saw it. I always thought that was just an expression, but when I said no to Michael, all his features sort of slid downward, as if the muscles had given up. I, Rebecca Olchowecki, made a guy's face fall, a guy who had just given me this long, intimate, meaningful kiss. A surge of power ran through me. It was so strong that I was almost scared, but it also felt fabulous.

"Listen, it was really fun tonight. I mean it." I started to get out of the car, stopped, and said over my shoulder, "Maybe some other time. I'll be in touch." I slammed the door and walked toward my house. I'd always wanted to say that to someone.

The week flew by. One day I brought a picture of my dad to school. He was pretty young and was holding a baby girl (my cousin Elise). I put the photo in a Ziploc bag and passed it around, asking people not to take it out because it was special and I didn't want it to get too marked up. I didn't even say anything about who it was. People love to come to their own conclusions.

Another day I brought a little pair of my scuffed baby shoes. Same thing. The girls touched them gently, making aahing noises. The boys just looked at them, but I could tell they were dying to touch them, too.

Every day at lunch I had to decide where to sit. It seemed like everyone wanted me at their table. I had become one of the major suns in the great school solar system. The others, the many little moons and comets and stars, just sort of drifted around, out in the emptiness, hoping to be touched by a warming ray.

The story was growing, with a little help from me, but mainly all by itself. Like I said, stories germinate fastest when they start in the dark, but once they've got into the light, the best thing to do is to step back and leave them alone. This one was growing at breakneck speed. I let it.

What could it hurt?

Friday lunchtime. The cafeteria had that great hum of excitement at the promise of weekend possibilities, and the relief of another week of school over. I was sitting at a table with Mary Louise Mafee and her friends. Mary Louise was talking about Saturday night.

"I'm so glad you're coming, Rebecca," she said. "Serge is really cool."

"Yeah. He seems okay."

"He and his girlfriend, this really snobby girl from St. Justine's, just broke up last month," a girl named Rhianne said. "They went out together for over four months and Serge was really bummed about the break-up. He hasn't taken anyone out since then. You're the first."

"He's in a band, too," Mary Louise added.

Why didn't that surprise me? I smiled brightly. "Really? Great."

Serge drove up at 8:30, right on time. As soon as I saw the car stop outside, I ran to the basement stairs and yelled down to my parents, who were sorting through holiday slides in the rec room.

"I'm going now. See you later."

"Don't be too late," I heard my father say. Suddenly his feet thumped up the stairs. I didn't think he'd come up. I opened the back door, trying to get outside before he got to the top of the stairs. I didn't want Serge to see him.

My dad's not abnormal looking or anything, but he definitely doesn't look like the kind of man who could have produced a daughter like Jessica Jann. Although genes are a tricky thing, and no one can prove anything by the size of a guy's ears or the fact that he's at least three inches shorter than his supposed famous daughter, I didn't want to take any chances. But I wasn't fast enough.

"Wait. Wait, Rebecca," Dad said, just as I was slipping out the screen door.

"What?"

"I'd like to meet this fellow. A father's prerogative, isn't it?" He gave a little chuckle. "The way the phone's been ringing lately, I'd say I'll be pretty busy, meeting all these boyfriends."

"Daaaaad."

"Come on, now. If he's a gentleman, he'll come to the door."

As if Serge had heard him, the doorbell chimed. Dad rubbed his hands together briskly and hurried from the back door to the front. He flung the door open with a flourish.

Serge looked down on him.

"Come in, young man, come in." Dad made a sweeping gesture in front of him with his arm.

"Dad, this is Serge. Serge, my father." My voice had a wooden, robotic quality. I didn't want to leave any openings for discussion.

Serge grabbed my father's hand and pumped it up and down. "A real pleasure, Mr. Olchowecki. Everyone is very excited to learn about your daughter."

Dad looked at me, then back down at Serge's hand. "Well. Yes. We're real proud of our little girl, too, uh . . . Surge."

"Serge, Dad," I said. "S-E-R-G-E. You say Sairj."

"Do you see her often?" Serge asked, obviously not bothered by Dad's pronunciation of his name.

Dad looked at me again. He had this earnest look, the kind a dog gets when you're trying to teach it something and it knows there's a treat in it if it can figure out what you want. He made a little "heh-heh" sound, then looked back at Serge. "Guess you could say I do. As much as any father, I guess." His head turned back in my direction. "Don't I, Rebecca?"

I pushed between the two of them, breaking their hands apart. "Come on, Serge, let's go."

"You two have a good time."

I pulled at Serge's arm. He was looking at the living room, his eyes darting around as if he were trying to spot something. His eyes passed over my dad once more and I saw them taking in Dad's slightly stooped shoulders in his old checked sweater, his baggy pants, the threadbare plaid slippers.

We walked to the car in silence.

"He's not exactly what I imagined," Serge said, as we pulled away from the curb.

I forced a laugh. "Well, whose parents are?"

"Yeah. I guess."

Serge didn't have a lot more to say on the way over to Mary Louise's, except to mention his band. "I play bass," he told me. "We've had a few gigs and we played in a band competition last month."

"Did you win?"

"Nah. It was rigged. One of the judges was the uncle of a guy in another band. Obviously they won."

"Too bad," I said. "What's your band called?"

"Scream of Love. Heard of it?"

"Uh, no. Not yet."

"Well, this time last year nobody had heard of Hot Spit either."

I still hadn't. I nodded.

"It was your sister who got them their start. They were knocking out crowds all over the west, but just couldn't get that break, you know. Just like us. But Jessica happened to be in Vancouver, caught them jamming at a club, and within a few weeks they had a mega contract. Right now they're over in Germany, booked solid for the next month. There's a big write-up about it in this month's *Rocking News*. Did you see it?"

I didn't want to appear totally out of it. "Oh, yeah. I think I read something about it."

"When do you think Jessica'll be coming to visit you next?" Serge asked, looking over at me.

I studied the billboard on my right. "She doesn't like me to tell people her schedule. You know how it is. She comes home to relax, just wants to lie low when she's here."

"I hear you." Serge nodded. "But listen, I'll give you our demo tape. Next time she's around, just slip it in, let her hear it without saying anything. Real casual. Get her reaction. Could you do that for me? Rebecca?"

My name sort of rolled off his lips. I liked the way he said it.

"Sure. Why not?"

There were twelve people at Mary Louise's. I was having a pretty good time with Serge when suddenly, at eleven o'clock, Mary Louise turned off the music.

"Okay, everyone, it's time!" she announced.

Everyone looked at me. "Time for what?" I asked. The whole room laughed as if I had said something funny.

"For Jessica's show, of course," Mary Louise replied. She turned on the TV, and everyone found a comfortable spot.

"Here she is. Look, she's got her hair different," Rhianne said. "I like it better down, like before."

"Shhh. Listen," someone scolded.

Jessica went in to her usual spiel, telling her viewers what was happening with the band scene around Canada. Her special guests were The Lasers. Then there were some taped dressing-room interviews and videos of the week's hits, from ten down to number one. Throughout the show Jessica was taking phone calls, reading notes, sending dedications out with songs.

"Sorry the switchboard gets so jammed, folks," Jessica purred, "but it seems like *everyone* has a question for me. Be patient. I'll get to as many of you as I can."

"I tried to talk to her once," Eric said. He was Mary Louise's boyfriend. "I started dialing at the beginning of the show and they actually picked up my call. They put me on hold, with those little taped messages repeating every sixty seconds. I waited forty-five minutes—and don't forget, this is long distance to Toronto—then they told me they didn't have time for my question. My parents killed me when they got the bill. It took me over a month to pay it off. It's just a joke, this phoning thing. It's impossible to get through. I think they have it all set up beforehand, like taped calls or something."

"Yeah, the calls are probably screened," Mary Louise agreed. "How else could they get those requests ready so soon?"

"I could get through to her." I don't know why I said it. Nobody was asking me to.

"Could you? Right now?" Serge put his arm around my shoulders. "All right."

"Well, not right now. The show's almost over. But she always takes my calls, whenever I phone."

"Could some of us talk to her, if you tell her we're your friends?" Rhianne asked.

I shrugged. "I don't see why not." Everyone waited. "I'll call her at home this week and get something set up for next week's show."

Mary Louise clapped her hands. "Okay, everyone. One week from tonight. Back here, to talk to Jessica on the air. Right, Rebecca?"

"Right," I said. Serge's arm tightened around me. I was feeling so good that I was sure I could swing something.

I had a whole seven days.

. . .

I had it worked out by Monday. Right after school I raced home and phoned the Toronto studio where Jessica's show was taped. The receptionist sounded bored, but said that, yes, they did take messages for Jessica, and if Jessica had the time, she would read it over the air.

"It's really, *really* important," I said. "And it's just a few lines."

"It doesn't matter to me how long it is," the woman said. "I don't read 'em. I just stick 'em in her mail bag."

"Well, maybe you could write Urgent or something on the top. In red ink. To make her notice." There was silence. "Hello? " I said.

"Look, just give me the message, okay?"

I read what I had written. "Hi to Rebecca and all her friends, watching from that little home town out west."

I could hear a scratching sound. "Okay," the woman said.

"Wait! Don't hang up. Could you . . . read it back to me?"

"Hi to Rebecca and all her little friends, watching from that home town out west." There was a touch of sarcasm in her voice.

"Good. Except it's not little friends, it's just friends. It's the home town that's little. That little home town out west. Or just leave out the little. It doesn't matter." I laughed, but it had an irritating shrillness, even to my own ears.

"Gotcha. Leave out little." There was more scratching. "Thank you for calling," she said mechanically, and there was a loud click, followed by the sound of the dial tone.

I phoned back on Thursday, praying it wouldn't be the same woman. It was a man this time.

"I left a message for Jessica Jann on Monday. I just wanted to make sure she got it. Is there any way I can—"

"I can't check on personal messages, but I can tell you that Jessica was in yesterday, and all her mail and messages were on her desk." The man's voice was kinder than the woman's.

"But you can't tell me if—"

"Sorry, I can't tell you anything for sure. But Jessica's pretty good about reading out as much as she can, and keeping in touch with her fans. She has a fan club. Would you like to join? I can mail you the information."

"No. That's okay. Thanks anyway." I hung up, feeling the first little bite of anxiety. Still, the worst that could happen was that she wouldn't read my message, and I could just make something else up. It was easy.

It was the same gang at Mary Louise's on Saturday. As soon as Serge and I walked in, everyone crowded around me.

"So, what's happening? Will we get to talk to her?" Rhianne asked.

"I'm not sure. When I talked to her this week, she said it was true, all her calls *are* screened beforehand. She doesn't even have that much choice about who she talks to. But she might say hi to us or something." I thought that would be enough to hold them.

The show had only been on for about ten minutes when Jessica read my message. She actually read it. She was reading lots of other stuff from a stack of papers in front of her, dates for shows, requests, that kind of thing. Then she looked right into the camera, smiled, and said, "For Rebecca and all my fans out west. Hi gang."

Everyone gave a sort of cheer and looked at me.

I shrugged. "Well, I guess that's all she was given permission to do this week." I reached for a nacho.

"I thought I'd get a chance to talk to her," Mary Louise said.

"I told you, Mary Louise, she doesn't have the final word," I said, dipping the nacho in some salsa. "You wouldn't believe how controlling the station managers are."

Mary Louise turned back to the TV, but a few minutes later she got up to go upstairs. I heard her say, "Be right back," to Eric.

I don't know how long she was gone, but it was near the end of the show, right after a commercial, when Jessica pushed one of the buttons on the phone in front of her. "This is a good one, folks," she said. "Somebody's on the line who claims she's friends with my sister." A camera zoomed in on her face and her voice dropped a tone. "My phantom sister out in Alberta. Scary."

My body went cold. I saw my hand, which was reaching for my drink, stop in midair. It just stayed there, as if it didn't belong to me. I kept watching it, waiting for it to either take the glass or come back, but it didn't move.

Jessica smiled prettily at the camera and shook her head. "It's not that unusual, people claiming to be related to celebrities. You wouldn't believe the letters and pictures I get. A lot, I mean, *a lot*." She winked and let go of the button. "Hello," she said. "You're on the air. What's your story?"

"Hi, Jessica." The girl's voice was breathy, excited, unmistakable. "My name is Mary Louise Mafee and I'm best friends with Rebecca. We all just wanted to say hi to you and tell you how much we love your show. And you. Maybe you'll come out and do a show from our school the next time you're here to see Rebecca and your dad."

"Whoa!" Jessica said, her lips pursed and one eyebrow arched the tiniest bit. "Hold on there, Mary. Just who is this Rebecca?"

Mary Louise's voice dropped to a sort of whisper. "You know. *Rebecca.* Your *sister.*"

"Sorry, kiddo. Some mistake. I don't go into too much personal stuff on the air, but let me tell you, I definitely haven't got a sister, and good old Pop won't be happy to hear he's got competition. Someone's feeding you a line. Now, have you got a video you'd like to see?" There was a loud buzz from the line. "No request that time. Well, we've just got time for the number three hit this week before our final interview. Catch you back."

Four jumping bodies filled the screen. I was able to force my hand back to my lap, but I didn't take my eyes off it. Nobody said anything. In a few seconds there were loud thumps on the stairs.

"Can you believe this? Did you guys see? What's going on, Rebecca?" Mary Louise demanded.

I looked up. Her eyes were catlike. Cruel. "It's a secret," I stammered. "She doesn't want to hurt her mother . . . her mother doesn't know she still sees Dad . . . I told Katelyn and Lauren and Mara . . . I . . ."

"Yeah. Right," Mary Louise said. "I go on national television and make a fool of myself, even tell my last name, all because you con us with some stupid lies. I can't believe we didn't see through you."

"No, I . . ." I turned to Serge. His arm wasn't around me anymore. He was staring at a bowl of popcorn on the table. I looked around at the rest of the faces, but they all looked like they had a few weeks ago. Perfect strangers.

Mary Louise picked up the remote and clicked off the television. The room was quiet, except for a few sounds. Someone crunching on a nacho. The muffled gurgling of water running down a pipe between the walls. The far-off drone of a distant plane. There was one more sound, too, but this one only I could hear. It was the tiniest of noises. Just a little "poof."

Probably the same one that old fishwife heard, too.

Maria's Gift

by

Jan Andrews

Maria's story is one in a collection of stories called Out of the Everywhere. *In this collection Jan Andrews takes traditional stories from all over the world and sets them in Canada, incorporating the old and the new, much in the way that peoples from all over the world change society and are themselves changed when they come to this new country.*

How far is it from a rugged island in Greece to a coal-mining village in the Rocky Mountains? Farther than Maria could have imagined. More carts and boats and ships and trains and wagons and weeks of traveling than she could ever have dreamed.

And why had they made the journey? Maria did not know the answer. She knew that in Greece they had been poor. She knew her father had said they must leave to find their fortune, but it seemed to her that if the family was better off at all, it was by little indeed.

Maria's mother had died on the journey. Now Maria was the mother to her brothers and sisters in their small shack. Each day she made her father's breakfast and a lunch for him to carry. She watched him set out with the other men toward the mine. Then she busied herself, doing what she could to raise the young ones.

She cooked and cleaned. She stitched and tended. Her life was hard. Somehow, however, she was not unhappy, for the mountains seemed to welcome her and she loved them. In summer, whenever there was some time with no work to be done, she would take the children to the high meadows and wander with them by the streams. In winter she would go outside and gaze toward the peaks.

As well she had her father's stories—the ones he told faithfully each evening no matter how tired he was from toiling with shovel and pick. They were the stories he had brought with him, and they made everyone feel better.

"You see!" he would say when the stories were finished. "There are such things as happy endings."

One day, Maria heard the shrilling of the whistle that told everyone in the village there had been an accident at the mine. Rocks had fallen.

Maria went as all did to wait at the mine entrance. She saw her father's body among the others, carried on stretchers through the gates.

What was she to do? Now that her father was dead there would be no money. The family would have nowhere to live and nothing to eat.

Day after day Maria went from door to door, but no one would hire her. Finally she found a place in the home of the mine owner.

The hours were long and the wages were low. At the end of the week Maria had only enough to pay the rent. Each day, then, she waited till the evening to mix the dough for the next day's bread. When the mixing was done, she left with the remnants of the dough still sticking to her fingers. At home she soaked the dough in water to make a kind of porridge to feed her brothers and sisters and herself.

So it went on. The strange thing was that while the children of the mine owner and his wife were thin and pale and weak and cranky, Maria's brothers and sisters were as strong and healthy, as rosy-checked and cheerful as anyone could wish.

One day the mine owner's wife noticed this as they were playing in the street. In her amazement, she went to consult her friends.

"You should see if the girl takes anything from you. Perhaps she is stealing," the friends told her.

The mine owner's wife kept watch. She saw the dough that went out of the house every day on Maria's fingers. When she mentioned this, her friends were all in agreement.

"With the dough she is stealing your children's luck," they said.

The mine owner's wife called Maria to her the next morning. She told Maria that from now on she was to clean off every scrap of dough before she left. Maria begged, she pleaded. The mine owner's wife would show no mercy. Indeed, that evening she sent Maria to wash her hands over and over. She inspected Maria's fingers to make sure that there was not a single speck of dough left on them.

When Maria's brothers and sisters greeted her, she had nothing to give them. They were so hungry they began to cry. Maria wept as well, but not for long. Pulling her shawl over her head, she went begging until she was given a few dry crusts.

When the crusts had been eaten, she put the children to bed and watched them fall asleep. She knew that although begging might do for one day, it would not do for another. She could not bear to watch the children starve. In despair, just at midnight, she went out into the darkness and began to walk.

As she followed the rough road that led out of the village, she saw a light shining in the hills above her. She started to climb toward it. The light was coming from a tent.

Maria went inside. In the middle of the tent there was a wonderful candelabra with twelve candles. Dangling from the center of the candelabra was a golden ball.

As well there were twelve young men seated in a circle. To the right of the entrance sat one who had his snow boots unbuckled. Next to him sat one who had his jacket open, and next to him one who was in his shirt sleeves. Each held something in his hands. One had a new green shoot that he was cradling, one a small bunch of crocus flowers, one a newborn calf.

Next to them sat three young men whose skins were bronzed from the sun. They wore wide-brimmed hats. They were bare-chested. They held the flowers of summer—daisies, lupine and clover. All had baskets of berries and early vegetables and hay stalks on their laps.

Beside them were three clothed for the time when the frosts come at night. One had a scythe and a sickle, a bundle of corn and a sheaf of ripe, gold wheat. One had his arms full of squash and pumpkins. The last was wearing a heavy jacket, but he had a gun and a pair of downed geese in his hands.

And next to them? Those young men were bundled up in furs and sheepskins. The ear flaps of their hats were pulled down low, and their collars were pulled up high. One had skis beside him and one snowshoes. One had a trapper's tools.

All the men welcomed Maria as if they had been expecting her, and they invited her to sit a while. They asked her how she had come and why. She told them of her troubles.

The young man who was closest to her on the left—the last of the ones dressed for winter—at once got to his feet. He had a limp, but he set a table before her and covered it with food and drink. When she had eaten her fill, one of the young men asked her to tell them what she thought about the months of the year.

"Tell us of March and April and May especially," the first young man said.

"They are good months," Maria replied at once. "By March we notice that the days are longer. We know that spring is coming. As the ice melts, there are puddles. We find flowers. By May the tracks in the hills are easier to walk on. People can work in their gardens, getting them ready for planting. As the snow leaves the mountain tops, water flows down. The rivers are full and the fish swim freely."

"You like those months, then?"

Maria nodded.

"What about June, July and August?" one of the next three young men asked.

"Those are the best months for the poor," she answered. "They are the season when it does not matter that our clothes are thin. We need no oil for the lamps because the daylight lasts so long. Food is more plentiful. Storms bring rain. The cattle fatten. Sometimes there is even milk."

"And September, October and November?" the next young men put in.

"It begins to be cold once more, but there has been the harvest. Supplies come from the farms. The elk and the sheep come down from the high places. People are joyous. They look forward to the holiday time to come."

"And now," asked the last three, "what about December and January and February? What do you think of them?"

"It is true," said Maria, "that those are the months when life is hardest—the months when some must die. But if we did not have those months, when would my brothers and my sisters be able to go sliding? How would the plants have time to rest? When would there be the long inside evenings when we can sit together, talking and singing songs?"

"You would not change the months? Not one of them?"

"No," said Maria. "I would not."

The young man who had been holding the wheat sheaf put it down beside him. He left the tent and came back carrying a great stoppered jar.

"Take it with you," he said to her. "But do not open it until you are home once more."

By dawn, as the miners were setting out for work, Maria stood again on her own doorstep. She went first to check on her brothers and sisters, although she did not wake them. When she was certain they were safe, she found a cloth and spread it on the floor. She opened the jar and turned it up to empty it. A stream of gold coins poured out.

Picking up just one gold coin, she ran out to the store. She bought bread and butter, eggs and cheese. As she was returning, she met the mine owner. He asked her what she was doing and she could see no reason not to tell him, for she was so delighted with her luck.

When the mine owner went home from work that day, he told his wife, and her eyes lit up at the thought of all that wealth.

She, too, set out at midnight. She, too, came to the tent with its wonderful candelabra. She entered and saw the twelve young men. She was welcomed and asked why she had come. She said she was poor and so they fed her. Then they asked her about the months.

"Each one is worse than the one before," she told them. "The summers are so hot, you'd think the skin would burn from our bones. Rain may come but it is hardly even enough to settle the dust. There is all that trouble of canning what has grown in the gardens. There is all that cooking. By November we are exhausted. There is no end to the work, though. I must have someone to carry in wood and coal for the fireplace. It is so cold that we can scarcely go outside. December and January are bad enough, but the worst of all is that Lame John of a February. That is when the temperatures sink the lowest. Maybe we could get used to it but, of course, we do not have the chance. March comes and April. Everything is sodden from snow melt. My children all have coughs and colds. They've hardly even recovered and the light begins to be blinding. The sun is beating on us once again."

"So there is not one month you can get on with?" the young men asked her.

"Not one," she told them. "Indeed, I would be rid of them all, if I could."

The young men turned to the one with the wheat sheaf. He went out and came in carrying a stoppered jar. The mine owner's wife took it eagerly, but she was careful to remember the instructions not to remove the stopper until she was home.

When she came to her house, she did not check on her children. She did not even tell her husband. She simply emptied the jar as quickly as she could. From it there came a great thick cloud of coal dust. The dust settled over everything and it settled on her. All her life she tried to wash that dust off, but she never could.

As for Maria, she spent the gold she had been given wisely and generously. She started with a sack of flour so she could bake bread instead of buying it. She planned and fig-ured and finally decided she would open a store of her own.

People came to shop and she was kind to them. She never let anyone go hungry. If a family had no money, she gave them extra time to pay.

Her brothers and sisters grew up and moved to other places, but Maria had no wish to go elsewhere. She kept walking in the mountains and gazing at their peaks.

She gathered the children of the village together and told them stories. They came to listen often.

"My father was right," she said to them. "There are such things as happy endings—in the end."

from

The Old Brown Suitcase

by

Lillian Boraks-Nemetz

Slava is a refugee. At thirteen years old she has experienced the terror, persecution, deprivation and hatred that Jews in Poland suffered at the hands of the Nazis in World War Two. Now she is safe. She and her parents and little sister have arrived in Montreal. They have been taken in by a Canadian family, Mr. and Mrs. Rosenberg and their daughter Ina. There is food, shelter, warmth. But safety is not that simple. Slava carries her memories of horror with her everywhere. As she says, "Sunshine and darkness can exist side by side."

The Sirens (Montreal, 1947)

The next morning, Ina avoided talking to me at breakfast. She quickly excused herself saying that she had to run or she would be late for tennis.

"I don't suppose you play tennis," she said to me as she rushed out the door. There was no time to reply.

"Slava has had to learn to survive for the past six years," said Father to Mr. and Mrs. Rosenberg. Did I hear a slight bit of annoyance in his voice echoing my own unspoken feeling? Father continued, "She has not even been to school yet, let alone learned how to play tennis."

The Rosenbergs looked at each other.

"Perhaps she should have an English tutor before school starts?" suggested Mrs. Rosenberg. This time my parents looked at each other, and I knew why. We could not afford it right now. All we had was a monthly check from my uncle in New York. It was just enough to cover our basic needs. Mother thanked Mrs. Rosenberg for her concern about my English, but said that this was not a good time for a tutor, since we might only be in Montreal a few weeks.

"Come on, Slava, let's get ready for our walk," said Father. For the moment I could forget learning English.

The quiet street was lined with trees. This area was called Westmount, Father explained, where wealthy English people lived. We walked past large brick houses like the Rosenbergs' that were set into spacious areas of land.

It seemed strange to see houses on the city streets, instead of apartment buildings. In Warsaw people lived in apartments, and houses were to be found only in the countryside. On Aleje Jerozolimskie, there were many shops and cafes. Warsaw's streets were always busy with people coming and going. But here in Westmount there were few people walking on the street.

We turned onto a street called Sherbrooke. It looked more like a proper city street with its larger buildings, dress shops, and streetcars. There were more people too.

I heard two languages spoken. I guessed that one of them was English. The other sounded similar to the French I had learned in Warsaw, but not quite the same. Still, just knowing that there was French spoken here made me feel closer to home.

Soon we came to another busy street called Peel Street. It was fun reading the different street names; some in French, others in English.

The streets were getting busier and Father announced that we were finally "downtown." We had been walking a long time, and decided to stop for lunch.

"There is a restaurant somewhere on Peel Street called Child's," said Father, consulting his map. "It was highly recommended by the Rosenbergs."

We found Child's along Peel Street just off St. Catherine's. It was a strange-looking restaurant, compared to the elegant cafes of Warsaw. The narrow tables had high-backed benches on either side. You had to slide into them, and ended up sitting next to a wall. A waitress came and asked us something in English. Father ordered, using a new word taught him by Mr. Rosenberg: "pancakes."

The waitress brought two plates, each filled with a stack of five flat round cakes. There was melted butter floating on top. Then she placed on the table a glass container filled with thick dark liquid. We looked at it, not knowing what it was for.

"Maple syrup," said the waitress, pointing at the dark-liquid container. "You put it on top of the pancakes like so," she said, tilting the container and pouring the liquid over my cakes. Father thanked her. She was kind, I thought, and must have understood that we were foreigners.

They were oozingly delicious, these "pancakes," covered with the sweet, golden "maple syrup." We also drank a dark sweet fizzy liquid, called Coca-Cola. After lunch, we continued our walk in downtown Montreal, passing movie theaters, shops, restaurants, and churches. Stopping at a street corner, I looked up and saw a mountain in the distance. On top stood an enormous cross, like a beacon in the bright July sun.

It was getting hot and crowded in the streets. Father was wiping his forehead with a hanky, and my clothes were sticking to my body, but we continued our walk. Soon we came to an older part of the city, with cobblestone streets. The buildings looked familiar to the ones in Warsaw before the War. They were narrow and very close together, built of grey stone and red brick with slatted wooden windows, high doors with arched entrances, and black iron gates.

Further down the street there was a throng of people in front of an old building. As we approached, we could smell smoke. There were flames shooting from the roof of the building and people in the windows, screaming and gesticulating. I grasped Father's hand and held it as tight as I could.

Then, above the noise of the crowd I heard a shrill and whining noise. A siren coming closer and closer.

"Papa, it's an air raid," I screamed, tugging at his hand. I wanted to drag him away, but we could not move because we were wedged in between the masses of fascinated onlookers. A long red truck pulled up across the street, and men in steel helmets began to unravel a long hose. Soon it squirted water at the furious flames, while more sirens sounded.

My head was exploding with visions of burning buildings and thunderous crashes. I caught a glimpse of a man who was laughing. Why was he laughing? I let go of Father's hand.

"Slava," he shouted, "this is Canada! There are no bombs here. It is only a fire, the war is over!" But all I could hear were sirens wailing in my ears.

I ran past blurred faces and windows, tripping over the holes in the pavement, seeing only dark cellars and faces of frightened children.

The Soldiers (Warsaw, 1939)

I am six.

I hear airplanes in the distance, and I am running towards a building for cover. I pass a baby in a carriage under a tree. I stop to look at her. She is wearing a pink bonnet, and her blue eyes look up at the sky. I can't see Father, where is he?

An airplane roars above, people are running. The baby starts crying. I don't know what to do. I try to stop several people to tell them about the baby, but they just rush past me.

Suddenly masses of planes thunder over the city. Father appears out of nowhere, running. He picks me up and carries me into the building and down the stairs to a cellar. Though there is whistling and crashing above us, it feels safer inside this dingy place, smelling of dampness and mould. The temporary shelter is crowded with people, some sitting on wooden benches, others on the floor. All look terrified. The men have their arms around the women and children. A woman is weeping, a child wails.

Someone says that when you hear a long whistle, a bomb is about to fall on a building. We hear a whistle now and I plug my ears and close my eyes. The whistle goes on and on. Will the bomb hit our building? There is a deafening crash, but when I open my eyes we are still here. The bomb must have fallen somewhere else.

As suddenly as it began, the grinding roar of the bombers subsides. All is still. No one moves.

A woman rushes into the shelter, carrying a bloody bundle with a pink bonnet. She is young and pretty in a polka dot dress, but her eyes are filled with tears.

"My baby is dead," she cries, crumpling to the floor.

We stare dumbly at her and at each other, while she wails from the dusty floor. I listen to her sorrow, still seeing the baby's blue innocent eyes looking up at the sky.

Father walks over to the woman and gently tries to help her up. Several women follow. One takes the bundle out of her arms. Another puts her arms around the woman's hunched shoulders, and leads her out of the shelter.

We walk out of the darkness of the cellar into daylight. It is the same warm autumn day outside, only now it's darker with the particles of grey dust and smoke from the burning buildings. The carriage under the tree is smashed, and pieces of fallen brick and steel lie all around us.

I am frightened. What has happened to the rest of our family?

We rush home to find that both Mother and Basia are safe. But my mother's pale face scares me. She looks almost ill.

"I was just having tea when the bombers came. We ran downstairs," she says. "Everyone was gathering in the courtyard, and some people ran down to the cellar so we followed. It was horrid, just like the raid this morning. Basia cried the whole time."

"I am sorry that we weren't home. I was very worried about you," replies Father, hugging her.

The German army is getting closer to Warsaw. Masha stays, but cook and maid leave for their homes in the villages. We are sad to see them go.

The radio calls for all Poles, young and able, to join the Polish army to fight the Germans who have invaded Poland. Father says that he must join up even though he doesn't want to leave his family. He promises to return soon. The day he leaves, Mother takes a thin gold bracelet off her wrist and gives it to him for good luck.

When Father kisses us good-bye, both he and Mother have tears in their eyes. I look at them through a mist of tears blurring my eyes also. We watch Father disappear down the corridor.

Mother tells me to pack my brown suitcase with my most important things and some clothes as well, because we may have to leave at any time. I take two of my favorite books and my sunflower costume. Mother helps me pack and shakes her head, unable to understand why I need the costume.

The days pass and there is no word from Father. I am not allowed to go outside. Mother brings home rationed bread and potatoes after standing in line for hours.

The air raids continue to devastate the city. We seem to be constantly running to the shelters as the sirens sound. There is no water or electricity. We burn candles and carefully ration cans of preserves we keep in the pantry. We drink the syrup from the jars of fruit preserves, which we dilute with the water that Masha brings in a pail from the Vistula River.

Everything seems to be in the state of terrible confusion. The windows are closed and the drapes drawn most of the time. It is so hot that I can hardly breathe. Often in the middle of the night I'd wake up from nightmares, screaming.

Booming sounds of guns are heard all the time in the distance. Mother says that half the city is in ruins. One evening we are sitting around the dining room table when someone knocks on the door. Masha goes up to the door and opens it.

A bearded man with dirty, tattered clothes stands on the threshold.

"Stefan!" Mother cries and rushes up to him.

It's Father. He looks worn and chalk-white. He tells us he has walked for miles, and has been without food for the last three days. Mother ushers him into another room. I want to go with them but Masha stops me. I wait impatiently for what seems a very long time, then the door opens and the "old Father," clean-shaven and elegant, comes in. I run to him and hug him.

Over tea and bread, Father tells us the story.

"We didn't have a chance. The German army is a powerful war machine and there was no way we could hold them back for very long. My leg was wounded on the second day. Our regiment ran out of ammunition and there were masses of casualties. The Poles fought bravely, but it was an impossible fight to win. Our army pulled back and fell apart. We were told to disperse and fend for ourselves." He sips his tea and continues.

"The roads were full of trucks and retreating infantry. I walked the fields and forests trying to avoid the road. My leg hurt and bled so I tried to stop at farmhouses to get help, but the peasants were suspicious and frightened, and didn't want to help me. One day I saw an old peasant riding in a cart full of hay drawn by a tired nag. With the last bit of strength I had left, I hopped on the cart from the back and hid in the hay, and rode part of the way to Warsaw. The old man didn't even know I was there. He was drinking vodka all the way."

We look at Father's leg. Mother has bandaged it with a clean dressing, but already there is some blood on it.

"Don't any of you worry, I'll be fine," says Father. "I am just so happy to be back."

Mother puts me to bed, and I have no bad dreams. Father is back at last.

A few days later, we hear marching feet, the screech of vehicles, and loud voices from the street. We rush up to the window: the street is crowded with German soldiers and tanks.

"Get away from the window," says Father. I look at him, not understanding.

"Jewish people are going to have to be very careful from now on," he says. "Hitler and his followers are out to get us."

I don't underseand why the Germans don't like us. And who is Hitler? I want to ask, but my parents look so upset that the questions freeze in my throat.

Several weeks later, we come home after visiting friends, and find our apartment in ruins. All the glassware and china lies shattered on the floor. My room's floor is littered with pages out of torn books and stuffing taken out of my animals. Most of the furniture is gone.

Father says that the Gestapo, the German police, must have traced our apartment as belonging to Jews. They are destroying Jewish shops in Warsaw, and evicting Jewish families from their homes.

My parents decide to restore the apartment the best they can and continue to live there despite the threat of possible eviction. There is no other place to go. Since there is now a housing shortage in Warsaw my room has been rented out. I sleep with Masha now and miss my own room. But soon Masha leaves for the country, and I have her room all to myself. She leaves me a long string of beads with a cross, and tells me to pray regularly.

Winter passes and then the spring. One day in late summer, Father and I venture out for a walk.

German soldiers in green uniforms are everywhere. They speak loudly in a language I don't understand and always seem to be marching rather than walking. Some have helmets and rifles. Others wear caps and pistols in black leather holsters, and tall, very shiny black leather boots. The worst are the ones in black uniforms and caps with the skull and bones on them. They look sullen and angry.

Father doesn't seem afraid, but he avoids main streets and we walk down the smaller narrow ones.

Through a space between two buildings I see men building a brick wall.

"What are they doing Papa?" I ask.

"They are making a Ghetto," Father replies. "The wall will close off a portion of the city and all the Jewish people of Warsaw will be forced to live there."

A bearded man in a black coat passes by. He wears a white arm band with a blue star on it. He is not the first person I have seen wearing the star. After the man has gone by I ask Father about it.

"These arm bands have been forced on the Jews. The star is the Star of David. Your mother and I already have ours, but we don't always wear them. If you don't and you are caught, you are badly punished," he says.

"Will I have to wear one?"

"No, children under twelve don't have to wear them." Father sounds tired and irritable.

I still don't know what a Star of David really is, so I ask.

"David was the king of the Jewish people a long time ago ..." Father doesn't finish.

A motorcade of Germans is passing by. Father takes my arm and quickly steers me into another side street. His step quickens and I run to keep up.

Later at home I think more about the blue star. The Star of David. I like the sound of it. Anyway, it looks much better than the swastikas, those twisted crosses the German SS wear on their uniforms. They are black and ugly.

In the months to come the wall grows higher. Father says that in some places it is already eight feet high, topped with barbed wire and jagged pieces of glass, to prevent people from climbing over to escape.

Sunlight
(Montreal and Ste. Adèle, Quebec, 1947)

"*La petite pauvre*," said an old man. People bent over me, exclaiming in French, as I sprawled, hot and out of breath, on the steps of a church. Father had finally caught up with me. He picked me up and took me to a nearby coffee shop. While I sipped a cold drink, he tried to assure me that the war was in the past, that there is peace now in the world, and I mustn't be frightened by the memory. But my memory of war lingered on the way home. I felt dazed. The past and the present seemed mated together.

The next day, Mother took me to a Polish doctor recommended by Mrs. Rosenberg. The doctor felt my stomach, listened to my heart and lungs, took a blood sample from my finger, and told my mother that I was anemic. He recommended vitamins and liver.

That evening I sat down to a plateful of liver and onions. Ina grimaced at the sight of it. "It's like a blob of mud topped by browned weeds," she said.

I couldn't eat it and my parents didn't force me to. Instead they gave me some tablets which fell into my throat like cement, and stayed there for several minutes resisting their passage into my stomach.

I forgot all about the tablets when dessert came, a banana split prepared by Mr. Rosenberg.

"Try *that*, young lady," he said, bowing, as he placed it in front of me. I had never seen anything like it: a glass dish full of vanilla ice cream, topped with whipped cream, chocolate sauce, cherries, and cut-up bananas. The mixture was unbearably delicious, and I couldn't stop eating. Before long Ina and I had our faces messy with ice cream. It seemed to me that Ina ate her banana split just as greedily as I ate my orange, the night before.

My parents decided to leave Montreal. Lodgings in the city were too expensive, and we couldn't stay on at the Rosenbergs' indefinitely. The Rosenbergs suggested a moderately priced *pension* in the village of Ste. Adèle and offered to drive us there.

I was glad to leave. Ina didn't want to come with us, so we said a polite but stiff good-bye in Montreal.

We had left the city's hot grey pavement and thick air for the gold and green fields of the Quebec countryside. Peaceful villages emerged, surrounded by wooded hills and farms.

As we went further into the Laurentians, we passed lakes that looked so clear and cool, I wished we could have stopped and jumped into their bluish-green water. Finally I saw a sign that read Ste. Adèle, and after another kilometer the car stopped in front of a large farm house.

It was nothing like the *pensions* my parents and I had visited at Polish summer resorts. The resort buildings were large, elegant, and white. Usually they were set inside orchards or surrounded by rose bushes and trees, and were close to the water and forest. In contrast, this Canadian *pension* was a sprawling rust-colored wooden farmhouse with a wrap-around veranda. A tawny cat sat in one of the windows while chickens cackled on the side of the yard behind a wire fence. Two trees graced the front yard, and several flower beds brightened the entrance. No one was in sight to greet us. We took our luggage from the car and went in, walking through a wood-panelled hallway into a lounge. Mrs. Rosenberg surveyed the room with a look of distaste that said it wasn't anything like her elegant home in Westmount. I liked it a lot.

Two large couches and three brown velvet chairs stood welcomingly on a worn rose-colored rug. The couches were covered in beige fabric with a faded pattern of red roses. The velvet of the chairs was quite bald in places. Here and there stood wooden tables with china animals and ashtrays, and several floor lamps with frilly shades bowed over the couches and the chairs. Above the mantel of a red brick fireplace hung a painting of a farmer loading his wooden cart with wheat, his horse standing patiently as several children looked on. Surrounding the farmer and the children were fields and wild flowers.

The room smelled of mildew, mothballs, and lemon, which brought back the memory of Babushka's cottage in the Polish countryside.

The Rosenbergs wanted to leave, so we followed them out onto the veranda. Mrs. Rosenberg and Mother exchanged good-byes with the usual niceties.

"You must come and stay with us again soon, my dear Lucy," said Mrs. Rosenberg sweetly, to which Mother replied with equal sweetness. But I got the impression that Mother didn't really want to stay there again. Of course she couldn't say that, could she?

Father and Mr. Rosenberg shook hands heartily, and Mr. Rosenberg offered his help if we needed anything. Somehow I felt he really meant it. We watched from the porch as they drove away in a cloud of dust, leaving us suddenly alone and apart from the rest of the world. At least with the Rosenbergs, we could communicate in our own language.

A small, slim woman came out of the house onto the veranda. Her blonde hair was done up in tight curls and she wore a dress patterned like the couches in the lounge. Her face was oval with a straight nose and wide blue eyes. She was attractive in an angelic sort of way. When she shook her head the curls bobbed up and down like springs.

I couldn't tell her age. I was fascinated by her red furry bedroom slippers.

"Please enter," she beckoned. "I speak no much English only *Français. Je m'appelle* Marie."

Father spoke to her in French, only twice having to look up a word in his French/Polish dictionary. I could understand her as she described the rules of the house and the meal times. It was wonderful to know that we could communicate with her, even if it meant using a dictionary.

Marie showed us upstairs to our rooms. In the room where my parents and Pyza were going to stay, everything was green from the wallpaper to the scatter rugs and bedspread. I followed Marie's furry slippers up a steep wooden staircase to an attic.

It was hot and stuffy, but when she opened the window the country air dispersed the heat. The room had blue-cornflower wallpaper, a wood-panelled sloping roof, a blue-patterned bedspread, and a desk and chair under the window. Above the bed hung a cross, and next to it a picture of the Madonna in a sky-blue robe, her hands gracefully folded and her face demure and peaceful. I had seen such pictures in Poland in the homes of Catholic country folk. Most of all, my eyes were drawn back to the window. There, below the azure sky lay an emerald field, and beyond it swelled the hills, luscious with forests.

Between the field and the forest stood a white church, its steeple gleaming gold in the sun. I stood enchanted, remembering the farm in *Anne of Green Gables*. Marie tried to tell me something in English but I didn't understand. I said, "No speak English," amazed that I knew enough to say anything. But when she pointed at the bedpan under my bed, I nodded in recognition. Of course I had seen one of these before. Then she pointed to a wash basin and white enamelled jug, standing on the desk. She explained in French that when I wanted to wash up, I could bring some water from the bathroom downstairs. I said *merci* and she smiled and said that she must go downstairs to get the dining room ready.

After Marie had left, Father came upstairs and announced that it was dinner time. I told him how well Marie and I had communicated, but I didn't mention my first attempt at English, which still felt like sticky rubber in my mouth. The dining room had two long tables for the guests, who lived either in the farmhouse or in the nearby cottages. A girl about my age came up and said something in English, but I couldn't answer, so she shrugged her shoulders and went away.

"See? You're going to have to try and learn English soon," said Father, watching us. Of course he was right.

Dinner was meat pie, vegetables and potatoes, followed by ice cream with chocolate sauce. I was hungry and ate very fast. I was glad that Ina wasn't there to watch me.

After dinner I wished that the girl would come over again. I tried to catch her eye, but she didn't seem interested.

Marie was busy clearing the tables. Her cheeks were flushed and her hair fell in limp wisps about her face. She looked over and smiled, and I wanted to go up to her, but instead I just sat there tied to my chair. If only I were as brave as that girl who came up to me before supper. So free and unafraid. All of a sudden Marie motioned me over to where she stood. Had she guessed my thoughts? She looked as if she could use a helper. I went over and offered myself. At first she hesitated. When I insisted, she gave me a tray and pointed to the dirty glasses on the table.

In no time the dining room was cleared and set for breakfast, and Marie invited me into the kitchen for milk and cookies. Before I knew it, I was learning French conversation and grammar.

"*C'est pour cela que je t'ai fait venir,*" said Marie, "teach you français," she added with a warm smile and closed the grammar book. Then she suggested that we go upstairs as it was getting on to bedtime.

She took up a jug of water and waited as I washed up and got ready for bed. Just as I was about to get into bed, she raised her finger, as if to say, not yet, and her eyes were raised to the cross above. She kneeled next to the bed and motioned me to do the same. Then she crossed herself, and looked at me as if I should be doing likewise. I did it only so as not to offend her.

Then she lowered her head and said, "*Prions.*"

I began the Lord's Prayer in Polish just as Masha had taught me, when I was little, without my parents knowing. Marie looked at me with surprise.

"What language?" she asked.

"Polish, *polonaise,*" I said in both languages.

"Oh . . . *polonaise,*" she exclaimed. "*Je suis canadienne-française, et vous êtes canadienne-polonaise.*"

"*Pas encore canadienne*," I replied.

"*Pas encore canadienne, mais vous êtes catholique, n'est ce pas?*"

I felt numb and couldn't answer.

"*Bon*," she said patting me on the back. She smiled at me warmly and left the room.

"I am Jewish," I said quietly. But the door had already closed behind Marie. Why hadn't I told her right away? I asked myself in the darkening attic. Anne of Green Gables would not have held back the truth. You're a coward, I told myself.

The moon had flooded my room with an eerie light. Its pale glow illuminated the face of the Madonna above my head . . .

I woke up in the morning to the sounds of chickens cackling, cows mooing, and bird-song. The room was filled with the smell of earth, a pungent blend of grass and manure.

Outside the attic window, sunlight bathed the corn field. The forest beyond the field stood dark and silent. I will explore the forest, I promised myself, and ran downstairs for breakfast. Marie, in a blue dress, hair tied back, served juice to the vacationers. She smiled in greeting when she saw me and said, "*Viens d'après-midi, je vais t'enseigner un peu de français.*" A French lesson in the afternoon? I nodded in agreement.

My parents were already seated at the table.

I told Father about the picture of the Madonna in my room and asked him what it meant to the Christians. He looked somewhat surprised and said, "In the Christian religion it is believed that Mary, the Virgin, had her son Jesus by Immaculate Conception. This means she didn't do what wives and husbands do together in order to have a child. She bore a child whose name was Jesus and who the Christians believe was the son of God. But the Jewish people believe only in the one Almighty God." Father finished and looked at me inquisitively.

I didn't really understand what he meant, and wanted to ask him more, but just then Pyza started to cry and my parents got busy.

I slipped out quietly into the garden and weaved through the corn to the adjoining field. It was full of poppies and dandelions, but nowhere could I find my beloved sunflowers. I walked across to the forest.

This shady place, with its soft green moss and ferns, could as well have been the forest in the village of Zalesie, where I lived with Babushka during the war.

How strange that happiness and sunlight could disappear from one day to the next, or one place to the next. Yet, sunshine and darkness can exist side by side, I decided, seeing my own shadow outlined against the grass, black, like that sunny day in Poland when the light in my life had suddenly dimmed.

The Ghetto (Warsaw, 1940)

I am seven.

It is a sunny November day, but I am cold.

An endless dark line of us moves slowly through a gate in the tall brick wall. People carry on their backs or push in carts all that remains of their life's belongings. They enter the Ghetto beneath the cold eyes of German soldiers and Polish police. A cruel silence reigns over us despite the voices, the shuffling of feet, the grinding of wooden carts against the cobblestone street, and the clanking of pots and pans. The faces of the people around us are frightened. Some are crying as they walk.

I walk with my parents, my hand is numb from the weight of the brown suitcase. It contains all I have: one chipped porcelain doll, two books, my ballet costume, and some clothes. My father carries two large cases, and a knapsack, while Mother holds my sister. Basia is only two years old.

We step through the gate away from sunlight, into the grey shadow of the Ghetto.

All of a sudden Mother stops as if she can't walk any further. A red-faced soldier yells "*Schnell! Schnell!*" into Mother's face and hits her on the back with a thick black baton. Mother stoops beneath the blow, her face twisted with pain, and moves on, with Father next to her, his face sickly white. Basia begins to wail. The soldiers are shooting at some people huddling in the doorway of a building. As we pass by one of the soldiers points his pistol at us. There are gunshots all around. Behind me I hear the footsteps of the soldier's boots, and another shot. My knees crumple and I sink to the ground. Am I dead? No, the bullet was for an old woman who fell to the ground behind us. Father pulls me up and whispers, "Quickly, these madmen will kill anyone who disobeys them." I look back. The old lady lies where she fell, and people step over her body.

As we get further away from that gate, the immediate feeling of terror only slightly wanes.

"I know how terrifying all this is," says Father, "but we must be brave, Slava." He is breathing hard under the weight of the luggage, and his face is still white. "You're not going to give up now, are you?"

"No, I am not giving up, Papa," I answer, still shuddering, my lips stiff and unwilling.

My mother walks in silence, staring ahead. Basia is quiet.

Finally, we arrive at our new home. The walls of the building are greyish and shabby. The stone facade is chipped and yellow in places and the windows are dirty. We enter through the courtyard, and find the inside even worse. Masses of people mill up and down the stairs and in the corridor of our apartment, pushing mattresses and suitcases.

Through the doors that bang open and shut, I see sheets being hung around the beds, the only way to create some privacy, as in a hospital. Wrinkled sheets hang on crooked rods or string, swaying in the breeze of human motion. The three bedrooms, dining room and living room of each apartment are occupied by five families, twenty-five people who must share the one kitchen and bathroom, and the stench throughout the place! It smells of old plumbing and sweat, of garbage lying around in corners, of dirt left behind by the previous occupants.

Our room is one of the large bedrooms of a common apartment, or maybe it's the parlor. Who knows? It is like the others, filled with the same stench and shabby furniture.

Black, torn shades hang against the windows like crows that have frozen in flight. On the table stands a naphtha lamp, our only source of light for the long winter nights to come. A red velvet chair huddles in a corner, its crevices filled with dirt and dust.

I sit exhausted in the red chair, and watch my parents make the best of what we have. They energetically clean, wipe and arrange our provisions on a shelf and put our clothes into a wardrobe. Meanwhile they give me the job of entertaining my baby sister, who is marvelously oblivious to our misfortune. I try to make funny faces, and then, quietly, tell her the story of Little Red Riding Hood and the Big Bad Wolf. She listens attentively then begins to chortle. Her laughter is the only bright moment of this unhappy day.

Mother makes tea and puts out bread for supper. The tea is hot and sweet. The coarse bread is black and stale, but we eat it thankfillly as if it were the best-tasting meal on earth.

Someone knocks on the door. It opens and an elderly woman enters our room. She is chubby and poorly dressed save for a beautiful hand-knitted shawl around her shoulders and arms. Her heavy beige stockings are held in place by elastics just below the knee, and they bag at the ankles.

"I am Mrs. Solomon," the woman says hoarsely. "I would like to invite you to the Sabbath dinner tomorrow evening. We will share what little we have. Anything you bring will be welcome."

Suddenly she begins to cough. At first the cough is normal, but gradually it becomes so violent that my parents rush to her side. They sit her down with difficulty as her large body heaves with spasms. Pulling a handkerchief from a soiled sleeve of her dress, she presses it against her lips. I offer her my cup of tea. She takes several sips, and when the cough subsides somewhat, she continues.

"These are terrible times for Jewish people. Before this terrible thing happened we lived in a big apartment on Marshalkowska Street. The Germans took everything from us, even the samovar my mother brought all the way from Petersburg in Russia. They killed my husband on the street because he refused to undress in public." She wipes tears from her eyes. "Now my daughter Sallye and I share one room with my brother and his wife and her sister. All in one room! They say that over a hundred thousand people entered the Ghetto today, and that there will be more to come. Where will they live?" she cries. "Where is the God of our people?"

Mrs. Solomon grows silent and her body rocks back and forth as if in a prayer. No one speaks. It is getting dark. Father lights the naphtha lamp and pulls down the blackout shades. Mother offers Mrs. Solomon a cup of tea but she declines.

"Thank you but I must go. Sallye, my daughter, has not been well lately. The doctor thinks it could be tuberculosis. But please come to our dinner tomorrow night." She smiles, and for a moment her tired face brightens, as if some inner light had turned on. "We must continue to live in spite of all this, at least until tomorrow," she says and leaves.

"What is tuberculosis Father?" I ask.

"It is a disease of the lungs," he replies, shaking his head sadly. "A very contagious disease. Her coughing makes me wonder if poor Mrs. Solomon doesn't have it too."

"Papa," I say, "I noticed blood on her handkerchief, after she coughed. She tried to hide it."

My parents look at each other sadly, but say nothing. I go to bed. The light of the naphtha lamp casts eerie shadows on the walls.

I sleep fitfully, half-dreaming about poor Mrs. Solomon and her daughter Sallye. Do I hear coughing across the hall? I want to say a prayer to God and include them. But I am uncertain after today, I wonder if Mrs. Solomon is right. Could it be that God no longer hears our prayers?

The morning brings with it a jumble of sounds. There are feet shuffling past our doors, voices behind the walls, cries, wailing, angry shouts, women's, men's and children's voices.

"There is a long lineup to the bathroom," announces my mother after looking out into the corridor. "What are we going to do?"

Father dresses and goes out for half an hour and returns with a bedpan and a pail. We all feel better in a while. He takes the pail out, while Mother washes out the bedpan with water taken from the kitchen, which she pours out later into the toilet.

Every Friday night my parents, Basia and I go to Mrs. Solomon's for a Shabbat dinner. The eight of us just fit around Mrs. Solomon's long brown table. I sit between my parents and Sallye.

Mrs. Solomon wears a black lace scarf on her head and lights the Shabbat candles. Her hand circles over the flames and she says a prayer in Hebrew, a language I don't understand. Afterwards, she looks up towards the ceiling as if it were heaven, her eyes full of tears. I like the sound of this language, and the solemnity of the prayer. Her daughter translates it into Polish for those of us who don't understand Hebrew. It is a prayer to God that gives thanks for the food and asks for His blessing and deliverance from our present condition. At the end of the prayer everyone says "Amen." Mrs. Solomon weeps. We are now given bowls of watery soup with dark bits swimming in it. Then potatoes are served with something that resembles chicken. It is boiled, mostly yellowed skin hanging from the meager bones. It tastes slimy. There are pickles and jam on the table. Mrs. Solomon tells us it is practically the last of her own preserves, which she brought to the Ghetto.

"Does the Lord hear our prayers?" I ask Sallye after the meal.

"Of course He does," she answers cheerfully.

"I like the idea of Shabbat," I confide in Sallye. "We never had it in our home, only sometimes at our friend's house, but I can barely remember it."

At night I say my own prayer to God.

I like Sallye very much. She treats me like an adult, and plays with me when she feels well. She sings Yiddish songs, some of which sound sad, some happy. She says that it doesn't much matter whether you understand the words, the Jewish soul comes through the sound. On this and other Friday nights we listen to Sallye after dinner and then clap, asking for more songs. Our lives become less dreary on Shabbat nights.

Sallye is becoming terribly skinny, and her skin is transparent like yellow tissue. She coughs more frequently now that winter is upon us, and sometimes stays in bed all week. I want her to get better, but one morning I awake to the news that Sallye has died during the night. I go back to bed and weep into my pillow. I vow never to pray again.

Mrs. Solomon is hysterical for days. Shortly after Sallye's death, she becomes very ill. As days go by I avoid looking at the soiled and smelly pile of sheets outside her room. One day they carry her body out on a stretcher. Our Shabbat dinners resume after a while in someone else's room, but they do not feel the same.

A sign appears in the courtyard and on the outside of our building: QUARANTINED–TYPHUS.

The gate to the courtyard remains open, because our whole street has been quarantined. But the food grows scarce because no one is allowed in or out beyond a certain point. Are we going to die? I wonder each night as I lie in bed. Often I hear a young boy cry out in pain from an apartment above us. I listen, helpless. In the mornings he sits in the window, white as a ghost. His mother tells everyone that he has a nervous stomach.

One night I hear nothing. Maybe he is better. But in the morning they carry him away. He died of typhus, and he was only fourteen.

A few days later I am playing hide-and-seek in the courtyard with the other children, when I am nailed to my spot by a scream. I look up. The mother of the boy who died stands in a window on the second floor. Her hair is wild about her face and she screams and screams. Suddenly she lunges forward and falls out of the window. She is falling towards me, but I can't move. Her body lands next to me with a thud.

Choking on tears, I run out of the courtyard into the street. But soon I am forced to stop, for the street ends abruptly at the high wall of the Ghetto a quarter of a block away from our building. I stand panting in front of the wall. This part of it is made of wood. Down below there is a space between the wood and the cobblestones, and through it I can see the soldiers' black polished boots, marching back and forth, back and forth. I hear men laugh and speak in their harsh-sounding language, which I have come to fear and hate. I turn around and walk back very slowly to the courtyard.

Life goes on.

from

The Onlyhouse

by

Teresa Toten

When Lucy Vakovik and her mother move into their own house, they discover that the new neighbourhood poses a steep learning curve for Lucy. It is tough to figure out the pecking order of the grade six girls, to find a strategy to avoid joining the Girl Guides and, most of all, how to get her mother to act like a "regular Canadian."

"Now *remember*, Mama," I warned, "don't improvise."

See, Jackie, Cindy and Jenny were all coming over after dinner. Mama baked for three nights straight. I kept explaining about how important it was not to look over-eager. "Nonchalant, Mama, nonchalant." She nodded and smiled at me between batches.

We rehearsed her English for days. The deal was that Mama was supposed to come into the living room and say in a real soft voice, "Hello, girls. How lovely to meet you all. Perhaps you would care for a cookie?" Then she would place the cookies on the coffee table, smile and leave. She'd spend the rest of the time in the kitchen pretending to read *A Tale of Two Cities* by Charles Dickens. He's from England. I borrowed it from the library at Emily McDonald's.

"Oh, and remember I've changed our name," I reminded her. "We don't say Vook-o-veech anymore, it's Vak-o-vik."

"Okay, okay," she muttered. "It sounds just as immigrant to me, but you *want* Vakovik, we'll *be* Vakovik."

The doorbell rang. I raced to get it. It was Cindy and Jackie. "Hi, guys," I said, real cool like. While they were taking off their coats and things, Jenny came tripping up the porch steps.

"I like your door," she said.

"Uh, thanks," I said. "We're thinking of getting it painted. Blue maybe."

"Blue's nice," said Cindy.

"Hey!" called Jackie from the living room. "Where the hell is the dining room? Whose bed is this?"

"Oh . . ." God. I forgot about that. Regular Canadians have dining room furniture in their dining rooms "Mine," I whispered. I was going to die. No, I was dying. How *could* I forget about dining rooms? They all have dining room furniture, dining room tables, dining room chairs, dining room china cabinets. I had a double bed and a dresser. They didn't even match.

"That's neat," she said, "you can see the TV from your bed."

"Yeah," I snorted, "it's great."

Just then Mama burst in with a huge platter of cookies, five different assortments. "Halloo everybodies, halloo! Nice to be lovely to meeting my lovely Lucija's lovely friends . . . is lovely."

Everyone gasped. You'd think she could get one lousy little sentence right.

"Wow, jeez!" they erupted at once.

"Did you make all those cookies, Mrs. Vakovik?" asked Jenny.

"I've seen bakeries with less stuff in them," said Jackie.

"Pa-da!" smiled Mama. "You be 'scusing my sometime English is broking."

Oh God . . . she was ad-libbing. If only they could speak Croatian. Mama is so good in Croatian.

"I be baking dis lovely cookies for visiting to making nice." She beamed at me. "You van it nice to drink someting? Eating, too? I got kolbasa, bread, milk, I getting 'na frige?"

"Milk, please," said Cindy.

"Me, too, please," nodded Jenny.

"What's a kolbasa?" asked Jackie.

"Come," Mama held out her hand, "I showing you 'na kitchen." Mama and Jackie came back with milk and meat.

This was all wrong and they were just pretending not to notice. Canadians don't sit around munching on kolbasa and almond mocha cookies. I had to think of something.

"Have I ever told you . . ." I said, "that . . . my great, great, great grandmother was an Iroquois Indian?"

"Get outta here! No way!" scoffed Jenny.

"No guff," I insisted, "I am actually one-eighth pure, adulterated, real, native Canadian."

"You mean one-eighth pure adultery," interrupted Jenny.

"No," said Cindy, "adultery has something to do with sex."

"It's pure *un*adulterated," groaned Jackie.

"Yeah, anyway . . ." I plugged on, "the Indian heritage gets passed down through the women, just like Jewishness. I'm full of Indian features like . . . like all Iroquois have uh . . . well . . . browny-black, black eyes. Not just regular brown eyes. Look at mine." I blinked at everyone. "See, these are Iroquois eyes."

"Well . . ." Jenny examined me carefully, "they're real dark all right."

"Sure," I nodded, "that's why Mama makes me wear braids and stuff."

"That's so neat," said Cindy. "We don't have anything interesting in our family, except my mother's grandmother was Welch."

"That's a grape juice, genius." Jackie rolled her eyes. Jenny giggled and I continued blinking at everyone. Jackie stared at me. "Your mom's unbelievable," she said. "We wouldn't even get this at Christmas. Do you think that, maybe, I could bring a couple of cookies home? You know, for Karen and Kyle and, well, really for Carole. She loves cookies. Maybe cookies would snap her out of it. She's starting to spook me, she's so bugged out."

"Men," sighed Jenny. We all nodded wisely.

I was so relieved that she didn't want to know what an Iroquois princess was doing coming from Zagreb, that I would have given her the whole platter. "Sure!" I said. "Cookies for everyone!" I ran to the kitchen and yelled at Mama to put the book down and make up gift packages. She tried to give me a hug, but I escaped. "Done!" I announced back in the living room.

"Thanks," smiled Jackie. "Okay, you guys, I have something to tell you. You know how we decided not to go out for Halloween?" Everyone nodded. I nodded—I didn't know what we were nodding about. "Well, it sort of leaves a hole, doesn't it? We need something. So . . . I have found it. I have found our clubhouse!"

"Clubhouse?" asked Jenny. "What for?"

"For our club, you goofs!" barked Jackie. "We're going to form a secret club, the Tomcats. You know the laneway behind Davisville?" We all nodded again. "Well, the third garage in from Bayview on the left-hand side is empty. Old lady Marshall lives there. She doesn't have a car and she never leaves the house. That garage will be our clubhouse. We'll be mutually exclusive."

"What's that?" asked Cindy.

"It means just us, stupid," said Jackie. "The whole school will be our minions. That means slaves."

"So how's that different from now?" Jenny just didn't know when to shut up. I'd seen this before when, for no reason, Jackie would rip into everything Jenny said or did. Cindy said it was like that since kindergarten. I guess Jenny didn't notice.

"Because, runt," Jackie glared at her, "we'll be a club! We're gonna be invincible. We'll have initiation and everything. That's a test, a test of loyalty—to prove you're worthy. I haven't figured out all the details yet. I'll work it all through for Susan Ambrose's birthday party. That's on November thirteenth. Yeah, I'll have it all figured out by then."

"Sounds great!" said Cindy.

"Yeah," nodded Jenny.

Party? What party? Well, who cares? Not me. I didn't want to go to a stupid party. I examined the ceiling and thought about my Iroquois heritage.

"What are you going to wear, Lucy? I made her invite you, too. You want to go, don't you?"

"You're kidding!" I bounced on the sofa. "Sure. Yeah. God, yeah."

We all agreed that, since we were eleven and everything, we would *not* wear party dresses. This was good since I didn't have one.

"So what do you want to be when you grow up?" asked Jackie. "You know, when I was a kid, I wanted to be a hairdresser. But now I think that sucks and I've decided I'd rather be a movie star."

"Yeah," nodded Jenny. "When I was a kid, I wanted to be a vet, but now I want to be a movie star, too."

"Yeah," agreed Cindy. "When I was a kid, I wanted to be a teacher, but now I want to be a movie star, too, but the kind that are on the TV soaps."

"Yeah," I nodded. "Well, I've got a really dumb one. See, when I was a kid, I wanted to be a mermaid. Isn't that a riot?

But now I really, really want to be a writer." Silence. No one nodded.

"Jeez, Lucy," said Jackie, "I don't know which one is dumber to tell you the truth."

"Yeah." Everyone nodded.

"Well . . ." My stomach twisted and untwisted "What I *mean* is that . . . I mean . . . I want to be an actor-writer. Like I'd write in all the best parts for me and my friends, I mean."

"Oh, okay," said Jackie. "That's cool!"

"Yeah!" nodded Jenny and Cindy.

We talked a bit more about what glamorous people we'd all be, and then they left. I pressed my face against the living-room window and watched them hip-checking one another down Cleveland Street. When they disappeared I ran to the phone.

"Hi, Emily? So how are you?"

"Lucy?"

"Yeah, it's me, Lucy. Look, Emily, are you going to Susan Ambrose's birthday party? Because I am."

"Oh, super! We can go together. That's great, Lucy. Susan has the best birthday parties."

"Yeah, well, I guess. Uh, Emily, what do you guys buy for each other, you know, for presents?"

"Oh . . . I see. . . . Well, I was going to get her a new Barbie."

"A Barbie?"

"Yeah, listen, she *collects* them. She's got the world's largest collection. Only she's always complaining that no one buys them for her anymore because she's too old.

"Oh. . . ."

"Look, Lucy, you go to Eaton's and buy her a Barbie. I guarantee she'll love it. I'll think of something else for me to get."

"Jeez. Thanks, Emily. You're a pal. Look, I'll meet you there because it's market day, but we'll walk back together, okay?"

"Sure, super. See you in the morning. Bye."

"Mama!" I yelled to the kitchen.

She came booming out, arms outstretched. "Did it go good? *I* think it went good. Do *you* think it went good?"

"Well, it sort of went good, bad, good, bad, great."

Mama stopped in her tracks.

"But see, the great part is that I'm going to Susan Ambrose's birthday party, and we have to buy a Barbie doll at Eaton's before November thirteenth. Isn't that great?"

"Did I do something bad?" she asked.

"No, Mama, no. You were . . . unbelievable."

She beamed.

"How many English classes have you had so far?" See, Mama's been going to night school at Northern Secondary every Thursday evening. English for New Canadians. She wasn't doing very well.

"Four," she said. "Why?"

"It shows," I lied. "You're doing much better, but maybe a little more practice, huh? Maybe we should talk in English together once a week or something. Like, every Friday could be an English-only day."

"Yah, yah. What was the bad part, Lucija?" Mama put her arm around me.

We walked back into the kitchen. "Oh, I don't know, Mama," I shrugged. "I blew it when we were talking about what we want to be when we grow up. I think I keep breaking a bunch of rules."

"You keep telling me about the rules here, Lucija," she frowned. "What *are* the rules?"

"That's the problem, Mama, I just don't know."

from

Sweetgrass

by

Jan Hudson

At the beginning of this novel Sweetgrass is a happy-go-lucky fifteen-year-old, picking berries with her friend, discussing boyfriends, complaining about her parents. But in the world of the Blackfoot people in the 1830s, fortunes can shift abruptly. The people are attacked by smallpox and the winter is bitter and hard. Sweetgrass and her family run out of food. In desperation, her father leaves to go hunting and Sweetgrass and her brother Otter are left behind with the family. The disease moves from person to person and soon Sweetgrass is their only hope of survival.

Death in the Tipi

In the deepest part of our sleep that night, the wind died down, and the tipi's air hung still and full of change. Was that what had awakened me? I lay there uneasy. Most of the tipi was still dark, but some gray dawn light was creeping down the smokehole. It was the dangerous time.

Soft lumps poked into my back as I wiggled to get comfortable under my sleeping robes. A buzz in my head was louder than the tipi's silence. Was somebody coming?

Then the scream began. Our baby's shrill voice ripped open the dark blanket of our nighttime. Fear squeezed my chest.

What was wrong? I could hear the baby, but I couldn't see her. I shook my head and fought the webs of sleep away.

There were running footsteps and confusion and a chill of voices. Through it all the baby kept on screaming. Her voice rose and fell. I lay still, and pulled my furry winter robes around me. Great shadows bent against the pale dawn light, stooping to touch the baby.

"Mother? Otter?"

They were the shadows. Good. If only I stayed still, everything would soon be all right. Mother would know how to quiet her baby. The shadows on the tipi walls bent and swayed, seemed to be untying the cradleboard cover. They freed the baby and bent to look at her.

She screamed even worse. The sound echoed sharp in my ears, like the evil voices in dreams. I sat up so I could see the baby, and see if she was really there. Maybe I was still asleep and dreaming. Little Brother wanted to see what was happening too, and scrambled up. He toddled across the tipi, arms outstretched to Almost-Mother who was bent over the baby with Otter. Little Brother gripped the leather fringe of his mother's dress tight and tried to pull her back to him. They stood that way for a long time.

She did nothing. Little Brother stood hesitating, one hand in the soft folds, until the baby wailed again, then he roared with her.

I sat straight up in my bed when Almost-Mother slapped Little Brother. His dark hair flew outward and he fell over.

Otter picked him up under the arms and carried him back to me, saying nothing. Little Brother stopped crying and looked at me with his mouth open. I noticed one tooth was black from eating too much honey.

"Otter?" I whispered. "What's wrong?"

"Nothing. The baby is sick."

"Sick? How is she sick?"

"She's hot. You can feel it."

My brother's eyes looked glittery to me. The rest of his face was in shadow. I knew what to do.

"You hold Little Brother."

I slid on my fur-lined moccasins and went outside to get some snow for making water. Our babies were often ill. We washed them with warm water and made them medicine teas. Often the medicine helped them. Sometimes it did not. Sometimes they died.

It was still cold out. The snowflakes sifted through the untouched darkness around me. Drifts of them wrapped around the bare skin of my ankles like a cold and gentle fur. The forest was quiet and so beautiful.

I didn't want to leave the clean coldness. The snow melted against my skin. There was almost no wind-sting to speak of. A gray dawn haze glowed over the eastern trees. Sun was coming. Sun was riding higher each day, and summer was riding close behind. Sun and Eagle Sun.

The tipi was silent now. Almost-Mother must have stopped the baby's crying. The newfallen snow was as hard as dust to gather. I brushed dry handfuls slowly into my bag. This snow would be clean. I stayed away from the crusted old snow underneath. No one could tell, in this faint light, where one of us might've squatted earlier.

Inside, Almost-Mother was bending over the fire, blowing at sparks hiding in the ashes. That made me feel happier. Now we would be warm. I carefully tied the tipi flap shut against the snow.

"Almost-Mother?"

She continued to blow, her face calm and cold as mountains. I scooped snow into the kettle with my stiff fingers.

"I'll use pine needles. Okay, Almost-Mother?"

But still she didn't answer. Maybe the baby was very sick, and she was worried and thinking of more powerful medicines.

Our tipi was quiet now, and there were no shadows of movement cast from the yellow light growing at the smokehole.

Maybe my brother would tell me what was wrong.

"Otter, is the little one asleep?"

"This little one is asleep," Otter said of Little Brother snuggled in his arms. "But he's hot."

Hot?

"How is the baby?"

"The baby?"

Otter did not look well himself. Not very calm, either. He held his eyes away from me. Something really was wrong with our baby.

"What came to the baby?"

"Sweetgrass, you know the way it is with babies. Any small sickness and they just. . . ."

I knew it.

"She is dead," Otter admitted.

So fast? Babies die, I knew, but never so fast. When we lost the one before Little Brother he cried and vomited for two long days. Our baby could not be dead.

But Otter nodded. It was so.

I swallowed against the dry hardness in my throat. The baby's medicine tea was still an unmelted lump of snow in the kettle. She hadn't even lived to see her first springtime.

And now Otter said our Little Brother was hot, too. What had come upon us?

A smell of decay, like the sweetness of too many meadow roses, wound around the familiar odours of our life. That also had come quickly. Someone must do something about the baby's body, and soon. But who?

Almost-Mother still sat there beside our fire, her hands unmoving. She just sat, without cooking or counting or sewing. She didn't cry for our baby, either.

She had cried for many babies, as is the way for a Blackfoot woman, but she didn't cry for this one. What was different about this death? I went to her and put my hand on her thin shoulder. She shrugged it off and refused to look me in the face. To stare silent at the fire was far stranger than any mourning. If she would only cry. . . .

Dawn light crept slowly down to reveal food bags, robes, a water-filled kettle, but it didn't touch the dead baby where it lay. In the darkness under the slope of our tipi I could see the edge of the baby's cradleboard. There was a dark shapeless thing beside it. I took a step forward.

The death smell flowed out—strong, and sweetly horrible, like a rotting animal under a summer rosebush. Maybe it'd be better if I didn't look? But how was I to know?

There were many birch bark cases to feel my way between—bags of clothing, dried food, mysterious ceremonial things of power. I approached carefully, hugging my breath to myself.

Where was she? There, lying beside her cradleboard, there she was. Of all the darkest gray things under the gray light of the farthest tipi edge, she was the only thing that was black.

She was truly black. And she was not smoothly shaped any more either. Her tiny tummy was swollen already, puffed out like that of a corpse of many days. She looked ready to pop. Soon her shape wouldn't be human at all.

I knew what had come amongst us, then. Only one sickness killed so fast and turned its victims to foul black dung. Smallpox. The white man's smallpox had stolen into our camp and was now bent, counting coup, over our little baby.

I stumbled out and puked into the snow.

Next morning I awoke to Little Brother's voice and the smell of death.

"Water, sister. Water," he pleaded, his fingers twisting the furry curls of my sleeping-robe. His fat baby face swam before me.

"Mother will get you water, Little Brother. Go away." I let my eyes close tight again, but he kept tugging at my robe. Tiny arrows of cold shot down into me with each tug. That woke me up enough to see his face.

Tears ran down his reddened cheeks. I brushed them off with my fingers, and felt why he was crying. Fever was burning inside Little Brother, yes, and pushing out in pimply spots on his skin. These were signs of smallpox—just as Grandmother's stories had said. Why had the spirits sent this evil thing to us?

"Maybe Mother will give you a drink." It was not much to ask. Little Brother was not quite weaned. "She doesn't even have to leave her warm bed." I needed a moment to wake up before going into the bitter world.

"Mother's sitting by the fire. She doesn't see me at all!"

Aiii. Still sitting by the fire. "What about Otter, then?"

He shook his head, and another tear blotch fell from his rounded chin. "Otter's hot."

"No! Not Otter?" I sat up right away.

"Yes, and he needs water, too. He says it hurts him all over to move. Please, Sweetgrass!"

I fetched the boys some water, promised them good medicine for their fevers, and tried to stir Almost-Mother. She just sat by that dead fire and stared at it. I touched her and tugged at her and, even though it was very disrespectful, shook her a little. But she only sat with her mouth queerly puckered up, not telling me what to do.

So I did each thing as I saw it. I put Little Brother back under his blankets, added some pemmican to the melted snow in the kettle, found a dry stick the right length for our fire, and on and on until all the tipi work was done. Still Almost-Mother would not look at me. This was awful.

"Maybe you'd better take that dead baby away," Otter suggested.

How sickening, but he was right. There was no one else but me to do it, and it had to be done. The dead should not be so close to the living. I would not leave that omen of decay near Otter and Little Brother. They were stronger; they would live.

I would fight for them! Where were the blankets? A robe or a blanket is always used for corpse wrapping. I chose an old gray one and folded it lengthways and widthways, laying it down beside the body. But it had swollen now to more than the size of Little Brother. This would not do. I hesitated, then unfolded the blanket once so it was just doubled.

"Otter, do you know how I'm supposed to wrap her?"

But my brother sat hunched over, guarding his sore head with his arms. I knew he was awake. He turned his face to glare at me and that was all. Almost-Mother continued to stare at the fire.

So I pulled the baby over onto the blanket myself. Not wanting to touch her softened flesh, I tugged at the buffalo robe she had been laid on. The tail of the blanket folded down to her neck where the bottom of the blanket folded up to meet it. The sides folded over her middle and tucked into the other pieces. According to custom, I ought to have sewn them all together, but surely an unsewn blanket was good enough.

Quickly I lifted the soft gray bundle and stepped backwards with it through the loosened tipi flap. Aiii, the wind blew sharp outside, but my sick lungs welcomed the clean air. Then I had another thought.

Properly we ought to move the tipi away from this death place into cleaner air. But how could I do it alone? And even if I rounded up the packhorses, took poles and hides down and moved a day's journey, how could I bring Otter and Almost-Mother to the new campsite?

I couldn't. Maybe the baby's evil spirit would come and hurt us. All I could do was find a far tree-grave for the body.

Around our campsite grew a tall set of poplars, but they were too near. Another stand, mostly poplars and spruce, grew across the river from us, maybe two rifle shots down. They would have to do.

At the farthest end of those trees, I tied her into the branches of a white birch tree. She was so small there was no need for a death platform. I simply laid her across a pair of forked branches. The naked poplars made whipping sounds with their tops swinging in the wind. It was a lonely place, good to leave her there alone.

"Do not haunt me, little sister," I whispered before I hurried away.

The last time the smallpox came, Grandmother said, many people left their dying families and ran away. I wanted to stay here in the forest, where everything smelled clear and good, and each white branch surged with cold power. The death of the baby had fouled our tipi air.

But Grandmother said those who left died too. I thought about that as I made my way slowly back to camp. Although it was longer, walking along the river was easier going than over in the deep hard snow of the trees.

I reached a clump of pussywillow bushes growing by the river. They smelled so green, I couldn't help stopping. Their buds were already beginning to fill with fuzzy rabbit tail promises of spring. I poked the top of one bud to reveal its inner fur. It reminded me of Pretty Girl's rounded belly.

I wondered where she was camping, if she were happy. Maybe springtime would let her blossom, give her some small cheer in being a mother. Springtime would also make me free—in not-too-long.

I remembered how once, when we were little, Pretty Girl picked early spring pussywillows with me. It had been a good, warm winter, with much game. Families and even small bands were camping close together. I remembered how Pretty Girl had frostbitten the smallest finger on her left hand and how cold it felt between my hands as we tried to warm it. We must have dropped our mittens in the snow. I remembered three of them lying on the ground, half curled, like three dead squirrels from a winter trapline. Almost-Mother scolded me later because the mittens were so wet.

Usually it had been Almost-Mother and I who had gathered the pussywillow buds in spring. She would boil them up to make a red dye. Little Otter would waste his pussywillow buds throwing them at me, and I'd chase him through the bushes, both of us yelling. Then Almost-Mother would scold us.

The buds were useless to me now. The willow's bark was what we needed. As I broke off the small twigs and stripped off their buds, my thoughts returned to the ghost I'd been avoiding. Had the evil that followed us here found Pretty Girl's camp also? And Eagle Sun's?

How does smallpox travel?

The old people say it comes with the white man's trade goods. A traveller from a southern tribe once said it was brought to his land first by white trappers, then by white missionaries. That Piegan said the smallpox had come from the far south, up the Missouri River on the American steamboat to our neighbouring tribe, the Assiniboin. And then somehow it made its way to us. Maybe its evil spirit rode on the southeast wind, touched the Piegans and then touched us. Maybe it came with Blood On Stone who brought us the bad news from the Piegans. Maybe it hid in our Hudson's Bay blankets. Assiniboin and Blood had traded together at the fort there.

Some even say smallpox snares you when you look at a blackened corpse. I shivered.

Who knows how evil spirits travel? Not even our wisest, oldest ones could say.

I broke from my thoughts when dull, puffed snow-clouds began to move down the mountainside. Gripping the pale green willow twigs, I turned again homeward.

The path was long and my eyes started to freeze as the cold wind swept down. The world seemed to get narrower. I walked stiff-legged across the ice to keep from falling.

Closer to camp, I scrambled up the stream's sharp banks, taking care not to drop the willow. Cold makes you clumsy. I reached shelter just as the clouds arrived with snow.

I unfastened our tipi flap with trembling fingers and swung into the warmth. It was still a stinking warmth, though.

"See what I've brought? Willow twig medicine to cool you off."

Almost-Mother looked at me but held onto her silence. She lay upright against a woven backrest. This would've been a good sign except that her fiery cheeks and bright eyes showed she was not restful. What if Father were dying somewhere out in the snow? Was I the last healthy person? How long would the smallpox wait to take me?

Maybe our ghosts would drift together through the shadow land of the Sand Hills. Maybe, but not yet. Not if I could slow it. Not ever, if I could stop it.

"Who wants willow for tea?"

Otter smiled at me, or tried to smile. He looked like a bad dream monster. Some of the pink spots on his face had swollen to yellow pus-filled blisters, and his skin had turned reddy-brown with fever. But he smiled at me.

"Willow tea would be good, sister," he whispered. "The water should be hot enough to make it. Mother has been keeping wood on the fire."

"Good. Are you stronger?"

"I hurt so much I want to die," said Otter. "Little Brother is very sick. Do you see him over there?"

Little Brother was curled up on my bed, throwing up on my sleeping-robes. I ran around the fire and across the tipi to him. "Little Brother! Stop," I yelled, and almost hit him.

But the light fell across his face, and I saw strange things. In the few hours I had been away, Little Brother's blisters had broken. They ran blood. His cheeks and his forehead were now one bloody scab.

Oh, poor baby. I had almost hit him.

I could ease his hotness, his headache, his body pains with willow tea, but nothing of mine could cure the smallpox. But I put the kettle on the fire all the same. And I prayed to the spirits. I prayed to Sun. Here are my fingers, here is my hand if you will only cure my youngest brother. Please don't let the dead baby's shadow find him. Take this sickness from his body, give me help!

Nobody—not Father, not Grandmother, nor the cruelest part of myself—would be able to say, if I lived and he died, that there was anything more I should have done for him!

But as I brewed the tea, I cried. All I wanted to do was leave all these sick people, go out on the clean snow and puke them all away.

The willow twigs made a strong medicine. Everyone drank it. Then I heated rocks for the sweathouse and dragged Otter and Little Brother out there. Steam is one of our long-time medicines. Many sicknesses sweat out of people—maybe smallpox too?

I boiled scraps of pemmican, roots and sour dried buffalo berries to make a soup. Soup is gentle in an empty belly. But for Little Brother it was not gentle enough. Over and over he threw up my offerings.

I tried again.

For several days in the early mornings, I stripped the poplars of their inner bark as high as I could reach. Otter had started to worry about his horses. So I fed his favourite horses, and Father's too. They were hobbled out in the back meadow. It meant a couple of trips each day, my arms heaped with bark, but it was good to get out.

Otter's gray stallion always whinnied when he heard me coming. The snow was too deep for the horses this winter. They couldn't paw through it for grass, and they were starving. If our horses died, we'd be almost *kimataps*. But maybe we would all die too, so it really didn't matter.

The willow tea helped some, but not enough. It didn't have enough power. Otter's blisters broke out in scabs, and Almost-Mother's skin turned purplish as well. They drank tea and more tea, all the while slipping closer and closer to death. I didn't want to do it, but there was only one thing left.

I took the dried calamus roots from my father's holy medicine bundle and began to peel them. Otter probably would have stopped me doing that, had he not been blind with fever. Never mind what my father might say later. I prepared my mind to use any of his other holy things too, if they held more power in them.

I raised each head in turn—my mother's, my brother's, the baby's small one—and poured calamus tea down each throat. A dangerous thing to do. If it goes down the wrong way, you can kill the person. But what else could I do? They all were dying. They all would have died for sure without it.

Almost-Mother and Otter looked a bit better after the medicine, but Little Brother seemed to burn away under my eyes. Some of his scabs became stinking ulcers. Pus gathered in their edges. I washed them and washed them but the ulcers kept spreading anyway. He could keep nothing down, not even the most powerful medicines. The covers of my bed became slimy with vomit so I threw them out. I gave him some of the new robes I had been making for Father.

Summer and the Sun Dance seemed dreams of long ago. I kept looking for signs and I prayed for my father to come, but Little Brother kept vomiting, and I had to sacrifice my last robes to his battle.

I was losing our last baby. Fear found nothing left in me to burn. I fought coldly without hope. Fighting had become my habit.

Then, six days after Father left and four days after the death of our girlchild, when the sun was a finger's width from its highest point in the hard blue sky, Little Brother died as well.

And at the sun's height the next day my brother Otter raised himself from his sickbed.

At first I did not hear his words, nor did I want to. I was sitting slouched by the fire, gazing into it. It was a very fierce fire—orange, red, and deep. But he called me again and again.

"Sweetgrass? My belly hurts. Can you, can you bring me some food to eat?"

The River Demon

There was no food for Otter and there was nobody to get any except me. All I wanted to do was sit and go into a fire trance like Almost-Mother had done. Our babies were dead. But if I surrendered to my lazy desire, we all would die of hunger. People coming out of sickness especially need food.

"I'll find something, Otter. Everything will be all right."

Father had taken the only working rifle, leaving an old musket. No one had fired it for years. It was a flintlock like our rifle, but it used a much larger and wilder bullet. A man of my tribe once killed his close friend with a gun like that, aiming at a buffalo only a spear's length away. I saw it.

A bow and some arrows would be better, if I knew how to handle them. But then I didn't know how to creep inside arrow range of an animal, either. The two skills have to go together. Using the musket was necessary.

"What do you do to this gun so it works?" I asked Otter.

My brother watched me, his eyes sparkling against his still-pale face.

"You'd kill yourself. Better not to ask!" He laughed and leaned back on his sleeping couch

I didn't know whether to be angry because be was teasing me or happy because he laughed. "Just tell me where the big bullets are, Hungry Otter."

"My sister, you can stop looking. There aren't any."

No big bullets?

"I melted them all down to use in that rifle Father gave me."

"Aiii, Otter! How am I to feed you?"

Almost-Mother would soon need to eat, too. She had been sleeping more quietly each day that passed.

Luckily there is always gathering—the woman's way of getting food. Somewhere out there, there must be some food for us. Though where, I didn't know. I picked up my Hudson's Bay blanket, my woven basket and digging stick, and left.

The sun shone down through a watery sky. The air was a bit cold, but quiet. In fact, the forest was one unearthly silence, broken only by my moccasins drumming out my stride atop an icy crust of snow. Walk carefully, I thought, or you'll crash through and cut your ankles. The group of poplars sheltering our tipi probably had wild roses blooming under them last summer.

I was right! Tips of several thorny branches poked through the snow. I dug down, and here and there hid withered rose hips. Thawed, the hips would be furry seeds and mushy fruit inside a brittle and tasteless skin. This meal would scratch all the way down your throat, but was welcome, so very welcome!

I gathered twigs and new little shoots from the younger trees. Many types of these boil into good, filling teas, although they are very bitter. Last I went down to the river, carrying my digging stick.

Along the widest banks were brown spikes of bulrushes as tall as a deer. Somewhere under each one were very tasty roots. But I soon found that river mud freezes as hard as rock. My digging stick only chipped the ground until it finally splintered in two.

All I got was one pale chunk of bulrush root. It looked more like a dirty icicle, certainly not much to carry home to my family.

On my way back, I spied a large white rabbit atop a hill across the river from our camp. My mouth watered as we locked eyes. But my hunger dreams were interrupted.

I heard a spooky noise, one that was new and wrong. Someone was crying inside our tipi. A woman's voice wailed out: it was Almost-Mother, sounding exactly like a woman in deep mourning.

I ran. The basket's high edge hit against my breasts with every footfall. My worst thoughts made me prickle with sweat.

I pushed everything through the tipi flap and dragged myself after.

"Almost-Mother? What's wrong?" Otter seemed okay.

She hadn't made any sound for days. She said nothing when our baby died, and didn't even blink when I told her Little Brother was gone too.

"Sweetgrass . . . Otter . . . aiii! My life, all my children," she wailed.

"What is it, Mother?"

"I have always done everything properly, your father will tell you so, and nothing, nothing has ever come back to me as I tried to make it be. Otter is dying, isn't he?"

"No," I said quickly, and looked toward my almost-brother. His bright eyes met mine. He looked as worried as I felt.

"He is, isn't he?" insisted Almost-Mother. "Isn't he, Sweetgrass?"

"Look for yourself."

"See, Mother," called Otter from his sleeping couch. "I'm fine."

"Everything, everything dies," she cried, "and I am going to die and so are you both and nothing of my life has made the way of anything be anything."

I pulled her body to me so that her head rested on my left shoulder and my mouth was full of her rotten smell of pus.

She was as hot to hold as a charcoal stick burning red at the core. Her cheeks shone a deep purple-brown under her stream of tears. Her thin hands fluttered over the pus and scabs of her face, blindly, fearfully, touching.

When she started calling me Shot With Metal, her long-dead sister, I realized her mind was not at all right. Her fever must be mounting. Maybe it would break soon or maybe. . . . I stroked her hair until she lay back down. Then I washed her gently, all over.

What a sickness. Here was my almost-mother burning up while her son in the next bed was shaking under mounds of blankets and robes. Now I know what Grandmother meant when she said with smallpox there's no sleep between ice and fire.

Was she dying? I rocked her gently and pushed away the thought. Her skin had blistered lightly, not close together, and the blisters were small. I felt strange, mothering our tiny mother. But then, was I not a full-grown woman and hadn't she taken care of me many times when I was sick?

"Is she all right?" asked Otter.

"Yes."

"Good." Pause. "Did you find anything for us to eat?"

The rose hips and the bulrush root made a few spoonfuls of stew. Otter ate most of it. I took some in the big carved-horn spoon Father had made and teased Almost-Mother into swallowing it. There was none left for me.

That was not important, because healthy people can live without food for many days. But I had to get food for my family—good food, enough, and soon. Otherwise only I would greet my father if . . . when he returned. I chewed the inside of my lips: the blood was comfort, and the pain sharpened my thoughts.

I needed wire. Father had traded for some this summer. What was left? I searched through his bags and found a piece as long as my arm. Not enough, but it must do.

Outside, the wind blew softly. If it were a little warmer the rabbits would wake and run. I slid my fingers down the chilly length of wire and began looking for a rabbit path. On top of the frozen stream were scattered little round scats, and some small trees nearby were nipped at a sharp-pointed angle. Ah, that soft groove worn in the snow down in the bushes. There I would set my snare.

My hands were already whitening, but I only thought of that rabbit I had seen earlier. I tied a loop in the length of wire, then fumbled its free end around the nearest poplar sapling. Finally I arranged the loop to hover over the little trail.

This is how it works. The rabbit comes hopping along his path. He does not understand what that wire is doing, and is not too worried. He hops and his head goes through the loop but his shoulders hit the wire. When he panics, the loop tightens around his furry neck, and he struggles harder and harder until it cuts off his air. The rabbit dies. Then he goes home for our stewpot.

That is a painful way to go. Sorry, rabbit, but you have to die for us to live, just as shoots and grasses earlier died for you to live. So it has always been for grasses, rabbits, and my people. In this pattern is comfort.

So I thought as I dragged my weary body home to bed.

"Sweetgrass, wake up. Sweetgrass!"

My mind surfaced lazily from its cool numb dream. Someone wanted me to do something. Again. Probably something I couldn't do.

"What is it?"

The mists of morning filled our tipi. Those big begging eyes looked like Little Brother's. Couldn't be. They were

Otter's eyes. Otter wouldn't beg. But I knew how hunger twists inside and drives you to things you think you'd never do.

Some scabs had fallen from my brother's face last night, leaving ugly pits in the skin. Who else would be pitted the next time I saw them? Inside me a deep voice answered: the lucky ones would be pitted. The others I would never see again.

"Sweetgrass? Are you awake?"

"I am now. What do you want?"

"Do you feel Mother is going to die? Am I going to die?"

I hesitated. "No, I do not feel it."

"Are you sure?"

"Pretty well. All the signs look good."

"But Mother is still burning inside."

"True, but you've both lived many days. Grandmother said that with smallpox most of our people die right away. They die and swell up like the baby." I tried to force a laugh through my tight throat. "Do you think I would stay here if you were dying?"

Otter smiled in a way I had never seen before. The softness around his eyes had nothing to do with smallpox.

"If I live, I will give you anything you want."

"Just be my good brother Otter."

He gave me his hand and I held it between mine in my lap.

"I tried to go hunting this morning," he said after a while.

"Otter!"

"You were asleep. Why not go?" he said.

"You are still too weak."

"I almost didn't get out of the tipi to relieve myself. You must have been doing some dirty nursing work these last days," he said, grinning unevenly.

I chose not to tell him about the buffalo robes. When their stink became too bad I threw the old sleeping-robes outside and rolled Otter and Almost-Mother onto ones I had been making ready for Father. So no one needed to feel any shame.

"Next hunt, Sweetgrass, every second buffalo hide is yours." He knew.

"I feel I must get well now, sister. Tomorrow I will try again to go hunting."

"Your spirit is rising, but it is still tender. Just rest."

Otter would not hear me. "I can hunt with the bow and arrow and you cannot."

"Just rest."

At long last he relaxed. Luckily he was still too weak to do more than talk.

"So you must not be sad," he continued. "I wanted you to hear me, not to worry, you know, if you. . . ."

If I got the smallpox.

I patted his hand and tucked him in. Otter was right. We had better be ready for the sickness coming to me, also. But he was wrong to think he could hunt tomorrow morning, or even the following morning. He must rest for many days, and most of all, if he was to care for us as I had done, he must eat well.

As I put on my mittens and prepared to go out, I couldn't help thinking. Why was the pox so slow coming to me?

Most of the time I didn't think of getting it. Me die? I would make Otter ready for it, but never would I give in! I would find power to live. *Ahksi Kiwa!* My heart sang with the warriors.

I fear nothing!

There was a ghostly world lying between our tipi and my rabbit snare. The night before, Chinook, the warm mountain wind, had melted each tree's robe of snow and then blew fast away to the south. Set free for a moment, the snow-water froze again as ice. Each tree, each twig and bud wore a shining shield that the arrows of the sun bounced off, so dazzling my eyes that there seemed to be no skeletons beneath their bright flesh. This was a spirit world—a world of clearest shadows, the shadows of light.

Axe in hand, I shuffled over the icy surface crust, feeling myself the only creature in this world. Where was the flashing silver of my snare? In the snow's light, it would be hard to see but I knew exactly where I had placed it. Right beneath those bushes bordering the stream.

The snare was empty! My heart jerked in disbelief at the sight. I shut my eyes and wished it full with a fat, white mound of rabbit.

I had to sit down. For the first time since Father left, I felt sick, really sick. A dizziness had caught me and left me weaker than I had ever been before. I had no choice but to lie back on a shiny crest of ice, and let come whatever was in store.

Overhead the sun hummed down from a pale blue sky. I lost myself in the vastness of it all. The world behind me could have vanished for all I knew.

A raven's laugh brought me back. The sun had wandered on, and a light blanket of cloud overcast the sky. It was getting colder.

I took off my mitten and felt my face for spots. There were none. One small relief.

But what could I do? I couldn't go back without food.

And there were those hungry horses to feed as well. Frustrated, I took up our big axe and swung hard at the last unstripped poplar on this side of the stream. I cut its bark off in rings. As I pulled the inside bark from the rings like I had so often done before, I realized how weak I was fast becoming.

I threw down what strips I had gathered and picked up our bright axe. I might not have much time, I heard myself say.

I headed towards where Otter had hobbled the mares and stallions in the woods behind our tipi, inside the lime meadow.

Stumbling through the fringing trees, I seemed to be in a dream where I knew what I had to do. I had to find the horses. We were starving. Horses. Meat. In this dream, the scattered tree stumps were helping me. All the tall ones were Father and the short ones were Little Brother. But the dark figures changed back into stumps when I looked straight at them. Visions come easy when a person is sick and hungry.

Move carefully now. I must not startle the horses. Into the bitter cold of my nose and mouth crept a faint, foul odour.

Something was wrong.

From my narrow edge of the meadow there were no standing shapes to be seen, except one gray faraway blur against the trees opposite. Maybe it was Otter's stallion. Evening wavered in front of me. Where were our other horses?

A stench rode on the wind twisting through the poplars. I had to spit a lot because it made me gag. And it got worse as I went on. In the snowy meadow, I came upon a heap of gray skin and long ragged bones, which once had been Otter's horse. A leather thong still hobbled what was left of one foreleg. Aiii, the wolves had been hungry, too. The unhobbled ones must have run off.

There was no eating here.

My family's ill luck had now fully ripened. There was nothing here for me to do.

I turned on my heel and hauled my clean axe home.

I chopped and boiled old pemmican sacks for soup while Otter rested on his elbow watching me. Almost-Mother was enjoying a much quieter sleep for the first time. She was getting better, but when she awoke she would need good food. This sack soup tasted of meat and grease, but it was pretty thin. If Otter didn't like it, he kept his comments to himself.

"What are we going to do?" he asked after he had eaten his share.

"There are many more pemmican sacks."

"Not enough. Have you thought about the dogs?"

"They left long ago. And the wolves beat us to the horses."

Otter's flushed skin darkened further. We sat silent together awhile, listening to our moaning from time to time.

"I'll check my snare tomorrow morning."

On the eighth morning after Father left us, Almost-Mother's blisters had hardened to scabs. I held her graying head on my lap and spooned pemmican-sack soup into her. She swallowed the watery broth greedily.

For the first time, she turned her face so that her eyes could look into mine. She smiled weakly. Her spirit flickered brighter, like coals being blown on.

Somewhere I would find food for my family.

Out I crept again under the cold dome of the world. Winter was coming back again, full force. Summer seemed only a lying dream to me. I couldn't shake mocking memories of food eaten for the taste of it, berries thrown on the grass in laughter. I forced my moccasined feet forward. Soon I would be too weak to move them at all. Without smallpox, I might live in this way another moon or longer, hoping for my father's return. But the others would die. Aiii, already I was so lonely.

Was Father alive? Pretty Girl? Grandmother? Eagle Sun? The thought of them alive somewhere was a small fire to warm my freezing spirit.

The world was black with shadow, blue-white with sky and snow today—nothing else. The light shimmered off the snow, making my eyes ache. I dragged my axe behind me. If my snare was still empty, there would at least be the untouched poplars on the far side of the stream. If horses ate the green inside bark, then so could we. I found it hard to control my trembling which came partly from desperation, partly from weakness.

I reached the snare, and its loop was empty. Always empty. So I took it apart.

My damp, mittenless fingers froze to the wire as I unwrapped it from the small tree. By the time I had the snare unsnarled, it was covered with bits of skin and iced with blood. Dragging axe and wire, I trudged up the river.

Under my feet the ice seemed to sway, and sometimes my eyes flooded with a gray fog. I would wait until I got some strength back before I went on. To walk blind on the ice is a good way to die.

Black Eagle did that once. It was long ago, in the year of the famine. He stepped on a rotten piece of ice, out on one of the rivers in the foothills. His wives never saw Black Eagle again, not even to bury his body. Here in front of me thrust a big stone. The dark patch on its sunny side was just like the patch Black Eagle stepped through.

I bent over and stared into that dark ice. It was almost clear, showing water beneath its brittle frozen layers. Something moved in the darkness. With a start, I stepped back a bit. Did the dead seek me to join them?

The movement came again, and I saw it to be a black and narrow slash of a shadow, floating under the ice. As long as my arm at least. It moved sideways again. A river demon's fish!

If I fell through the ice that fish would eat me.

I remembered a story. Sometimes fish were eaten by people. Not by the Blackfoot, but others like the Cree. Our warriors called them fish-eaters in insult.

I hadn't heard any stories of the Cree being wiped out by river demons.

The ice was very thin here. It felt like a sign to me, the sign I had been seeking.

An evil fish waited under the ice. I would catch him and cook him. I shook with fear and power and loathing. Now.

When I hit the axe on the ice, the demon was gone like a shot. If he wanted my spirit as much as I wanted his, he'd be back.

I chipped with the blade until a bowl-shaped sheet of ice broke out. I swung the axe high and gave the ice underneath a good blow. The metal sunk in sweetly, and the water made a sucking sound when I pulled out the axe. How good to hit something!

I chipped out a big enough hole.

What to do now? I sat on a snowdrift to rest. How do the Cree catch fish?

I shut my eyes and tried to picture, one by one, my dizzy thoughts. Could a fish be grabbed? Not likely with them being so quick and slimy.

Could a fish be shafted upon an axe blade? Maybe. But when my mind pictured it, the fish split, then sank out of sight.

Could a fish be caught like a rabbit in a wire?

I opened my eyes.

I pulled off my mittens again and forced my stiffening fingers to wrap the loose end of the snare around the axe handle. It was hard to get it tight. I cut myself a few times.

The snare must go quietly into the water. I lay down on my belly on the ice.

Down it dipped into the dark hole. Success. The whole loop went all the way under the water. I was afraid I wouldn't have enough wire. I got my mittens back on and prepared myself for a wait.

My plan was to let the fish get his head all the way through before yanking. I had a lot of time to think about it.

I never really noticed before how noisy a quiet forest can be. There's always a bird somewhere calling out to his friends. The wind is always there, rising and falling, talking to every tree. Even the ice groaned.

The ice. At first, it was just cold. Then it hurt. It sent out fingers under my blankets, up and down my spine. I got a little worried when a wash of numbness settled in, but I didn't dare move or make a sound.

Then a big pointed head glided into view right under my nose. It stopped short a hand's width from my snare. Dark, cold eyes on the sides of its head could see everywhere. I didn't move a muscle.

What now?

I held my breath, and he flicked his fins again. A shivering thought: fish needn't follow paths like rabbits do. This creature could swim here or there or even under, and miss my trap!

I knew I had to make my move, but nothing must frighten him. Steady now. I eased the snare over the evil head so gently that it made only an arrowhead ripple where the wire parted the water.

Then the fish shot forward!

I jerked back on the axe handle. I had him!

But how well? Jumping to my feet, I hauled up on the axe handle. The demon thrashed and thumped along on the bottom of the ice before it could get his head free. Then up!

A shower of drops rained down behind him as he landed splat on the ice. His eyes were fierce and he bared a mouthful of terrible tiny teeth. Another flip, a flop, and somehow the fish escaped the wire.

I felt my entire life fall with him in that moment.

The mottled green body arched this way and that. His tail gave the ice mighty slaps, skittering him back towards the hole.

He came to rest on the jagged edge of the icehole, his head only smelling-distance from the open water. I jumped fast to catch him. It was life against life. I sat on top of him, holding his slippery, writhing, slimy body between my legs, and grabbed his gill.

With my other hand, I stretched for the axe, caught the wire, pulled it over. Then I cracked him smartly between the eyes. I gave him another, and another.

I dared not loosen my grip until the fish was truly dead. At last it gave its final spasm, smearing blood and slime all over me and the ice.

Underneath us the river trembled. I froze. It should be a moon or more before the ice broke. Would the river demons take me?

But the air was full of nothing, nothing but a delicious slimy smell. The ice did not crack and the river didn't move any more.

I went home in triumph.

from

After Hamelin

by

Bill Richardson

In the whole village of Hamelin only two children are not lured away by the wicked Piper. Penelope is one of them. She is also the only person who can find the stolen children, rescue them and bring them home. Her quest takes her to an amazing world, a world where her cat Scally can talk, a world populated by such creatures as Belle, one of the "singing Trolavians," a world where an avalanche can transport you from winter to summer in an instant. Listen to 101-year-old Penelope tell part of her adventure, the adventure of the year that she was eleven.

Whackity

A sound woke me. Something both known and unknown. A distant, rhythmic clatter.

Whack, whack, whackity, whack!

I opened my eyes.

Whackity, whack! Whackity, whack! Whack, whack, whack!

I blinked. I looked around. I took stock. Everything had changed. I had traded a world of tumbling white for a world of dappled green. Green above. Green below. Lovely leaves. I had come to rest in a tall, broad tree. I sat astride a wide branch. The foliage was dense, but here and there a narrow yellow beam shone through. I reached out. It was warm. Sunlight! Whatever place this was, it was far removed from the land of the Trolavians. And whatever place this was, I seemed to be quite alone. I saw no sign of Scally or Belle. Nor could I see the source of the sound.

Whacka! Whacka! Whacka!

I felt remarkably well, all things considered. My limbs were still in place. So was Alloway's necklace. And the skipping rope was still knotted around my waist.

Whackity! Whackity! Whackity!

I knew that sound. Where had I heard it before? It was loud and getting louder. Whoever or whatever was responsible for making it was drawing nearer. The branch seemed very sturdy. It was wide enough to crawl along and didn't bend under my weight. I crept forward, parting leaves, until finally I was able to look down. So high! Far below was a forest floor. Some small drifts of snow and a few broken branches were the only evidence that the avalanche had passed this way.

Whack, whack, whackity whack!

A pretty footpath had been carved through the forest. It wound among the trees. From my vantage point, it looked like a fallen ribbon. Coming along this path, passing in and out of view, was the source of the rhythmic whacking. Again I blinked. I stared. At first, I couldn't believe my eyes. I had never seen such a creature before, but I knew right away what to name it, for its hide looked exactly like the cloak given me by the Magistrate. There was no doubt. This was a dragon. It was not much taller than I, and it was moving along at a brisk pace. To see a dragon was astonishing enough. More amazing still was that it was not merely walking, not merely promenading trippingly along like a happy Sunday stroller. It was skipping.

Whackity whack! Whackity whack! Whackity whackity whackity whack!

No wonder that sound had seemed so familiar. The dragon was jumping rope as it came along the path. It paused in its travels directly beneath my tree. It sang.

Once there was a dragon and her name was Mary Jane.
She skipped into the forest and was never seen again.
She skipped into the forest and she simply disappeared.
You'll never, ever find her if you search a hundred years.

Skip and never find her, skip and never see!
Mary Jane has vanished now and happy she will be.

Then, with a call of "one, two, three, jolly-o pepper!" the dragon began to skip very quickly. It doubled, then redoubled its speed. It did some fancy foot- and handwork and then proceeded once again—*whackity whack, whackity whack*—along the forest path.

Skip and never find her, skip and never see!
Mary Jane has vanished now and happy she will be.

Was this Mary Jane? I supposed so, although it seemed an unsatisfactory name for a dragon. Had anyone asked me what I thought a dragon might be called, I would have suggested Hermione or Rondella or Peregrine or Sybil. Whatever her name, she was an expert skipper. She would be a worthy opponent in a jumping contest.

The avalanche had thoughtfully deposited me in a tree with branches as evenly spaced as rungs on a ladder. I was down it in a flash and hurrying along the path in pursuit of the skipping dragon. It seemed the only thing to do. I had to find Scally and Belle. And Mary Jane might have seen some trace of them.

The shady woods were silent. Now and then, I heard the raucous shout of what sounded like a crow, but otherwise there was no bird song. Here and there, the thick canopy of leaves parted to allow some sunlight to reach the forest floor. It shone golden and round, as welcome and surprising as a found coin. I jogged along as quickly as I could behind Mary Jane, but the distance between us grew wider. The *whackity whack* of her skipping, which at first had made her easy to follow, was growing fainter and fainter. I supposed that she was picking up speed. The magistrate had said that dragons were fast. He had also said that they were given to getting lost. If that were so, where might she be leading me? Still, I scampered along, not pausing until I reached a fork in the path. Which way had she gone? I listened, but heard nothing. Had she gone left? Had she gone right? Which should I choose? My decision was made for me when a terrible scream rent the air. It had come from down the right-leading trail. Then again. The same bloodcurdling cry!

I ran as quickly as I could, jumping over roots and fallen branches. There was a sudden clearing. It was lit by sun. I squinted at the unaccustomed brightness. My attention was caught by something dangling from a branch of a tree at the glade's edge. A banner ? No. I looked closer. Of course! It was the dragon-skin wrap I had worn among the Trola-vians. And lying on the ground directly beneath it, with her feet in the air, in what looked to be a dead faint, was Mary Jane. I ran towards her and heard a welcome voice.

"Goose!"

I looked up.

"Oh, Goose. Thank goodness it's you."

"Scally!"

He leaped from his branch and into my arms. I kissed the top of his head.

"Goose, Goose. We thought we'd lost you for good."

"We? But where is Belle?" I asked. As if in answer to my question, a shower of twigs drew my attention upwards. A familiar face, but a frightened one, peered down from between the leaves. And a familiar voice, quavering but still tuneful, sang out.

"Trouble, trouble, trouble! I am going to be in so much trouble!"

The Dragon Swoons

Take a dozen people, each of whom can paint equally well. Ask them to imagine a cake. Ask them to paint it. When they are done, you will have twelve very different cakes. Flat cakes. Layer cakes. Brown cakes. Pink cakes. Cake is a simple word, but no two people imagine "cake" in the same way. Or else, say "dragon." Right away, a picture comes to mind. But of what? Some see enormous purple lizards. Some see fire-breathing monsters. Some see snakes with wings. As sure as I am 101, the picture you hold in your head of the dragon Mary Jane is different from the picture that your sister or brother or best friend would conjure.

"Is it dead?" asked Belle, peering down from the tree.

"I don't think so," I answered, kneeling for a closer look.

The creature who lay before me was small. Soft. Not scaly, but spotted and covered with a fine fur.

"Don't wake it!" hissed Belle. "Who knows what it might do? I'm already going to be in such trouble with the magistrate for not having taken better care. I'll never make corporal now. I'll probably get demoted to street cleaner, and Fergus and Bergus will never stop teasing me. And it'll be even worse if you go and get yourself killed by a dragon!"

"Don't be silly, Belle," I admonished. "This dragon is not going to hurt anyone."

"How can you be so sure?"

It was a good question. After all, I had no more personal experience of dragons than did Belle. Still, I was convinced that this was not a creature who was likely to misbehave. In the first place, I knew in my heart of hearts that anyone who could skip as well as Mary Jane could not be deeply evil. What was more, she had fainted, which did not suggest bloodthirstiness. I supposed that she must have been scared out of her wits by the sight of my wrap dangling from the tree.

"Believe me, Belle, she's even more frightened than you are. So you can come down from that tree."

"But I can't!"

"Of course you can. No one will harm you."

"I don't mean that I can't because I'm afraid. I am a soldier, after all. I mean that I can't because I *can't*. Trolavians were never designed for tree living. I'm stuck up here, just as the avalanche left me."

"She's quite right," said Scally. "Those long, skinny feet of hers are all wedged up among the branches. It's a terrible tangle. I don't see how we'll get her down without an axe."

"No! No axes. What if you miss the branch and hit my feet?"

"Do you have any better ideas?" asked Scally, tetchily.

"Calm down," I said, trying on a voice I hoped was authoritative.

"Very well for you to say calm down! No one is going to go after you with an axe!"

"We don't have an axe, Belle, so there's no need to worry."

Mary Jane moaned. She stirred. Scally yelped and jumped back up to a low branch.

"Look out!" shrieked Belle, who pulled her head back into the crown of branches.

"Hush. You'll only frighten her."

I knelt again beside the dragon.

"Mary Jane."

I held her by her dragon hand—it was surprisingly smooth and delicate—and shook it gently.

"Mary Jane. Wake up."

She opened her eyes. I watched her face register first bewilderment, then surprise, then alarm.

"Where am I? Where am I? And what are you?"

"My name is Penelope. I'm a visitor here. You fainted, Mary Jane."

"Mary Jane? Who is Mary Jane?"

Had I misheard her? Or had she hit her head when she fell? Did she no longer know herself?

"You're Mary Jane. Aren't you? That's the name you sang while you were skipping."

"I'm no more Mary Jane than I'm Polly-Put-the-Kettle-On. That was nothing more than a skipping rhyme! Do I look like a Mary Jane?"

"I don't know if you do or if you don't. I've never seen a dragon before. What is your name, then?"

"Quentin."

"Quentin?"

"Yes, Quentin! Are you deaf?"

Was I deaf? That was a question that would have taken much too long to answer.

"I'm just confused. Where I live, Quentin is a boy's name. Do you mean to say you're a boy dragon?"

"Of course I'm a boy dragon," he said, struggling to sit up. "If I weren't a boy dragon, I wouldn't be—"

But then he looked up into the tree. He saw again the dangling skin. His eyes widened, then rolled back in his head. And once again he collapsed in a deep, dead faint.

Taking Charge

I am Penelope. I am 101 years old. When people ask how I've managed to live so long, I answer that I have cultivated calmness of mind. I am untroubled by regret. I am sorry for nothing I have done. Nor do I pine for the things I've missed. And I can assure you I've missed a great deal. Why, I've never ridden a camel. I've never milked a yak. I've never smoked a pipe. What else? I've never learned to juggle, and I've never been to Paris, and I've never had tea with a duchess. I could write a very long catalog of things I've never done, but what would be the point? The world is full of magnificent possibilities, but even if you live to a very ripe old age you will never be able to explore them all. You must satisfy yourself with tasting as much as you can in the little time that you are given.

Regret will only wear you down. If ever I feel something like regret welling up, I need only remember that once in my life, if only in a dream, I did things to which no one else can lay claim. Once, I flew with a talking cat. Once, I revived a fainting dragon. When I remember that, even rid- ing a camel pales in comparison.

You may have heard it said that an emergency will bring out either the best or the worst in people. As it happens, the same rule applies to cats and to Trolavians. Quentin's sec- ond fainting threw Belle into a panic, and Scally's good sense seemed to have been toppled by the avalanche. He could do nothing more than look down from his tree branch and mutter, "Oh, my stars and garters! Oh, my stars and garters!"

A calmness of mind. Was this the first time the prized calmness settled on me in a crisis? I think so. What is cer- tain is that ever since that day in the dreamtime forest, I can be counted on to remain at ease when everyone around me is in a fretful flap. I would not call this a gift so much as a talent born of necessity. Maybe it was the shock of the ava- lanche. Maybe it was the sudden change of climate and the unaccustomed shine of sun. Whatever the reason, neither Scally nor Belle was in a position to be helpful when help was what was most required. There was no one else to turn to for assistance, no one else to make decisions. There was me, and me alone.

Do not think that by calmness I mean something passive and hazy. If this calmness had a color, it would not be minty green or misty blue, but a pure, hot white. It was not aimless. It was full of direction and purpose. Calmness came. My mind was clear.

"Scally!"

I was surprised by the ring of command in my own voice. Scally must have been as well. He stopped simpering and looked at me quizzically.

"Scally, listen to me. We have to do something about that dragon skin before Quentin wakes up. Can you hide it?"

He gave me a cattish grin and a nod.

"Hide the hide? Right you are!"

He took a corner in his jaws and hauled it up into the tree, where it was camouflaged by leaves.

"Belle," I said, with as much edge to my voice as I could muster, "I promise you, this dragon is not going to hurt you. When he wakes up I will need to talk to him. You must be quiet."

Scally sat beside her, and the two of them peered down from their high branch. I took the dragon by his hand. I gave him a gentle shake.

"Quentin. Wake up."

Again he stirred. Again he moaned. High in the tree I heard Belle gulp.

"Shhhhhhhhhh!" I warned, a finger to my lips. Quentin's eyelids were fluttering. For a moment I faltered. What if Belle was right? What if he was angry enough to want to harm me? But no. I could not let my mind stray in that direction. I unknotted the rope from around my waist. I measured its weight in my hands. I gave it an experimen-tal turn or two. I satisfied myself that I had not lost my knack. And then I began to skip in earnest.

A Duel

Wake up, Quentin, wake up now.
Don't lie around like a silly old sow.
Quentin, Quentin, dare to skip.
I can jump a thousand and never ever slip.
With a ha ha ha and a hoo hoo hoo
I can skip a thousand times better than you!

It felt good to be skipping again. It felt good to hear that satisfying whack of the rope as it met the earth and to feel the soft forest floor beneath my feet. It felt good to feel my heart quicken, to breathe hard, to find that the words I needed were waiting on my tongue.

Jump! Your name is Quentin.
Jump! That's plain to see.
Jump! I know you'll never skip
Fast like me!

Quentin was coming to, and I wanted to be the first thing he saw when he shook off his faint. Slowly, slowly, he opened his eyes. He shook his head to clear away the cob-webs. He blinked hard, three times.

Jump! My name's Penelope.
Jump! I never rest.
Jump! As far as skipping goes
I'm the best.
Hop and leap and skip and jump.
Jump and leap and whirl.
There's no one can skip as well
As this girl!

I hadn't recognized that Quentin was a boy. Perhaps he didn't know that I was a girl, and it was vital to my plan that he understand this. If boy dragons were like boy humans, nothing would make one angrier than being challenged by a girl.

Hop and leap and skip and jump.
Jump and leap and whirl.
There's no one can skip as well
As this girl!

By the narrowing of his eyes and the pursing of his lips, I could see that I had struck a nerve. Quentin got to his feet, a little shakily at first. He steadied himself. He picked up his rope from where it had fallen. He curled his lip in a look of defiance. He began to skip.

Jump! My name is Quentin.
Jump! That's plain to see.
Jump! And there is no one who can
Skip like me.

Coal turns into diamonds.
Oysters give us pearls.
You're as slow as treacle and you're
Just a girl!

I called up all my flintiness. I gave him a look of withering contempt and picked up speed.

Hickory dickory bickery bock
Knickety rickety flippity flip.
Dragons are nothing but wind and talk,
I am the one who will win this skip!

Quentin was quick to answer.

Whickity whackity nickery nack
Singity songity pippety pop.
Yours is the rope that will soon go slack
You are the one who will have to stop!

"Harpy, Harpy, Scarface!" That is what Mellon and the
others call when they see me plodding down the road, bent
over my cane. How is it possible that they don't know the
truth of me ? I have lived so long that I have outlasted my
own legend.

"Hail, great dragon slayer!"

That is what they should properly say.

Well.

Perhaps not quite.

Not slayer.

Not slayer, exactly.

But close.

Quentin and I matched each other, turn for turn and skip for skip. When one of us would quicken the rhythm, the other would keep pace. Every cross-handed flourish was met with another. Every feat of fancy footwork was answered in kind. One of us would call out a challenge, and it would always be met.

"Kick skip!"

"One leg skip!"

"Double skip!"

I had never met so skilled and tireless an opponent, and I had skipped against the best Hamelin had to offer. Nan and Elfleda. Bridget and Newlyn. All the girls from up and down our lane. All girls who were in the hands of the Piper, and whom I had to find unless I wanted to spend the rest of my life skipping alone. I quickened the tempo.

"Backward skip!"

"Turnaround skip!"

"Pepper skip!"

Neither of us could find a way to trip up the other. Our ropes hummed, and we skipped so fast that there was no rupture in the sound they made as they scuffed the earth. The forest rang with *whackitywhackitywhackitywhackity,* punctuated with the sound of our cries.

Jump! My name's Penelope.
Jump! I never rest.
Jump! As far as skipping goes
I'm the best!

Jump! My name is Quentin.
Jump! I can't be beat.
Jump! You're sure to finish up
In de - feat!

On and on we skipped, our ropes now nothing but blurs in the air.

"Shin cross skip!"

"Double jump back skip!"

"Spin around skip!"

"Click heels skip!"

"Ankle bend skip!"

Each was dispatched with equal aplomb.

"Give in," called Quentin. "You can't win against me. I can go forever."

"Forever?"

"And ever!"

"We'll see about that."

In a flash, I knew what I had to do.

"Somersault skip!"

He almost faltered.

"Somersault skip? No such thing."

"There is now!"

In all my skipping days I had never heard of such a maneuver, let alone attempted to bring it off. But I had to do this. If I could not best a dragon in a skipping contest, what chance would I have against the Piper?

"Go on!" panted Quentin. "I dare you!"

I put all my trust in my body. I left the ground. My head and heels traded place, then traded place again. The rope never stopped its spinning as the world went topsy turvy. I was filled with joy. And I did it! I landed with a riotous whoop and saw with satisfaction that Quentin's jaw had dropped nearly to his knees.

"Your turn," I said, merrily.

"That was cheating!"

"Fraidy dragon!

"Am not!"

"Then do it!"

His bulging eyes narrowed to tiny slits. He knew how much was riding on this.

"Somersault skip!" Quentin bellowed and up he flew, his every limb flailing, high, high, high into the air.

Roses Sing on New Snow

by
Paul Yee

Fairytales have always celebrated smart girls. In this original story Paul Yee uses that tradition in the character of Maylin, a young woman who is not only capable and smart, but wise as well.

Seven days a week, every week of the year, Maylin cooked in her father's restaurant. It was a spot well known throughout the New World for its fine food.

But when compliments and tips were sent to the chef, they never reached Maylin because her father kept the kitchen door closed and told everyone that it was his two sons who did all the cooking.

Maylin's father and brothers were fat and lazy from overeating, for they loved food.

Maylin loved food too, but for different reasons. To Chinatown came men lonely and cold and bone-tired. Their families and wives waited in China.

But a well-cooked meal would always make them smile. So Maylin worked to renew their spirits and used only the best ingredients in her cooking.

Then one day it was announced that the governor of South China was coming to town. For a special banquet, each restaurant in Chinatown was invited to bring its best dish.

Maylin's father ordered her to spare no expense and to use all her imagination on a new dish. She shopped in the market for fresh fish and knelt in her garden for herbs and greens.

In no time she had fashioned a dish of delectable flavors and aromas, which she named Roses Sing on New Snow.

Maylin's father sniffed happily and went off to the banquet, dressed in his best clothes and followed by his two sons.

Now the governor also loved to eat. His eyes lit up like lanterns at the array of platters that arrived. Every kind of meat, every color of vegetable, every bouquet of spices was present. His chopsticks dipped eagerly into every dish.

When he was done, he pointed to Maylin's bowl and said, "That one wins my warmest praise! It reminded me of China, and yet it transported me far beyond. Tell me, who cooked it?"

Maylin's father waddled forward and repeated the lie he had told so often before. "Your Highness, it was my two sons who prepared it."

"Is that so?" The governor stroked his beard thoughtfully. "Then show my cook how the dish is done. I will present it to my emperor in China and reward you well!"

Maylin's father and brothers rushed home. They burst into the kitchen and forced Maylin to list all her ingredients. Then they made her demonstrate how she had chopped the fish and carved the vegetables and blended the spices.

They piled everything into huge baskets and then hurried back.

A stove was set up before the governor and his cook. Maylin's brothers cut the fish and cleaned the vegetables and ground the spices. They stoked a fire and cooked the food. But with one taste, the governor threw down his chopsticks.

"You imposters! Do you take me for a fool?" he bellowed. "That is not Roses Sing on New Snow!"

Maylin's father tiptoed up and peeked. "Why . . . why, there is one spice not here," he stuttered.

"Name it and I will send for it!" roared the impatient governor.

But Maylin's father had no reply, for he knew nothing about spices.

Maylin's older brother took a quick taste and said, "Why, there's one vegetable missing!"

"Name it, and my men will fetch it!" ordered the govemor.

But no reply came, for Maylin's older brother knew nothing about food.

Maylin's other brother blamed the fishmonger. "He gave us the wrong kind of fish!" he cried.

"Then name the right one, and my men will fetch it!" said the governor.

Again there was no answer.

Maylin's father and brothers quaked with fear and fell to their knees. When the governor pounded his fist on the chair, the truth quickly spilled out. The guests were astounded to hear that a woman had cooked this dish. Maylin's father hung his head in shame as the governor sent for the real cook.

Maylin strode in and faced the governor and his men. "Your Excellency, you cannot take this dish to China!" she announced.

"What?" cried the governor. "You dare refuse the emperor a chance to taste this wonderful creation?"

"This is a dish of the New World," Maylin said. "You cannot recreate it in the Old."

But the governor ignored her words and scowled. "I can make your father's life miserable here," he threatened her. So she said, "Let you and I cook side by side, so you can see for yourself."

The guests gasped at her daring request. However, the governor nodded, rolled up his sleeves, and donned an apron. Together, Maylin and the governor cut and chopped. Side by side they heated two woks, and then stirred in identical ingredients.

When the two dishes were finally finished, the governor took a taste from both. His face paled, for they were different.

"What is your secret?" he demanded. "We selected the same ingredients and cooked side by side!"

"If you and I sat down with paper and brush and black ink, could we bring forth identical paintings?" asked Maylin.

From that day on Maylin was renowned in Chinatown as a great cook and a wise person. Her fame even reached as far as China.

But the emperor, despite the governor's best efforts, was never able to taste that most delicious New World dish, nor to hear Roses Sing on New Snow.

Copyright
Acknowledgements